The Crime of Olga Arbyelina

Also by Andreï Makine

Confessions of a Fallen Standard-Bearer
Dreams of My Russian Summers
The Earth and Sky of Jacques Dorme
A Hero's Daughter
Human Love
Music of a Life
Once upon the River Love
Requiem for a Lost Empire
The Woman Who Waited

The Crime of Olga Arbyelina

ANDREI MAKINE

TRANSLATED FROM THE FRENCH BY
GEOFFREY STRACHAN

ARCADE PUBLISHING · NEW YORK

Originally published in French under the title *Le Crime d'Olga Arbélina*

Visit our website at www.arcadepub.com.

10 9 8 7 6 5 4 3 2 1

Library of Congress Cataloging-in-Publication Data

Makine, Andreo, 1957-
[Crime d'Olga Arbelina. English]
The crime of Olga Arbyelina / Andrei Makine ; translated from the French by Geoffrey Strachan.
p. cm.
ISBN 978-1-61145-764-3 (pbk. : alk. paper) 1. Russians--France--Fiction. 2. Mothers and sons--Fiction. 3. Hemophiliacs--Family relationships--Fiction. 4. Princesses--Fiction. 5. France--History--20th century--Fiction. I. Strachan, Geoffrey. II. Title.
PQ2673.A38416C7513 2012
843'.914--dc23

2012025005

Printed in the United States of America

For You

"'My mother must have influenced God in my favor,' the accused states at the inquiry. . . ."

Fyodor Dostoyevsky
The Brothers Karamazov

"'What have you done to me! What have you done to me!' If we chose to think about it there is probably not one loving mother who could not, on her dying day, and often long before, address this reproach to her son."

Marcel Proust
Filial Sentiments of a Parracide

One

THOSE THAT COME FIRST LIE IN WAIT for his words like mere eavesdroppers. Those that follow seem to appreciate something more in them. And they can easily be identified: they are much rarer than the merely inquisitive ones and come alone. They dare to draw a little closer to the tall old man as he slowly patrols the labyrinth of avenues and they leave later than the first comers.

The words the old man murmurs are swiftly dispersed by the wind in the icy light of a late afternoon in winter. He stops beside a slab, stoops to lift a heavy branch that lies like a fissure across the inscription carved in the porous stone. The inquisitive visitors cock their heads slightly toward his voice, while pretending to examine monuments nearby. . . . They have just overheard an account of the last hours of a writer who was well-known in his day but is now forgotten. He died at night. His wife, her fingers wet with tears, closed his eyelids and then lay down in bed beside him to wait for morning. . . . Now from the parallel avenue, where the dates on the gravestones are more recent, comes another tale: of a ballet dancer dead well before the onset of old age, who met his end repeating over and over, like a sacred formula, the Christian name of the young man, his lover, who had infected him. . . . Next they steal some words spoken beside a squat pedestal surmounted with a cross: the story of a couple in the early nineteen twenties whose lives were tortured by the impossible hope of getting a visa to go abroad. He, a famous poet who no longer had a single line in print, she, an actress, long since banned from the stage. Living reclusively in their flat in St. Petersburg, they could already picture themselves being condemned, imprisoned, perhaps executed. On the day when, miraculously, their authorization to leave the country arrived, the woman went out, while her husband remained behind in a daze of happiness. To do some shopping in preparation for the journey, he thought. She went down, crossed a square (the passengers on a streetcar saw her smiling), emerged onto the quayside, and hurled herself into the sea-green water of a canal. . . .

The visitors who have been listening out of pure curiosity are beginning to leave. A moment ago one of them crunched a fragment of flint beneath his heel. The old man drew himself up to his full gigantic height and fixed them with a somber gaze, as if angered at seeing them all there around him, frozen in their falsely preoccupied poses. Clumsily they make off, in single file at first, dodging between the tombstones; then forming a little group in the avenue that leads to the exit. . . . During those few moments of discomfiture facing the old man they felt the whole disturbing strangeness of their situation. There they were beneath the bare trees at that cold, clear day's end, in the midst of all those Orthodox crosses, a few feet away from this man in his unbelievable greatcoat, black and disproportionately long. A man who, as if talking to himself, summoned up these beings in their very swift, very individual transition from life to death . . . It all felt pretty weird!

The little group hastens to dilute this feeling with words. Their voices grow steadier with lighthearted bravado; they joke; they suspect that the old man's stories will give rise to a fascinating discussion on the journey home. One of them remembers a surprising detail: the dancer, an obsessive collector, already hugely rich, used to buy up antiques and pictures at prices one malicious tongue called "obscene" and explained, half in earnest, half hamming it up, that he needed "to make provision for my old age." The debate is launched. They speak of the vanity of material things and the little caprices of great minds. Of the weakness of the flesh and of depravity. ("Let's face it, he was a genius killed by that nonentity of a gigolo," exclaims one.) And of how there was no perversion in it because love redeems all. "Love?!" A theatrically indignant voice reminds them that the wife whose fingers caressed the eyelids of the newly dead writer (yes, that faithful wife now at rest beneath the same stone as he) had been forced to tolerate a ménage à trois. The writer, already an old man, had needed the physical presence of a young woman for his inspiration. . . . The arguments come thick and fast: the sense of sacrifice; art justifying everything; men's visceral selfishness. . . .

The car taking them back toward the capital is filled with flashes of wit, laughter, and disillusioned sighs that accompany the occasional sanctimonious observation. They are happy to have succeeded in curbing the dread that recently held them in its grip. Dread has become an anecdote. And the old man, "a kind of enormous half-crazed priest, dressed in a surplice at least a hundred years old." Even the capricious drowned woman of St. Petersburg simply serves to illustrate the irrational nature of her fellow countrymen. Yes, that soul so given to excess, and so often described, with which, thanks to their Sunday outing, they have become better acquainted. They mention the names of various writers and a few long novels in which, if you looked carefully, you might well come across the drowned woman and the dancer, and the old man himself. . . . After experiencing disorientation in a remote spot amid a drab, chilly landscape, it is an almost physical pleasure for them to find themselves once more in the familiar twisting streets, to recognize this café and that crossroads in their very characteristic Parisian look and with all the lights making it seem like night already. . . . And when, a year later, or perhaps more, depending on the rhythm of their busy lives, a dinner party brings them together again, not one of the four visitors will dare to speak of those few moments of dread beneath the wintry sky. And this fear of admitting to it will greatly enhance the pleasure of their evening.

Their retreat has not deflected the old man from his regular round. You can see him now lifting a long tree trunk uprooted by last night's storm. The cross on one of the tombs has been turned into a kind of prop, bowed under the weight of the toppled tree. This task accomplished, the man remains motionless for a moment. Then nods his head several times and pours out his words once more, to melt in the cold transparency of the evening. The visitor now listening to him remains mesmerized by the power and appearance of the hands thrusting out from the sleeves of the greatcoat and grasping the tree's damp bark. Hands that themselves resemble powerful, knotty roots; marked with scars; lined with violet veins. This spectator would like to have been the only one gathering up the words scattered by the wind. To his annoyance a young woman with an indifferent and willful expression stops on the neighboring pathway, attempting to decipher upside down—or pretending to—the inscription on the tombstone that the old man has just liberated; then she begins listening as well. . . . The dead person, whose name she has just mentally spelled out, a certain Count Khodorsky, was a cheerful adventurer. He arrived in Paris after the revolution and spent a terrible year reduced to begging; painting his toenails with India ink to camouflage the holes in his shoes; and a prey at night to the hallucinations of a starving man. His only fortune consisted of the deeds to several estates long since confiscated by the new regime. To his great surprise he found a buyer one day, someone who believed that a return to the old order in Russia was quite likely. So Khodorsky began seeking out from his compatriots deeds that were at once worthless and valuable. The purchasers, impressed by the imperial two-headed eagles and attracted by the derisory prices, easily allowed themselves to be persuaded. The count secured several years of riotous living for himself. But in time as the rich seam became exhausted, one day he had to put up for sale a very modest country house, the family home where he had spent his childhood. The purchaser, suspicious, examined the papers for a long time, asked for more details. Khodorsky, with a painfully forced smile, praised the lands that surrounded the house, the little river with its white sand, the orchard where nightingales sang. He even showed a photograph, the only snapshot left to him from his youth. In it you could see a farm cart near the front steps, and a child holding out a wisp of hay to the horse, while gazing fixedly at the photographer. . . . This snapshot seemed to be the deciding factor. As was his habit, Khodorsky celebrated his temporary enrichment in a restaurant in the Passy district. His guests found him true to himself: brilliant, extravagant, able to take part in several conversations at the same time. The next day toward noon, one of them who called on the count discovered him lying in his best apparel, his head stuck to a pillow heavy with blood. . . .

The two visitors seem to pay little attention to the vicissitudes of these tales of broken lives. As if, without knowing the facts, they have already foreseen their endings, each as logical as it was absurd. Only certain details arouse their interest; it is hard to know why. They have just looked quickly at each other; both were struck by the presence on the suicide's nightstand of the photograph of the wooden house, the horse and cart, and the child—that mysterious being, almost frightening in his ignorance of the future. Yes, their glances almost met, then at once turned away impersonally, seeking no one's eye. They are watching more than listening. The sky is cut in two—to the west the cold crimson of the setting sun and in the other half a low, gray canopy of cloud, gradually spreading and spilling out sparkling hail, whose needle points sting the cheeks and fill the dead leaves with a dry whispering in the paths between the tombstones. And when this dark canopy furls back, the vivid coppery light gilds the brown earth and the tree roots and glints on the puddles—mirrors half buried here and there in the thickets of the shrubbery. A gust of wind, as cutting as a steel wire, assails the eyes with fragments of tears. The old man leans forward, picks up a ceramic urn that holds a long, dry chrysanthemum stem, and puts it back on the gravestone.

His voice begins again, calm and detached; a voice, it seems to the two tardy visitors, that seeks neither to persuade nor to prove. A voice quite different from the incessant hubbub of words that fills their minds; words that, in their daily lives, assault them, solicit them, and demand their allegiance, in an everlasting verbal hash made up of snatches from newspapers and items intoned by newscasters. Words that kill the rare moments of silence within them.

Moreover, the old keeper's tales are barely sketched in. It is in the visitors' minds that the words tell a story, become theater. "A certain adventurer used to sell noble estates," is what he said. "Yes, houses of cards. . . . One day it was the turn of his boyhood home. And in the small hours, he blew his brains out. . . ." Before the next slab exactly the same tone of voice. "You see this mistake here. It withstands time well. 'Cavallry officer'. With two 'l's. It's a good thing not everyone can read Cyrillic script. Cavalry officer. . . . Very talkative, always getting carried away. And always the same stories of fighting; decapitating reds with his saber. And the more he told his tales the better he got at imitating that short hiss when the blade slices into the neck and breaks the bones. 'S-s-shlim!' he would hiss. You could really see a head rolling in the grass. . . . When he grew old his face was paralyzed and he couldn't talk anymore. The only thing he could still get out was that 's-s-shlim!' He died in the spring. It was a warm night, they opened the window. Just before the end he pulled himself up on one elbow, took a breath with all the strength of his trembling lungs, and whispered, very distinctly, 'Lilac . . .'"

The young woman listening to the old man could well be one of those women of whom people say, as they approach forty: She's made it. A woman who finds herself one Sunday in winter confronting emptiness and despair so great that death suddenly seems like an invitation secretly longed for. . . . That morning she had begun to leaf through her address book. Her fingers slid over the pages, as if on ice, without being able to get a grip. A whole crowd and at the same time no one. Then finally a name that reminded her of a promise made at least ten years before: "You'll see, it's not like a cemetery at all; it's a real garden, run a little wild; where you get the feeling right away that they have quite a different concept of death from us . . ." In all of ten years she has not had a single moment free to go there.

The other visitor, the man in a dark blue overcoat with the collar turned up, showing the gleam of his shirt and the knot in his tie, this man, too, has heard of "the garden where you discover a different view of death." He has the look of someone who, half an hour before the family lunch, a gathering of a dozen relatives, gets up, dresses in haste as if he were on the run, and slips out without telling a soul, something he has never done before. The vision he is running away from is of the eyes, the mouths, the faces about to surround him, making the same grimaces, uttering the same remarks as last time, chewing, swallowing. He would have had to reply to them, smile. And, above all, to accept that he was happy because other people considered he had every reason to be happy: the blonde, sleek serenity of his wife; the feline grace of his two daughters, about whom the family banter would be repeated once more—"two beautiful girls, ready to be wed"; and the laden table, facing a bay window, through which, from this sixteenth story, you can study the topography of Paris, as if on a map; and his office located in the same apartment building, which will, by tradition, prompt a gruff observation from one relative ("some people have all the luck; they only have to cross the landing to go to work!"). . . . This man has pictured all the small blessings whose sum total is supposed to make him happy. A great panic has overtaken him. He has seized his coat, closed the door behind him, trying to avoid slamming it, and rushed toward the staircase, dreading that he might encounter the first of the guests outside the elevator. . . .

The old man picks up an armful of dead branches and adds it to a pile of leaves and dry stalks at the foot of a tree. The man and the woman listen to his slow footsteps on the gravel, louder on account of the cold and the silence. So all of this has always been here, they think. This life so different from theirs, a life filled with this calm, with actions that leave them time to notice the imperceptible fading of the light—coppery, pink, now mauve—and to watch it as their own musings ripple past. To let one's gaze roam amid the etched branches against the frozen sky, to sense, without really understanding it, that these moments are mysteriously significant and that even a distracted glance at the little tuft of grass between the stones of the old wall is a necessary part of this day's end, of its light, of its sky, of its unique life. And so intense is the sensation of already belonging to this life that they both resolve, in their own way, to engage in conversation with the keeper at the end of his tale. Indeed his voice seems slightly changed, less impersonal, taking account of their presence before this tombstone.

"The reds called this form of execution 'the hydra of counter-revolution.' They roped ten officers together in a closely packed group. Shoulder to shoulder, back to back. And they pushed them off the deck of a barge or from the top of a jetty. Some would struggle, others went rigid, trying to play dead even before dying. Still others wept, weakened by their wounds. . . . This one here managed to break free underwater, his feet already trapped in the mud. He forced the wire off his wrists and reached the surface hidden behind a block of granite from the jetty. It was only later that the faces of the others began to haunt him. Especially the eyes of the man whose body he pushed down brutally in order to escape from the water."

The old man looks at them as if he were awaiting a question, a response. And his look is no longer that of a strange genius of the place, "a kind of half-crazed priest and at least a hundred years old," but of a fellow human being. His words cut through several periods of history they have never known. So very human is his attitude that their prepared questions stick in their throats. All at once they notice dusk has fallen; only a narrow strip of the setting sun now casts its cloudy red light over this place bristling with crosses. They suddenly feel themselves to be face to face with some dizzying intuition, an insight that cuts into their lives with a blinding thrust. . . . The visitor in the dark blue overcoat notices that the woman has begun to walk down the avenue at a pace that is carefully restrained, so as not to seem hurried. Conversely, she sees him moving away discreetly, escaping by skirting the tombs. They arrive at the exit at the same moment, but avoid looking at each other, as people do who have witnessed an assault taking place but did not intervene. . . . Outside the wall there is still a little light, pink and watery. The man turns, sees the woman looking for her car key, her hand thrust into a little leather rucksack. For a moment he feels as if he were going back into the silent life that brought the two of them together beneath the trees in the cemetery. The woman's face seems intensely familiar to him. He is convinced he knows the timbre of her voice, without ever having heard it; that he has a deep understanding of the atmosphere of every one of her days and of today's unhappiness. As she opens the car door she looks up for a second. The man, some yards from her, smiles, takes a step in her direction. "It's the first time you've come here?" He smiles, draws closer. "It's the first time . . ." Smiles, takes another step toward her. . . .

No, their cars have already driven off a moment ago, edging their way rapidly into the hissing stream of the freeway. It is only as he drives along, musing, that the man goes over in his mind the scene that never took place. He walks up to her, smiles: "You know, this is the first time I've come here and . . ." Lost amid the hurtling thrusts of the headlights, on routes that diverge farther and farther, each of them recalls the account that brought them to such a remote spot, on this freezing day: "You'll see, it's a real garden, well, more like virgin forest, there are so many trees, plants, and flowers. And each cross has a kind of tiny window with a night-light in it." They are telling themselves they should have come in summer or autumn to see the garden; now is too late. Should I go back there one day? the man ponders. Next Sunday? Take another look at those deserted avenues, those dark branches against the evening sky, that woman who . . . He shakes himself. Too late. The city swallows him into its dark, shifting complexity, streaked with red and yellow. Before racking his brains for a pretext to justify his escapade in the eyes of his loved ones, he thinks about the woman who, at this very moment, is herself somewhere being sucked down into the mighty flood of streets and lights. "To see her again would be as impossible as resurrecting the dead invoked by that old madman," he tells himself, summoning a grain of melancholy cynicism so as to regain a firm foothold in reality. . . .

The old man accompanies them with his stare as far as the gate, then looks down at the name shown on the tombstone where the engraved letters stand out in the almost horizontal rays of sunlight. In the distance the sound of an engine dwindles and fades, like the trickle of sand in an hourglass.

Apart from the keeper only a tall figure remains; he seems to be vainly searching for a way out of the maze of intersecting paths and avenues. He is the very last of the visitors, quite a young man who has been coming here daily for the past three or four days. Despite the cold he is wearing a simple corduroy jacket which, with its narrow, elongated cut, recalls the dress of students in the old days. A white muffler, coarsely knitted, forms a kind of frilly ruff on his chest. He has the pale face of someone who, though chilled to the marrow, no longer feels any pain, his body having become as cold as the icy air.

He was the one just now, as he watched the visitors, who imagined their feelings, pictured their lives. First, the gawking group, then the two solitary ones who were on the brink of talking to one another and now will never meet again. He spends his own life guessing at other people's lives. . . . A moment ago he noticed that this birch tree with two trunks had been split by yesterday's storm just at the point of the fork and that there was a risk that at any minute now the wind might enlarge the deep gash and bring down the twin trunk in a rending crash of timber. He tells himself that all the silence of the day hangs upon that mute cry. Taking a notebook out of a big satchel like a postman's, he writes in it: "The silence whose depths are plumbed by this suspended crash."

The man in the student's jacket is one of those invisible Russian exiles, increasingly isolated and shy with advancing years, who pursue a fantasy of writing and end their days in attics piled high with books, almost buried beneath the pyramids of pages that no one will have the courage to decipher. He has known several like this but tells himself that such a fate only befalls other people. In his own pyramids there will be the story of the reckless count who sold his childhood home, and that of the dancer who, as he died, called out the name of his lover, his murderer. . . .

The old keeper lights the little night-light in the cross surmounting the grave where his evening round always concludes. It is the grave of the condemned man who wrenched himself free of "the hydra of counterrevolution." The man in the corduroy jacket heard this story yesterday, alone face to face with the old man. One detail intrigued him: the name marked on the tombstone is that of a woman. He has not dared to ask for an explanation. . . . Now he sees a match flame shielded in the hollow of the keeper's hands, lighting them up from inside, then flaring on the wick of the night-light at the heart of the cross. The tiny glazed door closes, the sinuous flame flickers, steadies itself. The light and the sheltered warmth remind the young man so much of a long remembered room that he shivers. He is only a few steps away from the old man.

"Could you tell me about this woman?"

The old man's gaze seems to travel across long stretches of darkness, nocturnal towns long since peopled by ghosts. He is clearly trying to size up who he is dealing with: one of the inquisitive ones who come to collect two or three anecdotes? A fugitive who has escaped a family lunch and taken refuge here to gain a breathing space? Or perhaps the one whose coming he had given up hoping for?

He begins talking as he makes his way slowly toward the entrance gate that should have been locked at least an hour ago. His words are permeated by great weariness.

"Everyone would have it they were lovers. And that the death of that dubious character was murder."

It is the usual style of his stories: blunt, clear-cut, flat. All the man in the student's jacket expects is just one more anecdote. He is longing to get away, to drink a glass of warm wine, to go to bed. . . . Suddenly the old man, as if he had sensed this desire to escape, cries out in urgent tones that can be heard almost as a plea and an apology for not knowing how to tell stories in any other way, "You're the first person I have ever told about her!"

EVERYONE IN VILLIERS-LA-FORÊT (the men perhaps more openly than the women) wanted it to be a murder. This theory corresponded to some inescapable cliché of the imagination on the part of people who had very little, to the classic scenario of a crime of passion. Or, much more simply, to a desire to picture two naked bodies, first of all joined in love and then separated by the violence of a brief struggle and death.

Fascinated, abnormally perceptive, the townspeople held forth about the crime, invented new theories about it, and were critical of the inquiry that was making no headway. But it was really the bodies that fascinated them. For all at once their appearance amid the sleepy rural calm of Villiers-la-Forêt had to be accepted; and their nakedness, whether erotic or criminal, had to be written into the record of those idle July days that smelled of dust baked in the sun and the warm mud of the river. For such was the soft, slow landscape they burst in on: the man, his clothes drenched, stretched out on the bank, his skull smashed in. And the woman with disordered, streaming hair, her breasts bare, a woman seated beside the dying man, as still as carved stone.

It was thus that the scene had been reported by a breathless witness—the man with a stammer whom the people of Villiers called "Loo-loo," on account of his everlasting "loo-loo-look," the introductory phrase that enabled him to embark on a conversation. This time he was so overwhelmed that his stuttering lasted longer than usual. The men on the little terrace of the Café Royal eyed him with indulgent smiles, the younger men began to parody him. His efforts and their mockery brought tears to his eyes. The combination of this frailty and his defective speech caused him to be taken for a simpleton. He managed to overcome the strangulation of his "loo-loos" sufficiently to alert the men to the presence of the two bodies beside the river. It was his tortured expression that convinced them. They got up and followed him, as you follow the barking of a dog that despairs of conveying the urgency of its summons.

For several minutes on the bank they were blinded. Everything around them was so radiant on this fine summer's afternoon. A heat haze enveloped the willow thickets in a soft, milky light. The water with flat glittering patches rippled under the tiny promontories of plants that overhung its flow here and there. The soft and dreamy sound of it made you want to stretch out in the grass and listen distractedly to the sparse notes of the birds, to the distant crowing of the cocks that carried all the way to this spot, as if better to measure its whole summery expanse. A hundred yards away a fisherman was casting his line. Even farther away along the bank you could see the old brewery building, all garlanded in strands of hops. And more distant still, toward the horizon, the first houses of the lower town clustered together; then, climbing above them, the familiar roofs of the upper town—with the dark point of the steeple, the green mass of plane trees above the station and the place where the road turned off to Paris.

People were arriving, alerted who knows how, greeting one another with furtive little nods; and the whole crowd, composed of neighbors, acquaintances, and relations, froze before this inconceivable sight: a man lying there with a broad brown mark on his bald head, his mouth open, his eyes glassy; and a woman seated on a great worm-eaten tree stump, washed up by the river, a woman whose beauty and lack of modesty hurt your eyes.

And this was the sensation experienced by everyone on that bank. An ocular discomfiture, as if an eyelash had slipped under your eyelid and blurred your vision. This dead man whom no one dared to touch before the police arrived, this woman with her breasts scarcely hidden by a few shreds of cloth—two extraterrestrials landed on this day in the summer of 1947, the summer which all the newspapers had proclaimed to be that of "the first real vacation of peacetime."

Amid this uneasy stasis a movement was finally made that broke the spell. An old lady bent forward and removed a long, fine strand of waterweed that clung to the dead man's brow. Releasing all its pent-up energy, the crowd erupted into an angry hissing: nothing must move before the police got there! And at last it became clear to them that the whole scene really was happening. In a book, as several people remarked, everything would have been resolved much more quickly. But in the reality of that banal July day there was this long wait, extending absurdly beyond any acceptable limit. There was the strand of weed and the shirt that finally dried on the victim's body. Groups formed; words even more pointless than usual were uttered; "Loo-loo" wept; the men directed increasingly bold stares at the half naked breasts of the unmoving woman. And when they managed to tear their eyes away from the drowned man, with his face covered in duckweed, to which they were attracted, as if magnetically, it was the figure of the postman on his bike that could be seen in the distance. Such was the nauseating equanimity of real life, that has no concern with plot development and often actually ruins it with its glutinous slowness.

This ponderousness of reality also extended as far as the identification of the couple. "But that woman," many were to murmur. "I've seen her hundreds of times! You know, she works in the library at that Russian old folks' home. . . . That's it. She's the one who came to Villiers later than the others, just before the war . . ."

As for the man, they recognized him as the elderly Russian who could sometimes be seen bent over a little vegetable garden that sloped down to the river. A man of few words who lived unobtrusively. His mouth, currently wide open, seemed like life's last joke at the expense of his taciturn character.

A few Russians among the crowd were also eager to contribute to the identification of the two individuals. So it was that in the whispering that passed from one group to another, the name of Olga Arbyelina came to be disclosed. Then that of Sergei Golets. With these titles: Princess Arbyelina; Golets, former officer in the White Army. For the French townspeople such minutiae had the old-fashioned ring of titles like "Marquis" and "Vicomtesse" in a forgotten play of the romantic era. They paid much more attention to the young fisherman. He came running up holding a shoe that was missing from Golets's left foot. Nobody knew what to do with the shoe. . . . As before, they could hear the rippling of the warm water, the distant crowing of cocks. And, without knowing how to formulate it, some of them were struck by this disconcerting thought: So, if it were me stretched out on the ground there, with my mouth open, instead of this poor Russian, yes, if like him I had just died, it would have had no effect on the sunshine, the grass, the lives of all these people, their Sunday-afternoon walk. This warm, sunny posthumous world, smelling of reeds and waterweed, seemed more terrifying than any hell. But there were very few to pursue this line of thought to its logical conclusion. In any case, the police were arriving at last.

The disquiet provoked in the people of Villiers by the excessive radiance of the day that had greeted the tragedy on the riverbank faded away with the first stages of the inquiry. Now they all turned to reconstructing the facts, but setting off in the opposite direction from that chosen by the investigating magistrate. He was seeking to discover if there had been a crime or not. For them, the murder was not in doubt. Thus all they had to do was to yoke together as a pair of lovers the man and woman they had come upon one Sunday in July thanks to Loo-loo. And it was the challenge of this emotional and physical pairing that set all their brains in a ferment at Villiers-la-Forêt. For, as with those married couples who provoke the question: "What on earth brought them together?" it was impossible to imagine a conjunction between two more dissimilar natures.

Even their faces, their complexions, the expressions in their eyes, were opposed, like fragments of a mosaic that do not fit and, if forced together, disrupt the whole picture. A woman of forty-six, tall and beautiful, her abundant hair tinged slightly with gray, with features whose regularity, cool and detached, matched those of cameo portraits. A man of sixty-four with a broad face, animated by complacent joviality, a bald pate, sunburned and glistening, and a look full of self-assurance: a stocky man, with short, broad forearms and square yellow fingernails.

But what is more, you had to picture them together (this was a fact the inquiry would subsequently establish) in a rowboat out on the sunlit river. You had to bring them together on this improbable amorous excursion, see them land and settle in the grass behind the willow thickets. See the man set down on the ground a large bottle of wine he had been shading from the heat under the seat of the boat in the water stagnating on the old timbers. An hour later they had climbed back into the boat and, with the oars abandoned, were drifting toward the fateful spot, level with the ruined bridge, where the tragedy was to occur: the spot where the woman, according to her own muddled confession, had caused the death of her companion; or where the latter, according to the theory favored by the inquiry, had drowned, the victim of his own clumsiness, the drink, and an unfortunate collision with a pillar.

For uninvolved spectators every crime of passion acquires a covertly theatrical interest. The townspeople of Villiers-la-Forêt, once the shock of the first minutes had passed, discovered this diverting aspect, although its attractions had to be concealed behind a grave exterior. They applied themselves to the game with a will. The tedium of their daily lives encouraged this but so did the progress of the inquiry itself. Examinations of witnesses, confrontations, searches, seizures—the mere use of these terms in breathless discussions offered each of them a new and unexpected role, uprooting them from their stations in life as baker, schoolteacher, or pharmacist. Indeed the pharmacist (who had remained idle since his pharmacy was destroyed by mistake in an Allied bombing raid) no longer spoke anything but this language, halfway between case law and a detective novel, as if it satisfied his taste for Latin terminology.

The fact of having to take the oath before giving evidence also had considerable importance. To the point where the youth who had been fishing at the moment of the tragedy emphatically insisted on repeating before the investigating magistrate the formula "the truth, the whole truth, and nothing but the truth," although his age exempted him from this.

The drowning of Golets, through accident or foul play, had quickly become an inexhaustible subject of conversation for the people of Villiers, since the progress of the inquiry always kept it fresh. In particular, it was a topic for all occasions, one that abolished the invisible frontier between upper town and lower town, between groups that hitherto had no contact with one another, and worked wonders in bringing strangers together. This whole verbal ferment was, in truth, based on few material facts. Thanks to the "no secrets" of small towns it was learned that the search of Golets's home had only brought to light a pistol with a single cartridge in the magazine, a collection of bow ties (some people mistakenly reported this as a collection of bows and arrows), and brief notes written on scraps of paper recording someone's visits to Paris. As for the Princess Arbyelina, no one had ever seen her in the company of this man. One witness, it is true, had seen them going together into the long shooting gallery, a kind of fairground booth in the big park in the upper town. But this visit, objected others, had only taken place shortly before the boat trip. Suddenly, within the space of a few hours, their adventure had become possible. What action, what word (coming from the man? from the woman?) had made it so?

The alleged rendezvous at the shooting gallery; the collection of bow ties that was so out of keeping with the image of a senior citizen tending his garden; the few rare visits made by a mysterious "Parisian friend" to the heroine of the tragedy: these meager details proved sufficient to unleash an endless avalanche of theories, hypotheses, and conjectures, to which were added some scraps that the preliminary investigation had apparently allowed to filter through. An excited, unquenchable chorus of voices combined in a wild round of truths, fabrications, and absurdities such as can only be trotted out in the course of the verbal orgy that follows a sensational crime in a provincial town.

During those summer months everyone at Villiers-la-Forêt tried out the roles of storyteller and sleuth. Every day, thanks to these countless mouths, the ghosts of the man and woman in the boat relived their last afternoon together. The townspeople discussed it standing in line at the baker's, on the terrace at the Café Royal, on the dusty square where they played boules, in the train during the hour-long journey that lay between them and Paris. They were on the alert for every new scrap of information, every little secret, without which their own picture of the crime might be left less complete than that of their neighbors.

And then, several days after the event, they discovered an article in a Paris newspaper. Two narrow columns in all, but in a context that took your breath away. The account of the local tragedy was sandwiched between Princess Elizabeth's engagement and this brief news item: "The plot against the Republic has been foiled. The Comte de Merwels and the Comte de Vulpian have been charged." Never before had the people of Villiers enjoyed so fully the feeling that they were making world news. The item about the tragedy that had taken place in their town ended with this observation: "It is now the task of the inquiry to establish whether what occurred was a mere accident or a premeditated and cunningly executed murder, a hypothesis that appears already to have won credence among the citizens of Villiers-la-Forêt."

The boating tragedy even altered certain deeply ingrained habits in the town. People who liked to saunter along the riverbank in the evening now continued their stroll a little farther, until they reached the glade amid the willows where the fatal rendezvous was said to have taken place. Young people, for their part, had abandoned their traditional bathing place and exhausted themselves diving at the spot where Golets had drowned, hoping to find his watch, a heavy gold timepiece with a two-headed eagle on the cover . . .

The fever for detection was universal. However, the two populations of Villiers-la-Forêt, French and Russian, were in fact piecing together quite distinct stories.

For the French, what the odd couple's adventure marked, above all, was the real start of the postwar era. If you could once more drift down the river in an old boat with your arms around a woman and a bottle of wine under the seat then peacetime had returned for good. The fatal turn of events only confirmed this impression. In one Paris paper a brief account of the drowning had succeeded for the first time in displacing the headline PURGED that recurred in issue after issue, often with news of death sentences. . . . Furthermore, in the same newspaper they were announcing the start of the Tour de France 47, the first since the war.

The Russians, too, saw Golets's death as what might be called a historic event. Those who that July afternoon had feasted their eyes on the man stretched out in the grass and his companion, whose body looked naked beneath the fine, wet fabric, all the Russian inhabitants of the lower part of the town felt, almost physically, that the passage of calm, predictable days had been shattered there on the riverbank. Indeed, they sensed the advent of a new before and after in their personal chronology.

The start of this chronology went back to the revolution, to the civil war, to the flight across a Russia set ablaze by the Bolsheviks. Next for them had come the period of putting down roots in Paris, in Nice, or, for some, in the sleepy monotony of Villiers-la-Forêt. Later, in 1924, came the terrible decision by the French to recognize the Soviet Union. In 1932, worse still: the Russian émigré Pavel Gorgulov assassinates the President, Paul Doumer! For several weeks the whole Russian part of the town had lived in fear of reprisals. . . . Then the war had broken out and, paradoxically, had somewhat rehabilitated them in the eyes of the French—thanks to the victory of those same Bolsheviks over Hitler. . . . And finally this latest event, this incredible coupling of the Princess Arbyelina with the ridiculous Golets.

This woman had made her mark on the Russian chronology of Villiers-la-Forêt by the simple fact of moving into the town in the spring of 1939. From the first day the émigrés had begun to look forward to a marvelous transformation, such as a princess must inevitably give rise to in their lives. They already knew that Olga Arbyelina belonged to one of the most illustrious families in Russia and bore the name of her husband, a certain Georgian prince who had recently abandoned her, leaving her alone, without means, and with a young child on her hands. Making her welcome among them all, people of modest origins, seemed to them like a kind of revenge on the Parisian diaspora, who took such a pride in their titles, arrogant and exclusive. They had a fleeting dream of figuring in a poignant melodrama, *The Exiled Princess* . . . . But this princess seemed to be showing a poor grasp of her role. She appeared not to be suffering from her relegation to Villiers, lived as modestly as themselves, and treated them with disappointing simplicity. They would have preferred her haughty; they would have liked to pardon her the pride of her caste; they were ready to share her loathing for the new masters of Russia! But she remained very discreet on the subject and had apparently even observed one day, to the great displeasure of the elderly inmates of the Russian retirement home, "The revolution was conceived not so much in the mud of the workers' districts as in the filth of the palaces. . . ."

There was yet more intense disappointment in store for them: her child's illness. Or rather the calm with which the princess endured it. In the minds of the Russian colony the word "hemophilia" had evoked the shade of the unfortunate Tsarevich. Everyone began to seek out some dynastic mystery; one by one the pensioners reeled off the names of those descendants of Queen Victoria guilty of introducing the scourge into so many noble houses. They expected an almost immediate tragedy: they were already decking out the Princess Arbyelina in the mourning of an inconsolable mother. But when one of them very circumspectly (with that studied circumspection that is worse than any tactlessness) alluded to this British lineage, Olga had replied, almost laughing, "No, no, we didn't need the Queen to bestow this treasure on us." Moreover, her child's case did not seem to be as serious, by a long shot, as the illness that had dogged the Tsar's son. And to crown it all, the boy showed no particular signs of suffering and spoke so little that he could easily have been taken for mute. . . .

Thus the miracle they had all been looking forward to went no further than the considerable enhancement of the library, of which the princess was now in charge, and the planting of a service tree by the front steps to the strange house where she alone had agreed to reside, the long redbrick annex, built against the wall of the former brewery in which the émigrés had made their home at the start of the twenties, dividing it up into apartments, a retirement home, a reading room, a canteen. . . . Yes, she had disappointed them cruelly!

However, none of these frustrations could match the latest one: her farcical assignation with this . . . someone recalled at that moment that Golets had worked as a horse butcher. With this horse butcher, then, who, no doubt so as to make them a laughingstock, had had the stupidity to get drowned!

The hypotheses advanced by the people of Villiers clearly erred on the side of unsubtlety. Where death is involved the seething mass of detail is obliterated and only the broad outline of human appearances is preserved. Thus sometimes Golets became "that dreary old Russian," sometimes "that horse butcher," and occasionally "the ex-officer." Princess Arbyelina's friend (one of his letters was said to have been found, signed "L.M.") was "a well known poet and journalist but afraid of his wife and of the wagging tongues of the émigrés in Paris." And Olga's husband "a hell of a fellow, a hero in spite of himself, a Georgian Don Juan." Death, like a harsh spotlight, picked out these three profiles—simplified but perhaps tolerably accurate, when all's said and done: the husband, the lover, and the suitor, as the apprentice detectives of Villiers-la-Forêt called them.

In the course of the inquiry the services of an interpreter, a Russian, had to be called on. And it was probably he who was responsible for several leaks, which the citizens were not slow to weave into their own fabrications. The rumors disclosed in this way seemed credible enough, in any case, and would be even more so when the affair was closed. One of them was quoted more often than the others. In passing it on they presented it in dialogue form, for greater authenticity:

"So you claim you always wished for the death of Monsieur Golets?"

"Yes, I did not intend to let a man like that remain alive."

"Can you tell me at what moment the idea of killing him came to you?"

"It was when he forced me to take a walk with him in the park."

"How could he force you to do it?"

"He knew that I would obey him. . . ."

And from this point the theories gushed forth in all directions, suggesting a thousand and one conceivable motives for the mysterious hold Golets had over Olga Arbyelina.

It also occurred that during the passionate debates at the Café Royal or under the poplar trees on the marketplace, someone would attempt to win credence for a completely far-fetched invention. According to one of these forgers the Russian princess had described her relationship with the horse butcher in these Delphic terms: "This man was an amalgam of all the ugliness in the world, while I was living at one with the beauty of last winter. I still had before my eyes the imprint of a hand on the windowpane, amid the hoarfrost flowers. . . ."

And what was most surprising was the extent to which this remark, doubtless invented from a lot of scraps, also nourished very reasonable suppositions. So who had left this imprint? The Parisian lover, the shadowy L.M.? Or an unknown person whose existence the investigator had failed to reveal? As for the readers at the Russian library, they interpreted this strange remark as a sign of incipient madness. "Oh, you know," the elderly inmates of the retirement home would exclaim. "The princess hasn't been all there for some time now."

In these tangled webs of personal interpretation there was, however, one matter that intrigued all the people of Villiers-la-Forêt equally, whether they were French or Russian: the impossibility of picturing the bodies of the two protagonists of the tragedy in carnal union. Their bodies were so physically incompatible. Such an act of love—for many of them almost against nature—led in their conversations, particularly among the men, to this disconcerting question, which subsequently spread through the town: "How could she give herself to him?" Which was, of course, the expurgated version of what they actually said . . .

Apart from that, picturing the Princess Arbyelina in the arms of this squat, bold, ungainly Russian allowed the men of Villiers-la-Forêt to have a kind of revenge on the woman. Most of them experienced jealous regret: this creature with her statuesque body must have been an easy catch, after all, given that this moujik had wooed her with such success! The bitterest of them harped on the fact that the woman was forty-six . . . thrusting her utterly inaccessible body toward old age, toward the unattractiveness of old age. Men can be pitiless toward a woman whose body has eluded them, particularly if this is thanks to their own cowardice.

Once male pride had been appeased, however, the key question returned: "But at the end of the day, what weird twist of fate brought them together?"

Be that as it may, by dint of tireless preliminaries, the whole scenario of the tragedy ended up being pinpointed with the conciseness of an epigram. And this was notably done in the observation attributed by rumor to the investigating magistrate: "This is the first time in my life I have had to convince a person that they are not guilty of murder." Another fragment, with the same aphoristic brevity, reported the riposte made by the magistrate to the interpreter. The latter had remarked in surprise: "But don't you think that, in accusing herself of one crime, she's trying to cover up another?"

The reply was trenchant.

"A killer breaks a shop window, admits it, goes to prison, and gets away with a murder. But you don't accuse yourself of murder in order to cover up a broken window."

That is how the affair was pictured during those summer months in Villiers-la-Forêt. The few who went away on vacation discovered new details on their return, strange revelations that their neighbors were eager to impart to them. Their game of a thousand voices resumed more merrily than ever. . . .

And it was after a great delay, early in the fall, that they learned this mind-boggling news: some time previously the case of the Russian lovers had been formally closed for want of evidence. It was only then that they realized Princess Arbyelina's house was empty and she and her son were no longer to be seen.

Yes, the curtain had been rung down just when their scenarios were taking on more and more substance, when they were so close to knowing the truth!

The people of Villiers found it hard to conceal their disappointment. They had grown so accustomed to the pleasantly fevered climate that the love and death of the horse butcher had caused to reign in their town. What they felt especially nostalgic for, though often without realizing it, was the secret life that the unfortunate passengers on that old boat had revealed to them. It had appeared that in their dull little town quite another life could be simmering away—devastating in its passions, criminal, multifarious. Unexpected. A life in which an obscure retired man was capable, heedless of the cost, of embracing a redoubtable beauty who, for obscure reasons, allowed herself to be seduced. A subterranean life, free, filled with promises and temptations. At least that was how most of the townspeople had perceived the blazing affair between the princess and the horse butcher.

★ ★ ★

But the most surprising event occurred a little later, when the first mists were beginning to filter through into the lower town in the mornings. One day, as if by magic, everybody forgot the boating tragedy, the woman sitting on the bank, the drowned man stretched out on the grass. As if they had never existed!

The people of Villiers talked about power cuts, the schedules for which were printed in the newspapers; about the meat shortages just starting, about Princess Elizabeth's wedding: about the stars in *The Best Years of Our Lives*. . . . And if anyone had taken it into his head to refer to the previous summer's inquiry, he would have committed an unpardonable gaffe, like telling an old joke that people no longer find funny.

Besides, soon the autumn floods covered the site of the ill-fated rendezvous and the bank where the man and woman had frozen in their involuntarily theatrical poses under the eyes of the spectators. The boat, whose side the people of Villiers had liked to poke their fingers into at the spot deeply torn by the collision, ended up among other wrecked vessels, its terrible singularity effaced among the peeling hulls, half hidden in the mist.

The expanse of meadowland covered in water was so bleak, the branches of the alders so trembling and tortured that it no longer occurred to anyone in Villiers-la-Forêt to ponder what kind of love or hate had brought two strange Russian summer folk together on this riverbank.

NIGHT HAS FALLEN. A moment ago the old keeper stopped talking. His hand resting on the lock of the gate, he is waiting for the man dressed in a student's jacket to go. But the latter seems not to notice this gesture. His eyes, unmoving, are filled with a torrent of shapes, places, grimacing faces; of cries; of days.

The tale has been told with the simplicity of the previous anecdotes: a man, a woman, an inexplicable pairing, a death or a murder. And oblivion. Nevertheless, this last visitor has managed to glimpse the fine strand of weed clinging to the drowned man's brow. He has sensed the disturbing intensity that the presence of the lifeless body bestowed on the scents of summer, the murmur of insects among the plants on the riverbank. He has heard the remarks whispered by the curious. He has experienced that delicious apprehension with which, later, they would come and thrust their fingers into the breach in the side of the boat.

His eyes dazzled by this imagined world, he stands transfixed, straining to hear the words that he still seems to make out down there: the strangely cadenced voice of the woman, replying to the magistrate. Now he thinks he can even understand the shackled sentences of the stammerer.

The old man takes out a heavy bunch of keys, shakes it. But the other does not hear. His vision isolates him in the night: "To be able to see what others do not see, do not wish to see, do not know how to see, are afraid to see—like all those visitors to the cemetery, who have been filing past this old man from time immemorial. Yes, to guess that the dress of the woman seated on the riverbank, the dress torn during a brief and appalling struggle, was gradually losing its transparency as it dried and beginning to conceal her body more fully. To see the increasing opacity of this fabric is already to enter into this woman's life. . . ."

The old man slowly draws the gate to and turns the key in the lock. The two of them remain inside the cemetery.

—Хотите чаю?

The invitation to drink tea seems to awaken the man in the corduroy jacket from his reverie. He accepts and, as he walks along beside the old man, notices that on the crosses several night-lights in their tiny glass cages are still shining, scattered through the darkness. In the distance the glowing window of the keeper's house also resembles a night-light, gradually growing broader as they approach, and admitting them, as a candle flame does if you stare at it for long enough, thereby entering its flickering, violent life.

Two

SHE KNEW THAT THE PAIN we feel, physical as well as mental, is partly due to our indignation at pain, our astonishment at it, our refusal to accept it. To avoid suffering, she always employed the same trick: making a mental list. What you have to do is take note, as dispassionately as possible, of the presence of things and people brought together by the painful situation. Name them very simply, one after the other, until their total improbability hits you in the eye. And so she was listing them now, first of all noticing the drawn curtains, the edges of which were fastened together by half a dozen clothespins. The dark curtains, the ceiling lit from the side by a lamp placed on a chair. And on the ceiling, as well as on the wall, those two angular shadows, dark and clear cut: the outline, like a capital M, of the legs of a woman lying on her back with her knees up. And another shape, this one moving; a gigantic head with two horns, appearing at intervals between the triangles of the bent legs. Yes, these two women linked by the silent work one of them was carrying out on the other one's body, in a stifling room, late one afternoon in August.

A precise pain, sharp as an injection, made her interrupt her list-making and close her eyes tightly. But she must start again quickly, so as to leave herself no time for indignation. So; the August sun, whose dusty indolence could be sensed, despite the drawn curtains and the closed shutters. Beyond the shutters, on the sidewalk, a few inches away from the insulated interior of the room, an encounter between two passersby, their conversation ("Mark my words, we won't be seeing a lot of meat next year"); then the clatter of a streetcar and the faint answering tinkle of the glasses in the cupboard. Then, like an amplification of that tenuous sound—the rattling of a metallic instrument on a tray.

The head swathed in a large white square with two horns reappeared at the end of the improvised operating table. "I'm not hurting you too much, am I?" And it dived in again between the patient's parted knees.

This silent smile too, must be added to the inventory. In resuming it she must strive for the greatest possible precision in the details. A cramped room, an incredible accumulation of furniture: that cupboard made of dark wood, almost black; a writing desk; a piano with candelabra fixed to it at each end of the keyboard; two armchairs close together like in a cinema auditorium; a pedestal table; sets of shelves—everything piled high with books, statuettes, knickknacks, vases with bunches of dried stems. On the walls a patchwork of pictures: antique portraits with barely visible features and bright, airy landscapes cheek by jowl with abstract geometry. In the corner, almost up against the ceiling, the brown, gilded rectangle of an icon, concealed beneath a long draped fabric . . . And in the middle of this chaos, straight, clean sheets, the smell of alcohol, a table that looks like an ice floe. Outside the window, some rhythmic chanting, those fleeting echoes that people carry away with them mechanically after a demonstration or a carnival. A snatch of music is woven into it—the joyful sob of an accordion, the sound of which conjures up a vision of the avenue in its August heat. . . .

The nature of the pain altered, becoming harsher, more humiliating in its physiological banality. Olga sensed that the words were already trembling in her mind and that, in an indignant, silent protest they were about to blame her own stupidity ("What an idiot! At my age!"); as well as the vigilant, petty perfidiousness of life ("The moment was well chosen, enough said! Or rather I was the one well chosen, otherwise I might have been able to cling to a few illusions about the best of all possible worlds . . ."). She hurriedly resumed her game of stocktaking. Yes, the festive shouts outside the window: the second anniversary of the Liberation of Paris . . . In the morning, on her way to her friend's house, she had noticed the profusion of flags on the fronts of buildings. . . . Yes, this city at once animated and drowsy; this one-story house at the edge of the fifteenth arrondissement; this sun beating against the closed shutters on the ground floor. And, in a room isolated from the world, two women. One of them stretched out on a table, covered by a sheet, the other bent over the first's lower abdomen, her head swollen by an enormous white headdress with horns, engaged in performing a clandestine abortion.

Olga felt her indignation thwarted by the absurdity of the situation. She could have been indignant if the pain had violated some logic, flown in the face of justice. But there was no logic to it. Just scattered fragments; unpleasant pricks that raised goose bumps on her thighs on that stifling afternoon of August 25, 1946; the room crammed with furniture; a woman subjecting another woman to an operation held to be criminal. "A clandestine abortion," Olga repeated mentally, thinking that the improbability of her situation might well have been even more striking. One had only to picture how close her half naked body was to the passersby outside the shutters. Her body that had been surgically amputated from the tiny life enclosed within it, a body now singular but which, from tomorrow onward, would melt back into the crowd of other bodies, indistinguishable from their mass.

She heard another click of metal on the tray. Her friend's horned head bobbed up at the end of the table.

"That's it?!" They spoke with one voice, one asking, one stating, in unintended unison, as often happens with people who have known one another for a very long time and end up unconsciously following the course of one another's thoughts. . . .

"And yet," thought Olga, "we'll never breathe a word about the most important things. I'll never even tell her how I make lists to help me forget the pain. The second anniversary of the Liberation; this tiny death in my womb; the portrait on the wall looking at me. How could I explain? I'd have to be able to ask her if she has thoughts of this kind; if trivia like this fill her mind, too, and seem important to her . . ." Those accordion notes just now; they brought on that sudden longing for an easy happiness, spine-tingling, very French, or at least what people imagine as French. The fleeting but burning desire to be without past, without thoughts, without weight; to be merry, intoxicated with being alive here and now. And all at once the shame at having had this longing. The vigilant censorship that watches over our happiness, a pitiless voice, always on the alert. A voice that reproaches her with the little life destroyed in her womb—as an immediate punishment for this longing to be happy. So many fragments of joy and fear we are made up of and never speak of.

But there had been no mention of any of this in their conversation at noon before the operation. They recalled the Parisian midwife who had been guillotined some years previously, for having practiced clandestine abortions. They chattered jokingly, making faces and feigning theatrical terror: "The French will guillotine us!" The anecdote allowed them to remain silent about what was on the tips of their tongues, in their eyes, their real lives, made up of little nothings that were serious, essential, inadmissible.

"I'm putting away my instruments of torture. You can get up. I've put your dressing gown here on the armchair."

Her friend touched her shoulder, smiling, then went out, taking with her the tray covered in a crumpled napkin. "That smile, I've already added it to my painkilling inventory." August 25, 1946. A room transformed into a used furniture store filled with Russian curios. The smiling face of a woman—a scarred face that since adolescence had borne a deep gash cut into her left cheek, like a pink butterfly with torn wings. Her smile made the butterfly move; the most childlike, the most vulnerable smile in the world, one from which strangers turned away, so as not to let their revulsion be seen. . . . The face of Li. Li, lily . . . At a party in the days of their childhood in Russia long ago a ten-year-old child weeps: the others are in fancy dress as flowers; her own costume, a lily-dress, has gone astray. People hear her lamenting: "Li-li-lia!" They laugh. They make up a nickname. The child becomes Li. She is consoled with a replacement costume—that of a magician: she has a turban with a peacock's feather, a star-spangled cape, a magic wand. She falls in love with the role. At every party from now on it is she who takes charge of the magic; she learns conjuring, knows how to set off fireworks. People have almost forgotten her real name, Alexandra. . . . One festive evening a many-colored rocket hits her in the face before falling into the grass and exploding in a shower of stars that makes the children shout with glee. Her own cry is lost amid the tumult of laughter and applause. She is fifteen. . . .

In her inventory just now Olga included that child. A child disfigured because someone had once found her a magician's costume. A child who would survive wars, famines, indifference, and disgust in the eyes of others and end up in a stifling room, lost in the midst of the Parisian ant-heap, on August 25, 1946, causing pain, while she tended it, to the bared body of a woman.

Along with the cool from the windows, opened at last, the evening also brought the marvelous sensation of the pain fading. Lying on a sofa squeezed between the piano and the armchairs, Olga heard her friend busying herself in the kitchen. The clatter of crockery, the swish of the water. Li . . . pleasantly distracted, as a woman can feel in the evening, soothed by the routine sequence of tasks. Li . . . so close, a friend for so long and at the same time unknowable. Other people are made up of questions that one dare not put to them. . . .

Li stuck her head through the half open door: "You're not bored?"

"So she was thinking about me. It's one of those questions you can never ask: What do you think of me? And yet we spend our days picturing how other people see us, picturing ourselves living in their minds. And I certainly have a life in hers. But what a strange creature that must be!"

She tried to picture Olga as imagined by Li, an Olga in love and very much loved, in the midst of a passionate affair with her lover. ("She doubtless calls him my 'lover.' ") For this imaginary Olga, pregnancy is a real disaster. The lover, a married man, is too prominent in the Russian colony in Paris to recognize an illegitimate child. Hence an abortion. The heroine of a pretty romantic tale . . .

She pricked up her ears. A little hummed tune was now mingled with the sound of the dishes being washed. "My dear old Li," thought Olga. "I must be something like that in her thoughts—a lover, passion, palpitations. If she only knew that the thing that really upset me in this business is that I can't remember when this 'lover' of mine last came to see me. That I'm almost sure he didn't come in June, nor more recently. So this pregnancy strongly resembles an immaculate conception. No, he must have come in June, the proof of it is . . . But I simply don't recall, I have no memory of it. And so where Li pictures a tragedy there is just this infuriating confrontation with forgotten dates, meetings that have slipped the memory . . . Other people make us live in surprising worlds. And we live in them; they go and see us down there; they talk to these doubles, who are their own invention. And in reality we do not meet at all in this life."

Li's laughter woke her in the night. Sleeping in two armchairs arranged face to face for the occasion, her friend gave a rather shrill, childish little laugh. It took Olga several seconds to realize that Li was weeping softly in her sleep. The moon was melting on the lid of the piano; the furniture and objects seemed to be in suspense, interrupting the existence they had been leading a moment before. And her friend's wail rang out both close at hand and in the infinite remoteness of the life that enfolded her dreams. . . . Olga remained awake for quite some time, listening as Li's breathing gradually calmed down.

In the morning, finding her friend neither in the room nor in the kitchen, Olga went out into the little yard at the back of the house. She sat down on an old stool in the soft, transparent sunlight and did not stir, her gaze fixed on a little stunted tree that persisted in growing in a crack under the gutter. It was important to her not to disturb the simple happiness, the absence of thoughts, the slow drifting of the air that still had the freshness of cold paving stones, of the night, but already carried the smell of grilled onions. Olga leaned the back of her neck against the rough surface of the wall. She suddenly felt she could live solely by following the permeation of these smells, live in this light, in the immediate physical sensation of happiness. On the wall facing her, several narrow windows, cut through at random, spoke of unknown lives that seemed touching to her in their simplicity. . . .

This happiness lasted for the time she needed to take stock of her own reality. It was still there, but yesterday's thoughts, the thoughts of every day, in the guise they had had yesterday, were already flooding in: that "lover," certainly the last man in her life; the tiny lethal operation in her body. During the coming days all of that would give rise to a long, futile inner debate, arguments that excused her and those that damned her. She could already hear words forming in her head, that vigilant voice that kept watch over her moments of happiness: "So, you've had your instant of bliss thanks to a little murder. Bliss in a backyard that smells of onions. Well done!"

She got up, went closer to the tree, inhaled the bright little blossoms scattered over its branches. . . . Her friend's words could be heard at the other end of the yard, coming from the cellar—Li's studio. Olga went down the steps: she could not yet imagine who might be on the receiving end of these cheerful and encouraging remarks.

"No no, my dear man, don't forget you're a satyr! Come on, give me a lewd grimace. Yes, very good, that's right, a look inflamed with desire, licking your lips with lust. Perfect! Hold it there. . . . And you, Madame, look alarmed, tremble! A nymph already feeling this lubricious monster's breath on her neck. . . . Good! Don't move . . ."

The cellar was lit with a sharp, theatrical light. Li, motionless behind a tripod, her eye glued to her camera, was pointing it at a huge plywood panel. Against an exuberant painted background of plants and leaves, it portrayed a beautiful nymph with a white, shapely body being embraced by a satyr surging up out of the rushes. The nymph blinked her eyes a little nervously. The satyr coughed.

"And-now-quite-still-everyone!" repeated Li in a magician's voice, and there was a click.

The faces of the satyr and the nymph detached themselves from the plywood and left two dark, empty circles in their place.

Li stood up, noticed Olga, and gave her a wink. A man and woman came out from behind the panel. It was comical to see their heads detach themselves from the painted figures and come down to earth on very correctly dressed bodies: a summer dress, a light shirt with a tie. They themselves seemed a little disconcerted by this sudden transformation.

"The photos will be ready the day after tomorrow, about noon," Li explained as she led them out.

They had lunch in this cellar where there were several painted panels arranged along the walls. On one of them Olga made out a castle in flames with a musketeer escaping out the window, clasping a swooning beauty in his arms. A little farther on a couple of suntanned bathers were basking at the edge of an expanse of blue, beneath the palm trees. The holes for their faces stood out oddly against the background of the tropical sky. In the foreground Olga was surprised to detect a streak of real sand, and a large seashell. . . . Li followed her gaze.

"Oh that's quite an old one. From the days when I was going all out for the illusion of depth, trompe l'oeil. I noticed that people very much enjoyed the realism. . . ."

Olga listened to her, amazed and touched, thinking: "This is Li. Elusive. Who is she? Conjurer. Painter. Photographer. Nurse. Three years at the front during the First World War. Imprisoned and tortured under the Occupation, yes, those hands covered in burns. . . . Last night she cried in her sleep. What was she dreaming about?"

Li got up, forgetting the meal, and took out one panel after another, placing them all on the stands. It was not the first time she had shown her collection to Olga, but, as with all great enthusiasts, her passion was rekindled each time and gave spectators the impression of experiencing anew things they had seen before.

"I just had to keep inventing," she explained, putting her head through a cutout circle. "This is my mythological period. Recognize it?"

A girl clad in a transparent tunic was approaching a bed, by the light of a candle. A winged cupid lay there asleep in voluptuous abandon. Li's face appeared now in the aura of the candle, now on the pillow.

"And after that, one day, a flash of inspiration. And my literary period begins. Look!"

This time it was a man with a bushy beard, wearing a long peasant blouse, a giant standing beside an izba and leaning on the handle of a swing plow. The character posed beside him seemed, in his city clothes, to be the very epitome of the average man.

"You see," exclaimed the photographer, thrusting her face into the cutout, "a certain Mr. N calling on Tolstoy at Yasnaya Polyana. And you can't imagine how many Mr. Ns have already succeeded in convincing people they were on intimate terms with the writer. And not only the French: even the Russians allow themselves to be taken in."

Olga was beginning to feel slightly drunk. It was not the taste, now forgotten, of the wine Li had served, but intoxication at the nonchalance with which her friend conducted her life.

"I've even concocted my little theory on the subject of all these fantasies. This Mr. N who wants (mainly as a joke, but not only as a joke) to have himself photographed in the company of Tolstoy. What stopped him from shaking hands with him in real life? Minor hazards of existence. Not even his modest origins. Tolstoy used to walk about on foot just like him and lived in Moscow in the next street. It was not even his age: this Mr. N was twenty when Tolstoy died. In short, what kept them apart was the most trivial bad luck. The same that causes one passerby to slip on a banana peel and break his leg, while the one before just misses it."

"So you decided to give fate a little helping hand?"

"No. I simply wanted people who come here to learn to defy chance. To liberate themselves. Not to assume their own lives are the only possible existence. You know, I've even found a motto: Listen to this! 'Tolstoy is walking by on the opposite side of the street. . . . Cross over!' They send one another these photos for April Fools' Day. But I want them to change their lives. I want to make them live waiting for the unexpected, miracles. I want . . ."

Olga nearly asked: "But Cupid and Psyche? Isn't it rather unlikely that your clients will meet them, even if they do cross the road? . . ." She held her peace. Despite Li's playful tone, she had sensed a vibrant, tense intonation in her voice. Which is how one presents one's credo to a friend, behind a smokescreen of jokes.

At that moment Li's face appeared in the next cutout, breathing life into a lady holding a white Pomeranian on a leash. The man who accompanied her had a pince-nez fixed in the empty oval of the face by means of a very fine wire. "Cunning, no?" exclaimed the photographer with a laugh, and . . . leaving the lady with her lapdog, she thrust her head into the hole with the pince-nez. When Olga went and placed herself behind the panel with the nymph laughter overcame them. They looked at each other from the two ends of the cellar—Li as the writer with his pince-nez and Olga as the satyr leaping out of the reeds. Then the satyr confronted the lady with the lapdog; after that it was Psyche and the huge vacationer in his striped bathing suit. . . . Laughing, they stuck their heads into different panels and improvised conversations between the characters. "The satyr is walking by on the opposite bank . . . Cross over," cried Li between two outbursts of laughter.

A client arrived for a simple passport photo. And, without admitting it to themselves, they both became aware that the presence of this man, motionless in his dark suit, with his serious expression in front of the lens, was in reality no less strange, in his anonymous personal mystery, than all the nymphs, satyrs, and musketeers. . . .

When the day drew to a close, and the sun's rays steadily lengthened, a feeling stole over them that their interlude of unreflecting laughter was coming to an end. Time was turned upside down, no longer flowing from its morning source but toward that moment when they would have to get up and say their good-byes, while trying to maintain a lighthearted, cheerful tone. It was that brief moment when solitudes are revealed; when one feels disarmed, incapable of checking the flight of the impalpable, gossamer stuff of happiness. Perhaps in an effort to hold onto the gaiety of the afternoon a little longer, Li gave a demonstration of a special camera. Its mechanism was concealed in a big book, a very clever simulation, with a thick binding and a gilded top. You could hardly see the reflection of the tiny lens. . . .

"I bought it from an American officer," explained Li. "You put it on a shelf. It reacts automatically to a change of light. It takes five pictures at three-second intervals. . . ."

Olga was hardly listening to her. When Li stopped talking and they could not let the silence continue any longer, they both spoke at the same time, in a swift collision of words, looks, and gestures:

"You know, I'm leaving L.M. for good."

"You know, I'm going back to live in Russia."

Their expressions of surprise, their comments, also clashed in a disorganized exchange of questions and answers.

"In Russia? Do you really think your fantastic photos will appeal to them over there? All those satyrs . . ."

"Olga, I'm sure he still loves you. Read his last book again, it's you he's talking about . . . Why rush to break it off like that?"

"But, of course they will. It'll be a breeze. You know, Olga, under that regime they've become too serious. They need to learn to laugh again."

"But you see, when there are some little things you can't stand any longer, it feels as if it's all over. We always see each other in hotel rooms. Every time he brings me a pair of embroidered slippers, a kind of pumps made of fabric. When we part in the morning he takes them back until the next time. It's his talisman. I suppose the pumps stay hidden in a drawer in his desk . . . Do you know what I mean?"

It was only in the street, on her way to the station, that Olga had this thought: for months each of them had been preparing to announce her break with the past. The man, this L.M., that she was going to leave. The Russia that Li was going to rediscover. And when the moment had come they had announced it as one, in a confused, breathless, false exchange. As they said their good-byes they were each in a hurry to return to solitude to explore the other's sudden future—the "tragedy" pictured by Li; Russia, that white gulf that had suddenly become a possible destination. They parted and the real conversation began, in their minds, the endless discussion with the other's ghost. "That exchange of words in which we spend half our lives," Olga said to herself as she left Li's house.

The street did not liberate her as she had hoped. The two days spent in Paris were concentrated into a dull weariness, filling her head with a buzz of obsessions, ones she had returned to a thousand times during the operation. Obsessions not easily brushed aside, massive as tablets of stone, that constantly tormented her mind: her age; this hollow sham of an exhausted love, very probably her last love; the need to consider this life as the only possible one . . . And now the vertiginous nothingness of Russia, which took her breath away; she did not even know what to think of it.

In a passageway in the Metro, when changing trains, she noticed a little gathering, their heads raised toward a commemorative plaque fixed to the wall. She went up to it, read the inscription: "At this spot on August 23, 1941, Colonel Fabien shot and killed the first German. . . ." The newspaper she unfolded in the train contained an account of the second anniversary of the Liberation of Paris. One of the photos showed Molotov with a sour expression on his face, leaving the official platform as a mark of protest. "That was yesterday," she thought, "while Li was operating on me. . . ." She felt she had her finger on the very essence of life: its chaotic improbability, the farcical absurdity of all this intermingling of destinies, dates, chances. . . .

She opened her bag and took out a thick leatherbound volume, the concealed camera that, with childish curiosity, she had asked Li to lend her as they said their good-byes. The leather smelled good and the object itself was alluring; it had the compact efficiency of an intelligent machine. Above all, it reminded her of the panels in

Li's studio. The marvelous simplicity of their subjects. "One should live like those characters on the plywood," thought Olga, suddenly happy. "I make everything complicated, I can't leave well enough alone. All that rubbish about embroidered slippers! No, Li's right: two characters, one situation. She ought to paint me: a woman leaving her lover. On plywood, with broad brushstrokes, without psychology: because that's where all the trouble starts!"

This brief explosion of cheerful indignation gave her the energy to climb the staircase at the exit, to cross the square without collapsing onto the seat her eye had spotted. And even to silence the poisonous little voice that was hissing inside her head. "You're a tired old woman: you're putting up a brave front and breaking it off first so your lover doesn't kick you out." She managed to resist this voice and even to answer it back. "You bitch!" It was a young voice, coming from another period of her life, one of her former selves, that had not grown old and often irritated her with these cynical remarks. They were always woundingly accurate. "Little bitch, I'm going to have to take her apart one day . . ." she repeated, and these words kept at bay the tears of weariness that were already burning her eyelids.

In the train with its almost empty coaches the two days spent in Paris seemed to her very remote, experienced by someone other than herself. Days filled with feverish, excessive words and thoughts. A kind of flight forward, a spiral of errors that then had to be corrected by making further mistaken gestures.

Outside the window a drowsy dusk was slowly spreading. On the platforms of the little stations the sky high above was reflected in the puddles of water, mauveish gray, a wintry sky, you might have said, despite the warmth of that August evening and the dark, heavy profusion of the greenery.

The names of the villages followed one another in the agreeable procession she knew by heart: Cléanty, Saint-Albin, Buissières. From time to time the smell of a fire of fallen branches, burning at the end of a kitchen garden, came in at the lowered window, evoking a gentle life, tempting in its imagined simplicity.

It was in the midst of this deep tranquillity that her child, her son, returned to her thoughts. During those two days in Paris he had been in her at every moment, in every stirring of her soul, but protected, separated from what she was living through. Now he was there and it was he who brought this calm, in which she was slowly catching her breath as if after a long escape. . . . She pictured him already returning next day at noon: with other children of Russian émigrés, from their holiday camp. More than a specific being, she felt him within herself rather like a very physical atmosphere, made up of a myriad delicate elements, a constant vibration of these delicate elements; a throbbing of the blood that must be listened to with a deep instinctive ear, on the alert for the slightest vacillation in this equilibrium. She heard his body; his blood; his life; the silent music, one false note of which could break the rhythm. She heard it, just as, on this return journey she heard the calm of the sky, the silence of the fields. . . . She forgot Paris.

And she remembered how one day in the spring she had been cleaning the windows and he had almost broken one of them, heaving himself up onto the sill of a window that he thought was open because of its new transparency. The glass had resounded vibrantly but resisted. With a rapid movement she had pushed open the two halves of the window, and recognized in the frightened eyes of the child the reflection of her own alarm. It was as if they could hear the shattering of the glass, see a shower of sharp fragments. They knew what that meant for a child like him. "I only wanted to give you a hug . . ." he said softly and sheepishly climbed down from the window. . . .

As she walked along the platform at Villiers-la-Forêt, where night had already fallen, Olga once more heard in her temples and in her throat (she never knew where it would be hiding) that mocking, aggressive voice she called the "little bitch." The voice told her this calm would be short lived, that new, petty, persistent worries would swiftly erode the serenity of the evening, and that . . . Olga managed to shake it off by tossing her hair back, as if all the better to feel the coolness of the rain on her brow.

IT WAS ONE EVENING in September (she was preparing her infusion of hop flowers) that Olga finally realized what memory it was that the painted characters in Li's studio had called up for her. The memory of that masked ball . . .

During the war this infusion that helped her to sleep also gave her the illusion of an evening meal or, at any rate, was a substitute for tea. Later on, preparing it was transformed into an evening ritual that, through the repetition of actions that had become routine, put her troubled thoughts to rest, let her live in silent intimacy with herself. She loved this vague hour, outside the measure of time, this floating in repose. The flowers looked like tiny pinecones, their petals swelled up in the boiling water, then cooled down and sank one by one to the bottom of the little copper saucepan. Her gaze was lost in the imperceptible transmutation of the golden liquid, becoming clear again after it was decanted. . . .

That evening the voice of the "little bitch" managed to disrupt the pleasant vacuity of her thoughts. At first Olga was almost pleased to hear the latest reproaches of her persecutrix, so anodyne were the comments. "You aren't consistent even in this stupid ritual. Sometimes you drink your infusion every evening, sometimes a week passes without you remembering. You drink it when you're upset. It's just another trick, a device for banishing unhappiness. . . ." Olga offered no retort, hoping that the reproaches would stop there. But, sensing this hope, the voice started again: "Given the life you've led, and the child that you have, you ought to have become marble long ago, invulnerable to all the little hurts of existence. You ought to be a *mater dolorosa* . . . smiling, yes a faint smile of disdain, in defiance of destiny. But look at you, mere words wound you; a remark made by some old madman at the library haunts you for weeks. You mentioned the embroidered slippers to Li and now you picture them each time you put on your own slippers. . . . Mater dolorosa in embroidered slippers. You've missed your vocation!"

This time Olga retorted, "But my life is almost entirely behind me." She knew that this argument silenced the voice of the little bitch when all other reasoning proved fruitless. "Yes. I'm approaching the age when nothing really new can happen to me before my death. No miracles. A highly improbable very last fling? The kind you embark on mainly to prove you still can. Yes, I'm a mater dolorosa in embroidered slippers. . . ."

The little bitch fell silent and in that innermost recess of her mind Olga experienced something of the quiet satisfaction of a person whose superiority has perforce been recognized. At least she could now resume her long drift through the evening. Distractedly she stirred the flowers in the infusion, made ready the drinking bowl and a little strainer. "And now it has to cool . . . ," she thought, relishing the delicious idleness of those minutes.

The boy was already asleep in his room. And the calm and the purity of this sleep seemed to be deepened by the distant chiming of the clock on the church tower in Villiers-la-Forêt. She ended up by matching her thoughts to this nocturnal rhythm. All that remained in these weary thoughts was resignation. Acceptance of this two-pronged house tacked on to the length of the wall of the former brewery where the other émigrés lived, which was known as the Caravanserai. The acceptance of her life here in this little town with no special charm; a completely random place and yet predestined; the only one that would take her in after her flight from Paris, her break with Parisian émigré society, and the departure of her husband.

The only place under heaven. This house between the wall of the Caravanserai and the riverbank. She smiled: her place here below.

Holding back the gilded sediment of the flowers with a spoon, she began to pour the infusion into the bowl. She was still smiling, thinking that Li might very well paint her as an old witch mixing her magic potion. . . .

Suddenly her mind made a rapid connection: the characters on those panels, Li and . . . that masked ball! How had she failed to notice the resemblance earlier?

A good many of the guests in costume were destined to crop up thirty years later on panels created by a whimsical photographer installed in the basement of an old house in Paris. In the feverish gyrations of that carnival long ago Olga had indeed glimpsed an operatic musketeer, a queen with her tall medieval headdress, a ghost making its white garb ripple. And even, in one of the little empty rooms in that mansion, an Othello, a fat man outrageously daubed with black, and drunk, no doubt, thundering out a desperate bravura melody on a piano, while smearing the white keys with muddy fingerprints . . .

. . . The twelve-year-old girl threading her way secretly across the great estate filled with music and laughter is herself, a distant reflection of herself. The adults are too busy with their masquerade to notice her shadow slipping along the walls, avoiding the costumed whirlpools. It is with a disturbing sharpness that the girl, who has just stolen out without permission from the little estate cottage where she was supposed to spend this festive night, experiences her autonomy, her liberty, her strangeness in a world clothed in merry madness. Above all, she is aware of the singularity of these, her childhood years: her father was killed in the Russo-Japanese War; her mother has "buried herself alive" (so say the grown-ups) in a fervent isolation made up of prayers, long hours spent upon her husband's grave, and nocturnal séances with a famous spiritualist, who gives her glimpses of the features of the dear departed and is ruining her. The girl lives in her uncle's family, a man who "will sell his last shirt to throw a party." This masked ball one fine June evening marks the start of a long series of festivities, hunting parties, amateur theatricals on a stage by the entrance to the garden. . . . The girl senses that the freedom she enjoys proves something is out of control in this great mansion. She knows that in her grandmother's time they would never have allowed a child to join in a grown-up party. This casual attitude disturbs her and at the same time excites her. . . . In a drawing room she comes upon a strange figure: an adolescent girl, dressed as a magician, sitting in the angle of a little sofa, fast asleep. Her tall headdress covered in stars sits beside her; her magic wand has slipped onto the floor. The girl picks up this instrument of magic and, not knowing what to do with it, touches the magician's forehead lightly with the end of it. The magician murmurs something in a whisper but does not wake up. The magician is "a daughter of poor parents" whom they put in charge of the fireworks and magic tricks at parties. . . . The girl steals the wand and goes off to continue her exploration. In the corridors she is jostled by groups of people in costume suddenly spilling out in an explosion of shouting, a fiery rustling of silks, a clattering of heels. . . . Exhausted at last, almost sleepwalking, she comes to a kind of small drawing room with no window, a remote corner: she has never known what it was for. It is lit by one candle, around which the melted wax is already forming a little glistening pool on the varnished surface of the table. The girl stops on the threshold. Her first impression fascinates her: she sees a man, a veritable colossus, dressed like a peasant in the folktales, half lying in a broad armchair and using his hands to manipulate a big puppet he has mounted on his stomach. But the puppet begins to speak with a woman's voice, musical, strangely musical and somehow tearful. . . . Yes, it is a woman straddling the huge body of the man, who has his arms stretched out along the armrests. From time to time the woman interrupts her murmuring and her face is transformed into that of a bird of prey: she peppers the somnolent face of the man with swift, insistent, stabbing kisses. . . . All of this is quite bizarre, especially in this room where it feels as if the coughing of the grandparents' old servant can still be heard. The girl would like to touch the woman's body, a very slender, nervous body swathed in a froth of muslin. This restless body seems to grow directly out of the man's stomach. It appears as if she has no legs, just this gauze of muslin that looks as if it covered the hollow trunk of a puppet. And the fine, long cigarette she holds in one hand extended far away from their bodies gives the impression of fluttering about on its own in the darkness. . . . Suddenly the man's face lights up, he utters a noisy gasp. His hands grip the armrests. And the girl realizes that they are not armrests but the woman's legs, her long thighs clad in gleaming black stockings. The man half stretched out in the chair moves heavily, plunges his hands into the muslin, and shakes the woman with such violence that the long cigarette rolls upon the ground. His huge hands plunge into the woman's flimsy dress as if it were a puppet's empty costume. The idea of this missing body is alarming. The girl prepares to run away, takes two steps backward, and suddenly, with a noise that seems to her deafening, drops the magician's wand. The woman turns, pivoting on the man's body. . . .

Olga drank the infusion in her room. As she put the bowl on her bedside table she heard the voice of the "little bitch" once more: "You've got all the quirks of an older woman. Your bowl; soon it'll be little medicine bottles, a shrine for your declining years. . . ." But the words hurt less than usual. For now she knew the hiding place of the mocking voice: in the great mansion during a party, where a twelve-year-old girl was discovering the cavernous complexity of life. As she ran through the corridors there was, among other things, the servant she caught drinking champagne from the guests' glasses. . . .

Now her thoughts were quite confused: "It's really effective, this infusion," she had time to say to herself. "I must recommend it to Li. She stuffs herself with sleeping pills and then cries in her nightmares . . ." Sleep overcame her so quickly that her hand, stretched out toward the lamp, stopped halfway.

On Monday morning at the library there was a constant procession of readers, as if they were deliberately conferring outside the door and coming in one after the other, each to tell her their story. And indeed for a number of them, solitary and often ashamed of their solitude, the library was the only place where there was someone, she, Olga Arbyelina, to listen to them.

The first to come was the nurse from the retirement home, the "Russian retreat" located on the ground floor of the former brewery. A tall, dry woman, whose youthfulness had been overlaid by the air of arrogant and peevish mourning she had imposed on herself. She wore mourning for a person who had never existed and who had been born by chance in conversation when, to conceal her loneliness, she had hinted at a distant loved one, an English fighter pilot, about whom she could not say very much in wartime, for obvious reasons. From one admission to the next this phantom had lived his invisible life, blossoming with a multitude of details, in the heart of the woman who had invented him, adding to his exploits, being promoted. . . . His life had inevitably come to an end at the end of the war. Otherwise she would either have had to admit the lie or else transform him into a lover who was in no hurry to return to his beloved. . . . None of the Russian émigrés at Villiers-la-Forêt was taken in but in the end they became rather fond of this pilot, shot down in one of the last battles of the war. . . .

Scarcely had the door closed behind her when it opened again. A man came in looking over his shoulder and continuing his conversation with someone in the corridor. He did not break it off but simply directed his remarks at Olga as she sat behind her display shelf. This made no difference to the sense of his tale because it was always the same story, with no beginning and no end, and could be heard at any given moment. The former cavalry officer was telling the tale of his fights with the Bolsheviks. Single combat; offensives involving several divisions; ambuscades; and the wounding and deaths of horses that grieved him, it seemed, even more than those of his best friends. . . . From time to time his interminable harangue was interrupted by the hiss of a saber cutting into the flesh of an enemy. His face contracted into a savage grimace and he shouted out a brief "s-s-shlim!" and rounded his eyes at the same time, imitating the expression of a decapitated head. . . .

The readers came in, leaned their elbows on the display shelves, commented on the books they were returning, asked for advice and embarked ineluctably on their own stories. . . . Not all, however. One of them, for example, was discreet and swift. Olga called him the "doctor-just-between-ourselves" in memory of their first encounter: one day he had treated her son, but as he left he had murmured, "I should like this to remain just between ourselves. You know, practicing illegally in this country . . ."

Shortly before closing time Olga had a visit from the pretty young woman, who two years previously had married an elderly art collector, the owner of several galleries. For a woman who had spent her youth in the poverty of the Caravanserai, had worked there as a waitress in the canteen, and had the banal name of Masha, this marriage seemed like the arrival of the handsome prince, even though her husband was neither handsome nor a prince but ugly and morose. The Russians of Villiers-la-Forêt tried to turn a blind eye to that side of things, knowing how rare miracles, even imperfect ones, were in this world. . . . Masha's tale consisted of a catalog of Parisian personalities whom she had met in her husband's galleries. The all-too-visible effort she had made to memorize all their names, often classy aristocratic names, was as great as the one she was making now to refer to them with worldly indifference. It seemed clear that if she came back to Villiers-la-Forêt and to the Caravanserai from time to time, it was to relish her wonderful deliverance from such places, and from her wretched past; to stroll about among all these people, as if through a bad dream, but one from which she could awaken at any time, by going back to Paris. . . .

The director of the retirement home was the last one to come that day. She had to wait patiently for Masha to finish her list of celebrities. When the latter had finally left the room, she exhaled a noisy sigh of relief.

"Phew! And I thought it was people of our generation who

couldn't stop talking. Looking forward to old age when there's nothing else to do. . . . But you heard that chatterbox. I'm sure it would take the two of us a week to get through as much gossip as that."

The director's words turned into a whispering inside Olga's head that nagged at her all evening. "People of our generation . . . looking forward to old age. . . ." It is in such trivial conversations, thanks to a chance remark, that the truth can be laid bare and wound us mortally. Of those two women, Masha and the director, she naturally felt she was closer to the former, who was thirty-five or thirty-six. Yet here was the latter, who had long since passed fifty, hustling her along, she who was only on the brink of forty-six, toward this "looking forward to old age.". . .

In the bathroom she spent a moment studying the mirror. "In fact it's very simple," she told herself. "Hair like mine turns gray quite early. I should explain to everybody: you see, I have hair of this type but I'm not as old as my hair looks. . . ." Then she shook her head to banish the stupid vision of a woman pleading that she had unusual hair.

As she went into the kitchen she saw her infusion cooling in the little copper saucepan and suddenly experienced a gentle sense of relief that came from resignation. Yes, to resign oneself, to settle down into "looking forward to old age," with little, slightly eccentric rituals. To grind down one's former desires into tiny particles, very light, readily accessible—live these evening moments of vagueness in the soul, like the slender trickle of liquid she will shortly pour into the bowl. . . .

Olga herself did not understand what it was that suddenly rebelled in her. She acted with the zest of the very first, still unconsidered impulse. The infusion was poured down the sink, the sediment of petals gathered into a lump and tossed through the open window. She thought of Li and said to herself that it was thinking of her that had provoked her rebellion: "She's older than me (again that arithmetic: three years older!) and yet she's embarking on a crazy project. On a new life!"

She was seized with the slightly nervous gaiety of someone who would have liked to thumb her nose at sober citizens. "Li really is a hell of a woman! She sure has guts," she kept repeating, pacing up and down her room. Then she stopped, snatched up an object, rubbed it, as if to remove the dust, adjusted the little cloth on the pedestal table, tugged hard on the corners of the pillow. "That Li!" Suddenly the great leatherbound volume caught her eye. The camera! The spy camera Li had lent her, forgotten since then, had almost been transformed, through the habit of looking at it, into a quite ordinary book in the row of other books. As her fingers manipulated the nickel-plated mechanism of the fake book Olga felt them tingling with gleeful excitement. She switched out the light, put the camera on the shelf, and pressed the smooth catch on the top as her friend had instructed her. . . .

She only remembered about it three days later when her rebellion, the night she threw away the infusion, already seemed remote and futile, as is often the case with big exalted decisions taken late at night about which you feel embarrassed next morning.

That day she had to go to Paris: someone had promised to introduce her to a leading specialist in diseases of the blood who could probably . . . Thus it was, going from pillar to post via slight acquaintances, that she continued her search for the miracle doctor that parents of doomed children never despair of finding. . . . She knew she would be calling on Li and decided to take the opportunity to return her spy camera to her.

A week later she was extremely surprised to receive a little note that came with three black-and-white snapshots. "The first two didn't come out; there wasn't enough light," Li commented.

Olga spread them out on the windowsill and saw a vision of her own body that for several seconds took her breath away.

On the first photograph, in point of fact, she was not seen. The space was lit from the side and in the part that had come out you could see the cat, which generally slept in the kitchen. This time it was awake and seemed to have been caught red-handed in some mysterious nocturnal activity. Its ears were pricked up, on the alert for sounds, its eyes with pupils like razor blades were outlined against the weak light shining on it. Its whole body was tensed in preparation for a velvety, leaping escape. . . . Olga was forced to utter a little laugh in order to rid herself of the disturbing impression left, for some unknown reason, by the attentive watchfulness of the cat.

As she examined the other two photos she remembered that on the night of her exuberant rebellion, when she had set the spy camera, she had had to get up to remove her nightgown and open the window, so warm was the September night. At that moment she had completely forgotten the camera hidden on the shelf. And yet the tiny lens had been activated and with perfect discretion had taken five pictures, at three-second intervals.

On the next photo Olga saw herself from behind, seated on the edge of the bed, her arm raised, her head swathed in the turban of the unwanted nightgown. . . . On the last she was standing up in front of the French door, her body leaning forward, one hand surrounding her breasts, as if to shield them from onlookers, the other resting on the handle. The features of her face were not clear. Of her eyes the snapshot had only retained a triangle of shadow. But you felt that her gaze was filled with the airy silence of the night and that along the white curve of her arm there flowed almost palpable coolness.

This naked woman in front of the open door seemed very different from herself, a stranger to her. She could easily perceive the beauty of this body, its youthfulness, even; when she caught sight of the photo, it had taken her breath away. And something else, a singular element she could not define, a secret beyond words, the taste of which, like that of mint, froze her nostrils, made her gorge rise. . . .

All the while she was examining the photos, the voice of the "little bitch" persisted in pointing out strange inconsistencies. "Why are the first two completely blank and the third one hardly lit while the last two came out?"

"Shut up. It's probably a defect in the camera."

"And why is the door open?"

"A draft."

"And the cat?"

"Shut up. I don't want to know anything about it."

This altercation did nothing to reduce her amazement at the woman in the photos. It was only late in the evening (she heard a slight sound from the direction of the boy's room and got up rapidly, ready to come at the slightest call) that the reproaches of the little bitch again reverberated in her mind: "All these photographs are very nice but you'd do better to think about your son once in a while. . . . "

Olga did not reply. She went to the door, opened it, listened to the silence along the corridor. Their strange house consisted of this corridor with her room, the kitchen, and the bathroom at one end, and the boy's room at the other. A storeroom furnished with a tiny window was located halfway along it and served as a library. The boy called it "the book room. . . ."

Hearing nothing, she went back to bed. What could she reply to the voice hounding her with its reproaches? Tell it that on the top shelf in the "book room," inaccessible to the boy, there were a good dozen volumes devoted to his illness. And that she knew every paragraph of them by heart, all the treatments described, the tiniest details of every stage in the progress of the illness. Reply that on occasion she had nightmares in which the course of the illness was speeded up and completed in a single day. But that to think about it all the time would not have been living; it would be losing one's reason and therefore not allowing the child to live. He needed a quite stupidly normal mother, that is to say unique, constant in her affection and her calm, constant in her youthfulness. . . .

The little bitch was silent. Olga got up again (she was already regretting not having brewed up her infusion), went to the mirror, gathered up her hair in a thick tress, and began to cut it shorter with a large pair of scissors. . . . She told herself that the photographs, the tales told by readers at the library, the endless arguments with the little bitch, the anxious arithmetic of women's ages, all this torrent that filled her days, was in fact the only way to avoid spending all her time thinking about the books perched on the top shelf in the book room out of bounds to the boy. To immerse herself in this torrent was her way of letting him see her as a mother like all the others. Of seeming to herself to be a woman like the others, in order better to play the part of that mother.

Before falling asleep she repeated several times in a silent whisper, trying to sound as natural as possible, "You know, perhaps we could go to Paris tomorrow or the day after, I'd like to show you . . . No! Look, we're going to Paris: I've been told about a doctor who . . . No. Someone who's a really nice man, a leading specialist in your . . . No. In your problems . . ." Generally her mind functioned without her being aware of it. Now she became conscious of this almost automatic mental process. "So I'm thinking about him all the time," she said to herself, as if she had won a bitterly disputed victory over the voice that persecuted her.

NEXT DAY AT THE LIBRARY she was eager to be over and done with the usual preparations for the start of the day. She could not resist the ludicrous impulse to spread out the three snapshots in secret behind her display shelf and examine them once more before the arrival of the first readers. Actually to examine them here in a neutral setting that ought to allow the photographs to be seen in an impartial light. An element in her desire to do this was that obsessive fascination of particular photos that one longs to keep looking at with the dependency of a morphine addict either to confirm that their mysterious charm has not vanished or, by contrast, in the hope of discovering some new detail in them that will transform their snapshot world.

She opened two parcels of new publications, but in her impatience decided to enter them later and began to clip the French and Russian newspapers into their rods. She generally took the trouble to leaf through them, though she was sure of learning their contents from the readers' interminable commentaries. This time she merely looked at the headlines on the first few pages. THEFT OF DUCHESS OF WINDSOR'S JEWELS . . . JOSEPHINE BAKER, OFFICER IN THE RESISTANCE . . . ALGERIAN UNREST: FEVER ATTACK OR GROWING PAINS . . . TRAINS TO RUN FASTER OCTOBER 7: NEW DRIVE BY SNCF, PARIS–BORDEAUX IN 6 HOURS 10 MINUTES; PARIS–MARSEILLES IN 10 HOURS 28 MINUTES.

At last she was able to examine the three snapshots in peace. The beauty and youthfulness of the woman in the photographs fascinated her yet again. While listening alertly for footsteps outside the door, she studied this body, striving to be pitiless. But the unknown woman casting off her nightgown and in the next photograph standing in front of the window had nothing about her that betrayed a sagging, a decline. The back revealed beneath the nightgown was of an almost juvenile suppleness. And although this instant in her life was captured at random, the camera had recorded what in her own eyes distinguished her body from those of other women she had observed: ankles with very slender Achilles tendons, as if pinched between the thumb and forefinger of a giant sculptor; and also the delicacy of the collarbones, that looked as if they were too slender to support the opulence of her full, heavy breasts. One never knows, often until one's dying day, whether other people notice such features and appreciate them or judge them to be graceless.

Yet more intensely than the day before, this woman surprised in front of the dark window gave the impression of trembling on the brink of an amazing revelation. "She is totally . . . how can I put it? Unrecognizable? Other? The fact is, at that moment I was—other . . ." She tilted the snapshot to change the angle of lighting, hoping that the words she sought might suddenly emerge from its surface and capture its mystery in a formula. . . . The first readers of the day were already arriving at the door.

To begin with, a very elderly boarder from the retirement home came into the room. Generally books were brought to her by the nurse. But that morning she had had the strength to come in person, quite amazed, quite radiant, to have managed to endure the long trek from one floor to the next, and quite dazzled, too, by the brilliance of the autumn sun that was shining through the windows. One could picture the feats this little body, almost transparent in its dressing gown, must have had to perform in order to climb stairs and walk down long corridors, filled with howling drafts that smelled of cooking, the street, and river damp. She had a long struggle with the door: as it closed it almost dragged her with it, almost wrenched her arm off by the force of its spring. In the look she leveled at Olga, along with her amazement, there was a reflection, at once anxious and proud, of all the dangers overcome. . . . As Olga escorted her back to her room she was addressing her, often breathlessly. "In the springtime . . . in spring I really must show you those flowers. You see they grow almost at the foot of the trees, coming up through the dead leaves. I'm sure even the French don't know them. In the spring. We'll go together. You'll see. They're pale white. And quite beautiful!"

Going to look for these white flowers in the woods in springtime was a promise Olga had been hearing for several years now. . . .

The round of the readers resumed. The cavalry officer told the story of his best horse, the one that was trained to lie down and stand up in obedience to a prearranged whistle. Then he acted out another saber fight and did his "S-s-shlim!" impression.

Then there were the readers whom Olga privately called "the climbers." These were the ones who had managed to leave their much-maligned quarters in the old brewery and had moved into the upper part of Villiers-la-Forêt while dreaming, secretly or openly, of one day going to live in Paris.

Masha came as well and, leaning on the display shelves, she murmured confidentially, "I won't be coming again for a couple of weeks now. I'm off to Nice. With him. . . ."

The significance of "with him" was already clear to Olga: not with the husband.

Into this intermittent sequence of conversationalists slipped the former pharmacist who lived in forced idleness following the destruction of his premises by Allied bombers. Since that catastrophe he had drawn closer to the émigré community in the lower town, had even begun to learn their language and had gradually assumed the role of the Frenchman par excellence that every Frenchman adopts when living among foreigners. Unconsciously perhaps, he exaggerated certain characteristics that are considered to be typically Gallic and was delighted if the inhabitants of the Caravanserai exclaimed, in response to his racy puns or his gallantry, "Oh, these French—they're incorrigible!"

When he had left, Olga said to herself with a smile, "Whatever they may say about him, he was the only one to notice that I'd cut my hair." And she went over the pharmacist's words in her mind: "Oh Madame! What a blow you strike at our hearts. *Quel coup!* 'Cou,' of course, without the final 'p.' The curve of your neck is exquisite. I hope this is not the last of your treasures you will lay bare for us to see. . . ." She went to put away the books the pharmacist had returned and, recalling the man's gestures and performance, thought, "You know, they really are incorrigible, these Frenchmen."

The tall, peevish nurse who was constantly in mourning came at the end of the morning and asked for a recently published book in which, she said, there should be maps that would enable her to establish the exact location of her British beloved's final air battle. . . .

Olga did not notice the day passing. Or rather it passed in the stories of all the readers, drowning her in their words. "They've driven me out of my own life," she said to herself bitterly.

Only at the end of the day, after closing time, did she feel she was returning into her own life. Generally she left at eight o'clock sharp, otherwise the library turned into a debating chamber: and the readers, particularly those who lived in the Caravanserai building itself, would only leave at midnight, after drinking several cups of tea, reliving all the revolutions and all the wars in the world and telling the stories of their lives for the umpteenth time. . . . That evening she locked the door and remained sitting there for a while behind the display shelves where the returned books were piled up. The faces of the day still hovered like ghosts in the half-light of the empty room. She saw herself just as all these visitors must see her: a librarian for life, a woman abandoned by her husband who had cut herself off from her own caste, the mother of a doomed child. . . .

A slight rattling interrupted this silent colloquy. She looked up. The handle of the door was slowly turning down. For no reason the slowness of this movement was alarming. A hand shook the door several times with the same strong, sure force. After a moment of silence, a man's voice, not speaking to anyone and yet not excluding the possibility that someone might have locked themselves into the library, almost hummed, "And the bird has flown! Forgetting to switch off the light. Strange . . ." And a moment later the same voice was replying to a tardy reader, "Too late, my dear! Madame Arbyelina is punctuality itself. It is a quarter past eight. Punctuality, as you know, is the politeness of kings . . . and of princesses . . ."

Olga tried to fit this or that face she knew to the voice, then abandoned the attempt. A voice she had never heard before. She took the last book to be put away, the volume that had been covering up that patch of ink on the light wood of her desk. It was unpleasant to look at because it resembled a potbellied man; she always hid it with a sheet of paper or a book. Suddenly, like a moth fluttering out of the folds of a curtain, the three snapshots slithered to the ground. Since that morning, amid the hubbub of words, she had forgotten all about them. The blood rushed to her cheeks. "Suppose a reader had taken this book out tomorrow?" She pictured the scene, the shame, the laughter, the tittle-tattle. . . .

And when her eyes peered deeply once more into the nocturnal room where a naked woman stood beside a French door in darkness, the mystery of this moment could be approached very simply. Nobody knew the woman was there, in the middle of the night, in the coolness that arose from the river. "Just as nobody knows that I am in this empty library now, lit only by this little table lamp. I have lived a half hour of my life they will never know about." She told herself the woman in the photograph could have walked out through the French door and taken a few steps across the meadow that sloped down to the river. . . . The freedom of it was heady. A naked woman walking on the grass, on a moonless night, no longer a librarian, nor an abandoned wife, nor a certain Princess Arbyelina. . . .

On her way home she stopped from time to time and looked about her: the little houses of the lower town, the trees, the first stars seen through their branches.

Her most intense amazement was at discovering the very close presence of a life that could remain unknown to other people.

Two days after that strange evening hidden from the others she received a letter from L.M. (her "Parisian lover," as she knew the inmates of the Caravanserai called him). It was in such half-page letters that he used to invite her to Paris. The latest one differed from previous ones in its serious and, it appeared, mildly vexed tone. Reading between the lines there was a kind of reproach: I'm just back from Germany where I've been given a guided tour of hell and here you are in France, living your little operetta of a life. The tone also meant: yes, I know we haven't seen one another for several months but you have no right to judge me: my work as a journalist takes precedence over all the tender sentiments in the world.

That evening she drafted a reply. A letter that put an end to this long sequence of meetings that they had referred to, for a certain time at least, as "love." In the lines she set down, crossed out, rewrote, this word no longer occurred. And once this linchpin was removed, all that they had lived through became simply a collection of dates, tones of voice, hotel rooms, ends of the street, different silences in the night, pleasures of which only the shell of the memory remained. She tried to tell him all that. . . . The rhythm of the sentences was transferred to her body and made her walk up and down mechanically in the corridor of her narrow house. In the hall her eye lingered on the old chest of drawers. The corner of the top had been sawed in an irregular curve. It was L.M. who had done that; so that the child should not cut himself when playing, he explained. He was very proud of this service rendered. "Like all men who give practical help to a single mother," she thought. Each time, as he came in, when he visited her at Villiers, he would finger the sawed-off corner, as if checking his work, and sometimes he would even ask her, "So it's doing the job? Don't hesitate to let me know if you need any other sawing done." Now, as she walked through the hall, she told herself that she should have risked the truth and mentioned that sawed-off corner in her letter—one of the real reasons for breaking with him! But would he have understood? She could just have written about that corner and nothing else. Or perhaps this scenario as well: a man with a pale torso, stretched out in the darkness beside her, talks without stopping, now spurred on by his desire, now deflated by the lack of it. . . . The whole truth could be summed up in those two fragments.

Having completed the draft she went to the kitchen where the wood stove had gone out and her infusion was cooling. It seemed to her that her letter breaking it off marked the start of a new era. Perhaps it would indeed be one spent "looking forward to old age" as the director had said. Everything that seemed transitory, still capable of changing, would become fixed—this kitchen with the familiar blisters on the tired paintwork of the walls; this long, low brick structure, her house; and her presence in Villiers-la-Forêt, daily less surprising to her amid a cycle of seasons, almost indistinguishable from one another, as they are in France, where the summer lingers long into the fall and where the winter, without snow, is merely a continuation of the fall. Henceforth her life would be rather like this vague slippage. . . . Before going to bed (that evening the infusion had no effect on her emotional state) she darned her son's shirt. Spread out on her knees, the fabric was rapidly impregnated with the warmth of her body, of her hands. The shirt with its frayed collar already belonged visibly to this new era in her life, when nothing extraneous would any longer come between her and her child. No visits, no affairs. She would drive away any thought that would take her further from him. But he would not notice this change, any more than next morning he would notice a cluster of stitches of blue thread on the collar of his shirt. . . .

Scarcely a few days after that evening when the final letter was written and the great decision taken with intense and tender bitterness, Olga was to forget all about it. Her resolutions, her mature collectedness, her resignation—all this would be swept away by a single gesture.

In the course of a light, cool evening in the last days of summer, in a moment of great serenity, she would catch her son unawares, standing beside the little copper vessel in which she brewed her infusion of hop flowers. She would spot him poised in the brief moment of tense alertness that follows one of those actions a person is trying to keep secret at all costs. The trancelike immobility that forms a bridge between a dangerous or criminal act and the exaggerated relaxation of movements and words that follows it. What she would think she had guessed at seemed to her such an improbably monstrous action that instinctively she stepped back several paces. As if she desired to turn time backward, already sensing that a return to their old life had at that moment become impossible.

LATER ON SHE WOULD FIND herself trembling to think that at the moment when she caught sight of him, he could himself have observed her through the slightly parted curtains at the kitchen window. . . .

The sky had still been light; and the trees stood out against its transparency with the clarity of an etching. The mauve luminosity of the air gave their silhouettes an unreal appearance. From time to time Olga would pick up a dead leaf or a fragment of spar and examine them by this deceptive, translucent light. Even her fingers, as they grasped the handle of a spade, had a supernatural glow in this fluid pink. The cold, pure start to the dusk, she knew, promised a calm and limpid night. A fine night at summer's end.

She was working slowly, following the rhythm of lights and colors that grew richer with an ever darkening blue before turning purple. The dry stalks she uprooted from the bed beside the wall came up comfortably, easily, with the resignation of summer flowers that are over. From the dug earth there arose a pungent, heady smell. It was dark now, but she continued the slow ceremony of simple tasks that left the mind at rest. . . .

It was a Saturday. During the afternoon she had recopied her farewell letter to L.M. for the second time. And to avoid the temptation of starting all over again she had put it in an envelope, deciding to mail it on Monday morning. For two days, now that the deed was done, she had had a sense of living in a soothing ebb of emotions. It was just as if she were walking at low tide on an uncovered seabed, distractedly picking up a pebble here and the fragment of a shell there. . . .

It was in this blissful, distracted state that she was working now. Bent low over the earth, she finally reached a spot below the kitchen window and stood up.

Too abruptly! Giddiness overcame her and made the lit window and the curtains sway. Her body was flooded with a dull, hazy weakness. As she leaned her hand against the wall it seemed to yield gently. To check this wavering she fixed her gaze on the bright gap between the curtains. And saw a stranger, a very young man standing beside the stove . . .

She saw his gesture. With the clarity that movements and objects have when observed at night from outside a window in cold weather. An almost incredible clarity, on account of her giddiness.

The young stranger's hand hovered rapidly above the little copper saucepan. Then his fingers crumpled up a thin rectangle of paper and slipped it into his pants pocket. He moved away from the kitchen range and glanced anxiously at the door. . . .

Still reeling, she took a few steps backward. A bush rose up behind her, repelling her with its springy branches. She stopped, hearing only the dull throbbing of the blood in her temples, seeing only the strip of light between the curtains.

Sensing everything, but as yet understanding nothing, she saw scattered fragments coalescing beneath her eyelids: the fingers hovering over the hop flowers; the three photographs of the naked woman; the open door the night when they were taken; two days spent at Li's; the abortion. . . . Her eyes, swimming with the thick fog of her giddiness, were already making horrified sense of this scattered mosaic. But her mind, numbed by her blood rising, held its peace.

Little by little, however, the mists cleared, the mosaic became more and more irremediable. Its colored fragments evoked a great dark red reptile, rapidly swelling in her brain. At that moment the giddiness vanished, clarity returned. Olga had a fraction of a second to understand. . . . But the reptile swollen with blood exploded, burned the back of her neck, froze her lips in a cry. The mosaic remained shattered: three photos; the open door; herself standing, quite naked; the infusion that occasionally made her sleep for so long. It was like a word at the back of your mind, the letters and sound of which are glimpsed for an instant and disappear immediately, leaving behind only the certainty of its existence.

True, this slimy reptile, swollen with brown blood, did exist. It was this that her mind, now cleared, retained, like the proof of a moment of madness. And even the voice of the "little bitch" had fallen silent, terrified by what had just been sensed.

Now her gaze was riveted on the young stranger who was nonchalantly leafing through a notebook open on the table in the brightly lit kitchen. It was her son!

But before she could grasp how he could have grown up to this extent, the child of seven that, after so many years, he still remained for her, there occurred in her vision a kind of rapid adjustment that hurt her eyes. The face of the young man bent over the notebook and the face of the child that lived within her mind trembled at the same instant, swam toward one another, and melted into intermediate features. Halfway between one thing and the other: those of a fourteen-year-old boy.

The young man, she now understood, had appeared at the moment of her giddiness, his face and body matured by the horror of the mosaic that had revealed the unthinkable. Yes, this very young man, slim, pale with the transparent, almost invisible shadow of his first mustache, belonged to the world of the mosaic that, once thought about, was transformed into a glistening reptile, with glassy, enigmatic eyes. A world that was horrifying but could neither be thought nor spoken.

The light between the curtains went out. In the darkness, following the wall with her hand, she made her way toward the door. She caught her foot against clods of earth and uprooted stalks. She felt as if she were returning to the house after several years. . . . In the hall the patterns on the wallpaper amazed her, as if she were seeing them for the first time. She bent down and automatically performed the action she repeated almost every day. Picking up a pair of dusty shoes she thrust her hand into first one, then the other, feeling the insides. To detect the point of any nail lurking in the sole. Suddenly she lost her grip on the shoe and it fell to the ground. Her hand had slipped inside the worn leather quite easily. She realized she was still living with the memory of her fingers, that used to have to wriggle painfully into the child's narrow shoes.

She stood up and her hand retained the sensation of the shoes growing gradually broader. "Fourteen. He's fourteen. . . ," she caught herself murmuring softly. The face of the adolescent whom she had recognized as her son was very deeply embedded in her eyes. She perceived in it the invisible mutation linking the face of the child to that of the young man. Everything in his features was still malleable, everything still had the softness of childhood. . . . And yet he was a new being. And almost as tall as she! Indeed, in a few weeks he would be the same height. . . . So a whole period in her son's life must have passed unnoticed!

She put the shoes away and went out into the darkness again. "I didn't notice him growing up . . . He was an endlessly silent, discreet child. . . . An absent child. When his father left it froze him at the age he was then. And after that there was the war, those four empty years. And, above all, there was his illness: I paid more attention to a scratch than to him growing three inches. And his shy independence. And his isolation. And this benighted spot, this Villiers-la-Forêt. . . ."

The words reassured her. She prolonged their exaggeratedly reasonable flow because she did not know what she was going to be able to do when they dried up. She simply did not know. She was walking in the dark on the grassy slope that lay between their house and the river. And whispering these explanations that, she sensed, would never express the essence of the bond between them, her and her child. The branch of a willow tree suddenly checked her. A branch that stroked her cheek with a caress that felt alive. Olga stopped. There was the willow with its silent cascade of branches. In their net a few stars. The reflection of the moon in the hollow of a footprint filled with water. The fresh, nocturnal scent of the reeds, asleep at the water's edge, the scent of the wet clay . . .

"Suppose I stayed here? Not to return, not to go back into the life of that house. . . . To walk endlessly on this silvery grass. . . ." But her footsteps were already leading her back toward the door. As she climbed the little wooden steps she pictured again the strip of freshly dug earth along the wall where she had been gardening scarcely an hour earlier. That time now seemed remote to her and filled with a paradisiacal happiness and simplicity.

In the hall, hooked onto the coatrack, hung her son's jacket, one of its sleeves screwed up comically short. Olga gave it a rapid tug, as if discreetly to correct a blunder. No gesture could have been more innocent. . . .

She pressed the switch and put her hand to her mouth to stifle a gasp, so reduced in size did the interior of the kitchen seem to her. The figure of the young man, even when invisible, imposed itself on the walls and the furniture, shrinking them, as in those bad dreams where you are propelled into a familiar apartment, which contracts as you watch and ends up like a little house for the figures on a music box. . . . Indeed, halting in the middle of the kitchen she felt as if she were examining the inside of a dolls' house, whose smallness, at once enchanting and unnatural, was obscurely menacing. Even the little saucepan on the range looked smaller than before and at last revealed its true shape—slightly bell-shaped, potbellied.

Olga knew that she would shortly strain off the infusion's brownish liquid and throw away the sediment of the flowers. She turned on the tap, preparing to wash her hands, but at that moment her eye lit upon the orange crayon that had been slipped as a bookmark into the notebook left on the table by mistake. She took it out, and studied the color. "No action could be more innocent," she repeated in a whispered echo. And swiftly, without her being able to offer the least resistance, the fragments of the mosaic, seen when she had her attack of giddiness, began to come together: a nervous hand hovering over the range; the cat in the first snapshot watching a woman asleep; the open door through which the animal had slipped in; the young man who from now on would be living under the same roof as she. . . . She felt a great mass of slimy, lumpy skin swelling in her head. The reptile . . . The mosaic coalesced more and more quickly: the hand above the infusion; her deathlike sleep on certain days; the child who was as tall as she was; the orange crayon. . . . One more round and these fragments were going to become fixed in an inescapable certainty.

She glanced at the range. The flowers that had been steeped for too long, had turned brown: under a shallow layer of liquid they resembled the damp skin of a hunched beast, the same one that, grotesquely bloated, was tearing at her brain. The mosaic began its round again: the hand; the young man near the range; the sleep. . . .

Olga seized the little vessel and with a febrile gesture poured the infusion into the big bowl and gulped it down. . . . The mosaic vanished. The reptile in her brain died noiselessly, thrusting a multitude of red needles under her eyelids. The kitchen resumed its normal dimensions. She felt pathetically relieved, as if she had just convinced a skeptical interlocutor.

Walking along the corridor, she noticed a light inside the book room. A lamp on a narrow table squeezed between the sets of shelves had been left switched on. Her eye was caught by an engraving on the page of a large old book that had been left open. It was one of the volumes of the zoological encyclopedia her son liked to leaf through. She leaned over the engraving and read the caption: "A boa constrictor attacking an antelope." The engraving, punctilious in its realism, had an unexpected effect, like all excesses of zeal. For even though the smallest tufts of hair on the antelope's spotted hide were visible, its whole aspect was evocative of a vaguely human form: the expression of the eyes, the position of the body surrounded by the coils of the gigantic snake. As for the boa constrictor: its muscular body, covered in arabesques and prodigiously thick, resembled the broad thigh of a woman, a rounded leg, indecently plump and clad in a stocking ornamented with patterns. . . .

She sat down to study it better. The engraving amused her: the boy certainly did not suspect this double vision of boa-woman. It was reassuring. So she was wrong to have been so alarmed just now. As long as all he saw was this huge, gaudy snake . . .

As she looked at it the picture began to sway slowly. The tiredness was pleasant, soft, as it touched her eyes. She wanted to lower her lids, to go on enjoying these peaceful moments. Her eyes were already closing of their own accord. Still believing it was no more than the lassitude of evening, she tried to shake herself but only succeeded in provoking this last thought: "I must get up; my hands are still covered in earth, I shall make the book dirty. . . ."

Sleep rapidly overcame her with calm, irresistible violence, mingling with the pleasant, delicate aroma of the old pages. Pages you smell with closed eyes, inhaling deeply.

IT WAS THE LAST FEW KNOCKS on the front door that woke her. That type of insistent hammering into which people annoyed by waiting weave a kind of drumming melody, in the hope that the variations in the rhythm will attract attention.

She leaped up from the chair, trying to make sense of her immediate surroundings: the dazzling sun at the tiny window; the clock with its hands in an odd position, showing almost eleven o'clock; and above all, herself, this woman in a crumpled dress, her hands covered in streaks of earth, a woman turning around in a tiny storeroom, knocking books over and unable to find a mirror. . . .

The hammering rose to a climax with the measures of a military drum roll and fell silent. Olga went out into the corridor then came back and, without really knowing why, closed the volume of the encyclopedia.

"What if they've guessed?" she asked herself in perplexity. "But guessed what?" The absurd notion occurred to her that the others might discover she had concealed her son's age from them. The senseless fear crossed her still drowsy mind that they would suddenly notice the boy was no longer a child, but an adolescent, almost as tall as she. . . .

In front of the mirror in the hall she quickly straightened her dress, tidied her hair, and seemed to recover the use of her features. Nevertheless, as she opened the door she was expecting, in spite of herself, to see a whole cluster of faces animated by malevolent and mocking curiosity.

The door opened on the luminous void of the sky. There was nobody on the steps; the meadow that sloped down to the river sparkled with drops of melted frost, and was also deserted. The sunny freshness of the air cleansed the lungs, penetrated the body. If only it could be possible! To have this morning as it was, but free of all the rest: the voices in her head contradicting one another from one moment to the next; other people's stares emptying her out of herself; numberless fears, above all, those of the previous evening. . . .

Her hope did not last longer than the deep breath she took, inhaling the scent of the frozen grass. . . . Then her gaze slipped along the wall and she saw a woman leaning on the windowsill, trying to look inside. Fear returned to her so abruptly that it gave rise to an improbable idea: "But that's me! Yesterday. . . ." In a veritable flash of madness, Olga saw the woman leaning toward the window as herself. But at once another thought, less fantastic and still more distressing, banished the resemblance: "She's spying on me!"

The woman began tapping on the window with a bent forefinger, shading her eyes with the other hand to avoid the reflection. . . .

Olga called to her. The woman straightened up: it was the nurse from the retirement home. "Something's happened to the child." This panic, like a squall of wind, raised a maelstrom of further anxious reflexes: "If something's happened to him it's my fault, it's because of that moment of bliss there on the steps . . ." They were not even thoughts but a sequence of images—the flow of blood that would have to be stanched on the child's body; and the blame she would have to take upon herself in order to pacify fate.

The nurse came up to her and greeted her mournfully and coldly. "No, it's something else, otherwise she would have spoken straight away," thought Olga. She had seen these bringers of bad tidings arriving so many times. . . .

At that moment she sensed an inquisitive stare on the part of the nurse. The latter must have noticed the residue of sleep on her face, the traces of earth on her hands. Olga clenched her fists, hid them behind her back, and with a nod invited the nurse to come in. In the corridor her anxiety increased. The nurse stopped, her hand resting on the chest of drawers, precisely at the spot where the dangerous corner had been sawed off. "She has guessed something," Olga thought again, and shook herself immediately: "Idiot! What is there to guess in this hovel?"

"I hope you'll have a cup of tea with me?"

Olga's voice sounded like a line from a role too well learned.

In the kitchen she saw the little copper saucepan and on the table the orange crayon. The nurse followed her look. She felt the visitor had not taken her eyes off her once and experienced an improper desire to call her to order: "All this is none of your business!"

"No tea, thank you, I don't have time. I've come to tell you . . . to tell you that last night . . . Xenia Yefimovna . . ."

Xenia, the elderly boarder who for years had been promising Olga to show her the famous "white flowers" that nobody knew about, had just died. . . . And now someone must go to Paris, the nurse said, to see her son and her daughter-in-law and let them know. In her role as the Princess Arbyelina, Olga had already carried out such delicate missions on several occasions.

"I know it's Sunday today," apologized the young woman. "It will spoil your whole day. I know . . . But no one but you could find the right words . . ."

Listening to her, Olga tasted the delicious simplicity of life. The wholesome, robust common sense of life, in which death, too, has its place.

In the train it was the memory of the white flowers beneath the trees in a fantasy woodland that saved her from the thought that suddenly assailed her: "Supposing I had waked up of my own accord this morning after that abnormally long sleep."

She understood that with all her strength she must hang on to the clear, dull appearances of life.

In Paris she carried out her mission with a kind of fervor. On this occasion the solemn murmuring of condolences, the son's contrite expression, his wife's sighs had the value of a proof. Yes, the interlude they were all three of them applying themselves to acting out demonstrated that in other people's eyes she remained uniquely the "Princess Arbyelina." And that no one had any inkling of the existence within her of the woman who, only the previous evening, rooted to the spot under the window of her own house, had been observing the actions of an adolescent boy. . . .

Another proof was the street. Olga walked through the crowd scrutinizing the expressions on people's faces, like someone on her first outing after an operation, trying to guess from the looks of the passersby if the aftereffects are visible or not.

She also called on Li. That Sunday her friend was painting. The features of a pair of characters were already emerging on a plywood panel: a woman in a white dress, with bare shoulders, and a man slightly shorter than she, with curly hair framing the round hole for his face. . . .

"By the way, I meant to ask you." Olga's voice was tinged with careful nonchalance. "That infusion I recommended to you, does it have any effect on your insomnia?"

"Oh yes! It certainly does. . . ."

Li replied in the same absentminded tone without lifting her brush from the surface of the painting. . . .

During the return journey, it seemed to Olga as if all the passengers had their newspapers open at the same page. She glanced at the one her neighbor was reading. It was the same twelve portraits that fascinated them all. NUREMBERG TRIBUNAL: THE VERDICT ran the headline above the photos. The condemned men had their eyes shut: their portraits were there as evidence of their deaths. At the bottom of the page an American soldier could be seen demonstrating the noose that was used in the executions. The thickness of the rope, very white, even beautiful, seemed out of proportion. It looked like the rigging of a ship or a long roll of dough for some gigantic pretzel. . . . Olga's neighbor got off the train, leaving his newspaper on the seat. She glanced at the article. Two columns of figures in a box indicated the precise time at which the hanging of each of the condemned men had started and the time death had occurred. "In other words, the amount of time they were struggling in that pretzel," thought Olga.

The numbers reminded her of the boring, enigmatic figures showing stock market prices.

	Trap Opened At:	*Pronounced Dead At:*
Ribbentrop	1:14 P.M.	1:32 P.M.
Keitel	1:20 P.M.	1:34 P.M.
Rosenberg	1:49 P.M.	1:59 P.M.

She looked up. The passengers were discussing the story as they read it, calling out comments to one another from one seat to the next, pointing their fingers at this or that part of the report. "No, not the stock market prices," Olga said to herself, watching this animation. "More like the results of a game." On her right a man reminiscent of a poorly acted father in a character comedy was leaning toward the person across from him, undoubtedly his wife, and reading the report of the trial aloud to her. For her part the woman seemed visibly embarrassed by her husband's overexcited declamation. She sat very upright, her handbag on her knees, looking down onto the bowed head of the man as he read, raising her eyebrows from time to time, sighing and lifting her eyes heavenward. Her husband failed to notice these condescending little grimaces, and kept wagging his finger to lend emphasis to his reading:

"'They all died with dignity'—Dignity! Who are they kidding?—'apart from Streicher, who shouted abuse at those present. . . . Only Hermann Goering succeeded in escaping the shame of the gallows. . . . Emmy Sonnemann, Frau Goering, kissed her husband through the mesh of the grill and transferred the vial of potassium cyanide from her mouth to his . . .' Look, there's a picture of the vial. . . ."

The little station at Villiers-la-Forêt was deserted. The arrival and departure times on the timetable board reminded her with cruel grotesqueness of the figures in the box about the hangings. She crossed the square, which was surrounded by plane trees, and turned toward the lower town. The vibration of the rails hung for a moment in the silence of the evening. . . .

The day she had just lived through was overflowing with complete madness. A madness that was nevertheless reassuring because everyone accepted it as life. You had to do as they did. To be happy, as she had been that morning, playing the role of the Princess Arbyelina offering her condolences. To tolerate those passengers who got a thrill from the vial passing through the mesh in a prison visiting room during a long, wet kiss. For months they had been learning in their newspapers about the countless millions of people killed, burned alive, gassed. And now all History had boiled down to a woman pushing a tiny vial between a man's lips with her tongue. . . .

She went home almost serene. As she climbed up the little wooden steps she managed to look at the flower bed beside the wall with no special emotion. . . .

That same evening, however, an apparently inoffensive detail upset her equilibrium. . . . She was combing her hair in front of the mirror in her room. The smooth action of the comb was pleasantly emptying her mind. And as she gazed, lulled by her own reflection, she saw the door shudder softly and stop halfway. This silent half-opening caused by a gust of air from an open window created a strange expectation. Olga remembered that night when a draft had awoken her as it made her bedroom door creak, yes, it was the night of the three snapshots taken by the book-camera. For as long as she could recall, that door had always creaked slightly (in any house there is always one knife that cuts better than the others and one chair that you avoid giving to guests). But this time the door had opened noiselessly. . . . Olga put down the comb and, with a keen sense of wantonly committing a dangerous act, she went out into the corridor, pulled the handle toward her, then pushed the door open again. It swung through its arc and came to rest against the little doorstop nailed to the floor. In silence. Without emitting the slightest creak. Olga became aware of an icy tension in her temples, as if her hair were stuffed with snow. She repeated the action. The door swung, opened wide. Without a murmur. Olga had the feeling that all this was happening outside her normal life. In one of life's strange back rooms. She bent down and touched the lower hinge, then the hinge at the top. In the glow of the lamp her fingers glistened. The oil was clear, almost without any trace of grease. Recent . . . The snow in her hair seemed to melt into a ferment of little burning sparks. She pushed against the door one more time with a slow, sleepwalker's action. Her eyes fixed on the hinges, holding her breath, she waited for an interminable second. The door swung smoothly, neatly shrinking its shadow on the wall, like a hand reducing its angle on a clock face. . . . Just before it touched the doorstop it emitted a brief groan. Olga leaned her hand against the wall and sat down on a little low stool in the corridor. She was breathing jerkily. Her bedroom beyond the open door had an unfamiliar look. It was like a hotel room, whose interior can be pictured in advance, but which, despite this, seems alien. The bed, the lamp on a shelf, the wardrobe with a mirror . . . She herself, seated outside the threshold, seemed on the point of leaving again. It took a muscular effort to banish the tense smile from her face—the delight at having rejected, or at least delayed, the final conclusion. . . .

That evening she did not dare touch the door handle again and slept with the door wide open.

SHE SPENT THE DAYS that followed belatedly entering books in the catalog. And this mechanical work matched the tidying up that was gradually taking place in her mind. Even the daily routine of clipping together the newspapers, which had always been a burden to her, helped in coming to terms with life. She now found herself quickly reading through complete passages from one article or another. She enjoyed the sheer absurdity of them, which seemed to her the best possible proof that nothing could upset the common sense of human routine. . . .

"The Führer pretended to have a fit of hysterics every time anyone opposed him . . ." Interrupted by a visitor, she did not immediately find her place again in the text where she had broken off. Her eyes strayed over the neighboring columns. The complaint of the Parisian woman who in "Letters to the Editor" expressed indignation that "the plaques indicating street names are hidden by café awnings." Then a feature about a young actress: "Educated at the Des Oiseaux convent, she is currently appearing in *Antoine and Antoinette*. . . ." Locating the earlier article again, she discovered that it was the last confessions of Ribbentrop: "I cannot understand it. Hitler was a vegetarian. He could not bear to eat the flesh of a dead animal. He called us *Leichefresser*, 'corpse eaters.' When I went hunting I even had to do it in secret because he disapproved of the sport. So how could such a man have ordered mass murders?". . . The following page was devoted to a big diagram of a "plutonium bomb," with almost lip-smacking explanations of its murderous power. Before the next reader arrived Olga also had time to notice the photo of a young musician with a gleaming permanent wave. The caption read: "Romano Mussolini is a fine guitar player. The Duce's son is a young man who has forgotten all about the past and would like the whole world to do the same."...

The readers came in and deposited their books on the display shelves: this action served as a pretext for embarking on conversations. The former cavalry officer blamed the Americans for "letting Goering get away." Masha gave a whispered account of her secret trip to Nice, glancing repeatedly toward the door with exaggerated alarm. They all took the librarian's smile to be a sign of interest, but Olga was unaware that she was smiling as she responded inwardly to the deep echoes of her own thoughts. "I always thought wisdom consisted of pointing a finger at all the madness that escaped other people's attention. And it turns out that quite the opposite is true. You are wise if in some way you can turn a blind eye. If you don't eat your heart out tilting at this daily folly. If you can live with the reassuring falseness of words: war; criminals; triumph of justice; this innocent young guitarist who has forgotten the past; oh, and Masha, who doesn't care a hoot for the past because she has a beautiful body that gives and takes pleasure. . . ."

Abruptly she surfaced from her thoughts. In front of the display shelves the director of the old people's home was talking about Xenia's funeral the next morning. "Well you know, Olga my dear, at our age (you're much younger than me, of course) one can't help wondering: Will I be the next to go?"...

During these days of tidying up she also managed to explain how her son's sudden maturing had passed her by unnoticed. The excuse of the war took on an arithmetical simplicity: '39–'45, six years. Six years of strange survival when everything that could protect her child had disappeared. Medicines, food, the increasingly grudging sympathy of other people . . . One particular memory came back insistently: returning from the market one bleak day chilled with rain. A dreary market, deserted, where a hunter had sold her—at an unbelievably high price, like all food at that time—a bird with speckled plumage and a beak stained with dried blood. Wrapped in a piece of paper, the bird seemed still warm, despite the fall wind. Its body was supple, almost fluid, on account of the very smooth feathers and the paucity of the flesh that lay beneath them. . . . At one moment on the road Olga had to scramble onto the roadside to avoid the mud splashing up from the wheels of a convoy of army trucks. The strident laughter of a harmonica lashed her ears. She continued on her way under the low sky, in the rain. The body of the bird that had grown warm in the hollow of her hand was the only particle of life surviving in this universe of mud and cold. . . . She had enough time to prepare the meal before the child, lying with his leg in a plaster cast, should ask her to show him the bird. . . .

Yes, the whole of the war came down to that return from the market, to her fear lest the child should see the beautiful bird transformed into a piece of food. . . . He had been seven years old when they left Paris and came to Villiers-la-Forêt in the spring of 1939. Seven years plus six more, lost in the war. Plus this year, '46, that would soon be finished. Fourteen.

In any case, the émigrés, especially those living at the Caravanserai, inhabited a very singular time. A time made up of their Russian past, from which they emerged sometimes, into the midst of French life, distraught, clumsy, and continuing, as soliloquies, conversations begun in their former lives. They were all stuck at the age of their last years in Russia. And nobody was surprised to see a man with gray hair leaping about like a little boy as he acted out saber fights, fiery cavalry charges, and decapitations. . . .

Thinking one day about the child who had not changed in her mind over so many years, she pictured him dressed up as a young sentry. . . . Some time before their separation her husband had taught the child to stand guard in the hall of their apartment in Paris. The child put on a tunic she had made for him out of her husband's old uniform, took his wooden rifle, and stood solemnly at attention, rooted to the spot, listening for the sound of footsteps on the staircase. After their split and his father's departure, he had continued to mount guard for several weeks. She would see his little silhouette, motionless in the dark hall, and longed to explain everything to him, but her courage failed her: his father had supposedly gone away on a long trip, a very long one. The child had guessed for himself and had abandoned his guard duties. As if he had perceived his mother's unease and wanted to protect her from any further pain . . .

For her, since then, he had always been that silent child on secret and desperate sentry duty.

On the day of Xenia's funeral everyone in the little Russian church at Villiers-la-Forêt made a surprising discovery, apparently banal, but all the more striking for that: people at the Caravanserai died just like everywhere else, they grew up and became old there—and a whole generation of Russians had been born on this foreign soil, all these young people who had never seen Russia. Like Princess Arbyelina's son, for example, standing there behind a pillar, staring curiously at an icon turned brown by the candle flames. . . .

Olga listened, without really hearing, to the voice of the priest and the vibrant resonance of the choir and was amazed at the triviality of the thoughts that such a solemn moment could not banish. Again she recalled Xenia's dream: of going to pick the mysterious white flowers in the woods behind the Caravanserai in springtime. "But what is left of that dream now?" The question seemed stupid. And yet Olga sensed that by replying "Nothing!" she would have betrayed someone who was listening to her thoughts. She saw the outline of Xenia's pale face in the midst of the white ornamentation of the coffin. And this question whose naïveté had irritated her—"What will be left of the woods in spring?"—suddenly touched the very essence of her life; of the lives of all these people, who were so different, packed together beneath the low vault of the church; of the life of this blue fall day, whose sky could be glimpsed when a latecomer timidly opened the door. . . .

At that moment she saw her son half hidden by a pillar. The sight of this young adolescent mingling with the others, detached from her, independent and lost in his own thoughts, caused such radiant and poignant tenderness to well up in her that she had to close her eyes.

That same evening, as night was falling, Olga noticed underneath the kitchen sideboard an orange crayon that had rolled into a narrow and dusty corner, out of reach of the coming and going of the dustmop. . . .

The infusion of hop flowers was cooling in its little copper saucepan. As before . . . The hour was striking in the distance, but the trees around the Caravanserai, now bare, had lost their musical resonance. While she was waiting Olga was cleaning the floor: coming into a spruce kitchen in the morning would make it easier to begin her day, she thought. However, she was also angry with herself over all these little weaknesses that were destined to fill her days from now on.

She saw the crayon without immediately noticing its color. Her hand patted the dust a couple of inches away from its hiding place but could not reach it. She crouched down even lower, her face almost on the ground, her arm outstretched, her shoulder pressed against the corner of the sideboard. Some kind of superstitious whim impelled her on this quest. . . . Several broad swings of the floor cloth finally swept out the crayon. It rolled across the floor with a thin rattling sound. It was the crayon she had seen slipped into her son's notebook. An orange crayon. She removed the dust from it, washed her hands. And suddenly the gleaming color blinded her. "But it's the same as . . . ," she murmured, and in a trice she was walking down the corridor and pushing open the door into the book room.

She climbed onto a chair and took down several volumes at random from the farthest corner of the bookshelf. Opened one, then another. Here a paragraph was marked with a vertical line, there a sentence with a horizontal line, almost on every page. They were medical books dealing with diseases of the blood. Her son's illness in particular.

She had always thought the lines on it, drawn with heavy pressure, were the result of her husband's readings. She had often pictured him thus: a man with his brow furrowed by grief, his eyes raw, scanning these paragraphs for reasons to hope. She had forgiven him a good deal, almost everything, because of those pages marked with orange. . . . The last two books on that shelf had been purchased after they split up. Standing on tiptoe she managed to grasp them. The pages fluttered in a hasty fan beneath her hands. They, too, carried the marks of the orange crayon.

The contents of these two books were well known to her, down to the very chapter divisions, and in one of them down to the transparent mark on page 42, which looked like melted candle grease. She was not reading but hearing the intonation of her own voice that had silently pronounced every one of these words so many times, hoping to come upon an encouraging prognosis, a new treatment. . . . And now she could feel her son's eyes resting on these pages. She looked up, still incredulous, and murmured: "So he knows all this . . ." Then looked again at the sentences he had underlined.

"A hemophiliac should work in an office and should not undertake heavy manual work. . . ."

"Ninety per cent of hemophiliacs do not reach the age of twenty. . . ."

"Transmission can skip one or two generations. . . ."

"One of the hemophiliacs followed up by Professor Lacombe had developed ankylosis of all four knee and elbow joints, to the extent of being effectively incapacitated. . . ."

"Without repeated transfusions these losses of blood would have caused death. . . ."

"He attended a different department where he was not transfused and died of a hemorrhage. . . ."

"Injection of calcium chloride causes no problems whatever in man, though intravenous injection of as little as 50 cg of this salt may be enough to kill off a large dog within a few seconds. . . ."

"Following the taking of an ordinary blood sample a hematoma developed, extending from the shoulder to the middle of the forearm. . . ."

"Sufferers must be forbidden to marry. . . ."

"According to Carrière, 45 percent of hemophiliacs die before reaching the age of four, and only 11 percent reach the age of twenty. . . ."

"In the night the patient several times vomited black blood. . . ."

On one of the pages a big mark had been made, still in orange crayon, against a strange genealogical tree: the hereditary and familial antecedents of a hemophiliac. Olga knew this anonymous family like her own, with which she had often compared it.

Her eyes took in at a glance the lines of relationship which resembled vessels that transmitted the diseased blood:

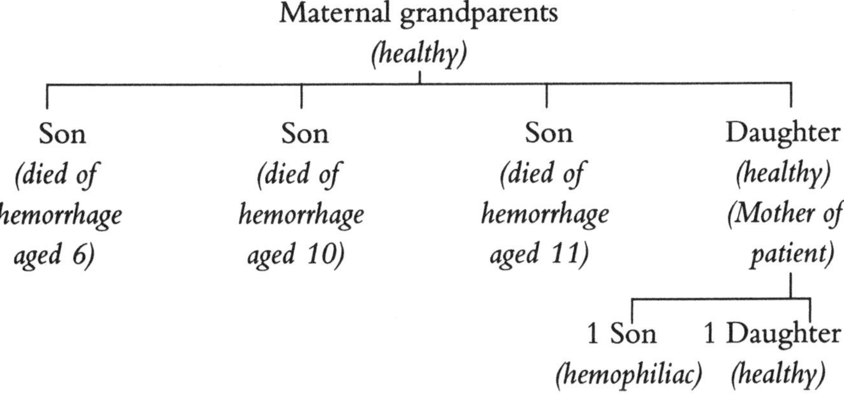

She looked up above the lamp and felt as if she were meeting a young, calm gaze with no illusions. "So he knew everything. He knows everything," she repeated. The eyes seemed to signify acquiescence with a slight flutter of the eyelids.

If she had not guessed the secret of these markings with the orange crayon, she would certainly have passed a remark the following evening when she once again surprised this delicate and very young man, who moved like a dancer, wheeling about near the kitchen range.

The stranger's actions repeated the scene she had observed before as precisely as a hallucination: a rapid quivering of his hand above the copper vessel; an about-turn toward the table, toward the notebook, his alibi; a moment of stillness, the exaggerated nonchalance with which his fingers turned the pages. . . .

Yes, when she noticed these fluttering movements through the half open bathroom door she would have interrupted him with a cry of reproach, a remonstration. . . . Or rather with some trivial comment to spare him the shame.

But now she remained silent. And yet the similarity with that September evening, the evening when she was gardening, was total. Save for one nuance, perhaps: this time it took her only a second to recognize the young stranger as her son. No more than a second, the time it took to suppress the cry that rose to her lips, to transform it into anodyne words and then, finally, into silence. But this time, above all, there was no longer any doubt.

LATER ON SHE WOULD REALIZE that the cry had stuck in her throat because of one memory in particular. . . .

It was two years ago. The last spring under the Occupation. Through the open kitchen window she sees her son running toward the house. All that she sees is his hand pressed to his chest. He has been swimming and has collided with one of the timbers of the old landing stage. . . . He bolts into his room. She goes in, makes him show her what he was trying to hide. "It's nothing serious, honestly." His childish voice is desperately calm. But he lifts his hand. On his chest, above his heart, there is a bruise, turning into a purple swelling, then a whole pouch of blood, almost before her eyes. This hematoma is reminiscent of a woman's breast, smooth, black. She senses that in a confused way the boy is embarrassed by this similarity. . . . During the healing process she recalls the advice given by one of the books that sit on the top shelf in the book room. The parents of a hemophiliac child must, says the author, "win his trust," let him understand that he is "no different from his schoolmates"; they must know how to "disarm fear" with a friendly tone of voice. . . . She tries talking to her son in these borrowed tones that have always been alien to them both. Politely, he remains silent, avoids her eye. With each fresh word she feels she is floundering deeper into a lie it will be difficult to put behind them. In order to break away from the falseness of this dialogue invented for an abstract parent and child, she wills herself to a more confident tone. "So, were you scared? I've written to your father, you know . . ." He leaps up and rushes out. Ten minutes later a resident of the Caravanserai arrives all out of breath to alert her. They run toward the ruined bridge. Her son, a slim elongated figure, is stepping out, like a tightrope walker, along a steel girder that overhangs the river. A heterogeneous little crowd is following his shaky progress. Olga stops, her gaze hypnotized by the swaying of this body as it makes its way above the void. The cry freezes on her lips. He is a sleepwalker whose tread is supported by the held breaths of everyone else. . . . Reaching the end of the girder he turns round, teeters, waves his arms, clinging at the air that solidifies beneath the petrified gaze of the onlookers, stands up straight again, returns to his starting point, comes down. . . . They return home without exchanging a word. It is only when the door has closed behind them that he says very softly, "I'm not scared of anything." She does not listen to him. She is watching the tiny red trickle snaking between the beauty spots on his forearm, slender and speckled with rust. A quite fresh little scratch that she will compress, recognizing beneath her fingers the unique consistency of his blood.

It was seeing that sleepwalker above the void, in a flash of memory, that made her repress her cry. . . .

That evening she could not help understanding. It was all too evident: the copper vessel; a hand hovering over it with the tingling precision of a criminal act, shaking a little rectangle of paper over the brown liquid; his shadow, already moving away from the range, pivoting and taking refuge in a deliberately neutral pose.

She closed the bathroom door. A second later rapid footsteps went along the corridor. She caught sight of her own face in the slightly misted mirror. What struck her about this oval framed with wet braids was the unrecognizable expression of frightened youthfulness. But it was the ease of her whole body that was particularly distressing; the fine tone of each of her muscles beneath the fabric of the dressing gown. It was almost with terror that she sensed the supple weight of her breasts, the moist warmth of her skin. . . .

In the kitchen she drank the infusion in a few drafts, pausing only to remove the petals that stuck to her tongue. . . . Then, settled in the book room, she began to wait, like one condemned, for sleep to come flooding over her. The tension only lasted for a few minutes, in fact. A very natural thought, but natural to insanity, made her tremble. "But . . . before going to sleep, I absolutely must . . . if not . . ." She saw her hands clenched on the table in an unaccustomed rigidity, as if they did not belong to her. In the middle of that narrow space her glance hovered against the tight rows of books, against the window layered with opaque darkness. Yes, before she gave way she must at all costs understand how what was happening to her had become possible. The young man with black hair, his features refined by long, secret suffering; the hands that hovered over the kitchen range . . . Her mind gave way without her being able to put a name to what that action signified for her and for him. Again she saw the plump reptile swollen with blood. She urgently needed to understand how this creature could have invaded her life, their lives. Already she felt the first waves of sleep clouding her vision. She must understand. Otherwise waking up again would be unthinkable. Waking up to what life? How could it be lived? How could she live alongside this mysterious being who had just walked down the corridor with furtive steps? During these last minutes of wakefulness she must find the guilty party. Identify the person, the action, the day that had warped the normal course of things.

She was no longer capable of thinking or remembering. The past assaulted her eyes, her face, with brief clusters of lights and sounds. . . .

A man, handsome, and with a giant's frame, getting into a taxi. The guilty one. Her husband . . . Before slipping into the vehicle he turned and, guessing with ruthless accuracy the window from which she was secretly watching his departure, gave her a military salute as a clownish gesture of good-bye. And in the days that followed, a child dressed up as a soldier stood at attention in the hall of that Parisian apartment, listening for the familiar footsteps on the stairs. . . .

She did not even have time to grasp how the departure of this man and his mocking salute were connected with the terrifying night she was living through. Already another fragment from an even more distant past was surging up. A man who thought he was dying struggled to master the trembling of his cracked lips and confess his crime to her; he had escaped execution (the hydra of the counter-revolution, he whispered) by thrusting a comrade to his death. . . . Yet this deathbed penitent was the same character as the one who only months after that confession would be directing his ironic military salute at the woman hidden behind the curtains. And the same who in earlier times leaned with all his weight on a roulette table in a room where the smell of cigars mingled with that of the sea at night. The same, only a little younger, who wore an officer's uniform, four St. George's Crosses on his heart, and listened with a solemn and bitter air to the singing at the Russian church in Paris, clutching a candle too slender for his powerful fingers. The same who . . .

Other masks slipped onto the face of the officer listening to the funeral service. They came around again more and more rapidly. The man saluted the woman behind the curtains, settled onto the seat in the taxi, and closed his eyes, letting his head tilt gently backward, following the motion of the vehicle. . . . No, it is no longer he but the dying man, his head tilting back as he slumps onto the pillows with a mournful groan. . . . No, it is the man at the casino, emitting a guttural laugh, his head flung back, his fingers clutching the last bill left to him. . . . These same fingers knead the wax of a candle, for it is now the officer, tilting his head back to contain the tears in his eyes that are like two brimming lakes. . . .

Olga tore herself violently away from these memories; the sequence of these metamorphoses was already becoming lost in sleep. "Both of us are guilty," she heard herself whispering. Once again, no thought could explain when, how, or by what error she had ended up surprising that young adolescent as he pranced nervously beside the kitchen range. And then, quite simply, those words, "both of us," suddenly brought back to her the sour smell that lingered on the ground floor of an apartment building in Paris and floated heavily upward as far as their apartment on the third floor: a pungent smell, suggestive of pieces of fish vitrified in the fierce hissing of rancid oil. . . . They are returning from the hospital. The child has finally been able to get up and take several steps, with outstretched arms to give him better balance. They have promised to go back the next day. . . . On the staircase there is this smell. "It's always going to be like this," they each tell themselves inwardly. Each suspects the other of thinking the same. The apartment door has hardly closed before the argument erupts. "A wasted life," "cowardice," "patience," "after so many years," "melodramatic," "for the sake of the child," "you're free," "death." The words, too familiar to wound, are marked this time by their tone of finality. If only their weary fury could be interrupted by a single second of truth they would have to tell one another: we are at each other's throats because of the foul smell of frying on the staircase. . . .

So everything had been prefigured in that greasy stench. A week later her husband would become that man giving her a farcical salute before plunging into the taxi.

"We are both guilty.". . . The proof had been found. With an instinct as deeply rooted as the instinct for survival, she grasped that she must leave it at that. Not seek anything else. And already the reek of burned fat that still lingered in her nostrils was fading, becoming distilled, taking on the perfume of fine cigar smoke, swirling in nacreous spirals in the vast hotel room with windows open onto the Mediterranean night, onto a eucalyptus tree whose foliage rustles in a warm wind glutted with rain. . . . He has laid his cigar down on the marble of the fireplace, he laughs. His whole giant's body is shaking with very youthful laughter. Youthful with drunkenness, with carelessness, with his desire for her. He pulls wads of bills out of his pockets, they litter the carpet at his feet, slip under the bed, whirl in the breeze that stirs the air in the room that is lit by a great glass chandelier. "Did you win?" she asks him, also infected by his merriment. "At first I won; then I lost everything and was ready to hang myself—or at any rate to drown myself, that would be a better joke! And suddenly that brigand Khodorsky arrives, bringing all this! A month ago we sold a house near Moscow to an Englishman, do you remember?

Ha ha ha! And what kept me from going straight back to the tables was that I was too hungry for you. . . ."

She is only half dressed, as she often is when awaiting his return, not knowing if he will come back with the hangdog expression of a bankrupt or drunk with gambling and laughter, like today, unloading from his pockets the booty that will grant them a lease of another week or two of the airy and frivolous merrymaking that is their life. . . . She keeps some garments on her to the end, others—like the corset with snaps that click as they open—are hurled away, and land on the carpet of crumpled bills. Lifted into the air by this giant, she, who looks tall, suddenly feels weightless, fragile, and totally engulfed by him. Standing there he appears to be pounding his own belly with this woman's body and it now seems slight and compact in his enormous arms. A pump dangles, suspended at the end of her foot, and falls, turning over several times. That evening, like so many others, will only remain in her memory because of a thought that suddenly rips into the pulp of her pleasure: "All this will have to be paid for one day. . . ." She utters an even more vibrant moan to drive the specter away. The man lets her fall back onto him in the frenzy of a climax reaching its peak. . . .

"Both guilty". . . The long eucalyptus leaves rustle as the wind gets up again. The smell of the cigar grows lighter, refines its substance, changes into the smell of incense. The candle he is holding drips wax on his fingers. He tilts his head back, his eyes brimming with tears. She watches him out of the corner of her eye and cannot forestall that mocking young voice that rings out inside her head: "Are you sure he's not acting?". . . A year later he throws back his head, collapses onto the bed, dragging her with him, still bound to him by pleasure. On top of this great male body, still tumultuous with love, she surfaces, slowly draws away from him, observes his fearsomely powerful hands, abandoned in the folds of the sheets. One of them comes to life, gropes toward her, finds her breast, squeezes it with blind and loving violence. . . . The fingers knead the wax of the burnt-out candle. Then they gather to slap her and lash her cheek. Still later they mime a military salute. And make a rapid sign of the cross over a child stretched out on his hospital bed. And . . .

All she could see now was this flotsam of gestures, bodies, lights. Everything grew fluid as she looked at it. Herself? In her rambling she now latched on to this ultimately certain, indisputable point. "I am the only guilty one." She and the youth caught in his criminal act; there was nothing else, no intermediary. She was guilty of rejecting the apologies of the man on his knees who had just struck her. And before that guilty of not saying, "It's the smell of frying fish that's making us get mad at each other: let's drop this pointless argument." Guilty at the hospital of not saying to herself, "I could forgive this man a great deal for that sign of the cross coming from a nonbeliever like him." And before that, guilty of enjoying the warm evening breeze that stirred the noisy eucalyptus leaves, and guessing that the blind hand was approaching to bring erotic torment to her breast. And a few minutes earlier when she heard a voice within her saying, "This will have to be paid for one day," guilty of thinking, "I don't care," in reply to somebody who seemed to be waiting for her reply. Guilty of not believing in those eyes uplifted toward the roof of the church. Guilty of being herself, as she was.

But who was she? The woman hiding behind the curtains to watch a man leaving her. She, who later walked along that muddy road clutching the supple body of a slain bird in her hand. She, who felt as if she had spent long years rooted to the spot as she compressed the blood of an everlastingly fresh wound with paralyzed fingers. A woman who, years before this interminable vigil began, used to enjoy watching the movements of her companion's hands in restaurants, as they grasped a glass, prepared a cigar—hands that had just now been lifting her own body. A woman who when she saw the man in his officer's uniform tilting back his head could not prevent herself saying, "What little devil lurks within me? I have this mad urge to burst out laughing and hear the echo and see their shocked faces!" A woman in rags, covered in filth and lice, barefoot, swaying on an unstable gangway, staring at the water crammed with dead fish and rotten timbers, unable to understand that she is leaving Russia forever. . . .

She felt as if she were running from one woman to the next; recognizing them; running straight through a day, a room, a compartment in a railroad car.

It was as she continued running that she realized she was still not asleep. . . .

Then she pushed open the little window between the bookshelves. The freshness of the night made her nostrils tingle. The yellow light of the lampshade sealed off the darkness, made it gleam. There was just this bare branch reaching toward the window that emerged from the night, surprised her with its living, watching presence. And from this branch, from this breathing of the night air she derived a timid but intense happiness, like the end of an illness. The clock read: five past midnight. She was still not asleep. She had not fallen asleep. She was not sleepy. The young man whirling about by the kitchen range, the infusion, the reptile—so all that was no more than a delirium. Born in the head of a woman who would not accept her used-up life. A woman who still hoped. A woman who refused to look forward to old age and die before death came. It was a madness that had lasted for less than an hour and had taken her to the frontier of a deformed world from which there is no return. The bizarre and suspicious movement of the boy in the kitchen? No more than one of those eccentric, often crazy gestures people make when they think they are alone in a room. "The potbellied man on my desk, that ink blot I always hide under a book, is a little whim of the same kind. Our solitary hours are made up of such routines. . . ."

She closed the window and sat down at the narrow table once more. The night spread out before her and seemed endless. An ample amount of unoccupied time, that was offered to her personally. Her thoughts now had the limpidity of extreme insomnia. It remained for her to understand how she could have imagined what she had imagined behind that harmless gesture of an adolescent boy. To understand her own life at last.

* * *

A very few days after this sleepless night that seemed to have dissipated her oppressive doubts for good, Olga was to guess why the sleeping draft had not taken effect on that November evening. She realized that the powder the boy emptied into her infusion had not had time to dissolve and that, in her haste to give the lie to her horrible intuition, she had swallowed the liquid without stirring it. . . . She realized everything.

But such were the intensity and richness of her passion already, the immensity and purity of her grief, that the unveiling of this little secret merely surprised her by its materialistic futility. A ridiculous chemical curiosity, a superfluous piece of evidence. A petty detail that was now quite meaningless within the wholly fresh surge of days and nights—that she no longer even dared to call "my life."

Three

A GREAT ARISTOCRATIC MANSION on two floors, a facade with four white columns and, most remarkable of all, the strange garden where they fasten pillows to the trunks of the trees. Yes, apple trees in blossom and white pillows bound with thick ropes . . . She is six; she already knows that the pillows are there to protect not the trees but this pale, capricious ten-year-old boy, her cousin. She has already noticed that the scratches and bruises she inflicts on herself when playing attract much less attention than a simple mosquito bite on the boy's arm. These oddities do not prevent her relishing the great sweetness of days that pass without seeming to. Every evening, at the moment when the sun lingers in the branches of the apple trees, the aroma of tea spreads over the terrace. An old servant strolls slowly from one tree to the next, collecting the pillows. . . .

The other joys of her early life she notices too late, when only the memory of them remains. She grows up. . . . And through overhearing the conversations of adults, discovers three astonishing things at almost the same time. The first: her mother will never get over the death of her husband, for "she loves him," they say, "even more than when he was alive." The second: she comes to grasp, very vaguely for the moment, the nature of her cousin's condition and senses that she herself is an unconscious participant in a mystery that is both disturbing and rare. And finally the third: she learns that her grandmother, whom they bury one fine day in spring, has always been "conservative and reactionary," words that her adolescent's tongue finds it hard to articulate but which she likes the sound of. . . . The changes that ensue almost immediately after the funeral draw her attention to the simple pleasures now vanished: they no longer tie pillows to the trees; her cousin is fifteen; there is less fear for his health, and in the evening she no longer experiences that blissful moment when the old servant wandered slowly about in the garden untying the ropes, the moment when the smell of tea and the first coolness of the forest hung in the air. . . .

But the new life has its advantages. Nobody pays attention anymore to this adolescent girl spending the summer here at Ostrov, on the estate inherited by her uncle. She is free to go to the village where the peasants no longer raise their caps when they encounter their former masters. The grown-ups congratulate themselves on this; in the days of the grandmother, the old reactionary, they say, the villagers used to bow down to the ground when they greeted her. . . . They often talk about "the People" whom "all decent men" should enlighten, assist, and serve. This is a novelty too. Grandmother would speak of Zakhar, the shoemaker; the blacksmith, Vassily; or Stiopka the drunkard, who stole chickens. She also knew the Christian names of all their children. But she never spoke of "the People." Ostrov was one of the rare estates not to be set fire to during the uprising of the previous year. The adults see this as a consequence of the grandmother's despotism. . . .

But the principal novelty is that they are living their lives in nervous, stimulating anticipation of novelty itself. It is the start of the new century, the "new era," as some of her uncle's friends call it. They rack their brains about how to accelerate the onward march—too slow for their taste—of a country that is itself too ponderous.

No doubt it is thanks to this impatience, this desire for transformations, that the idea of costume balls comes to them. Her uncle's best friend, the one who talks about the People more often than the others, generally dresses as a peasant. Moreover, Olga notices that they all talk about them with the greatest fervor on the eve of the celebrations that bring together the owners of the neighboring estates and city folk from the capital. It is really as if by indulging in this worthy talk they are seeking to excuse themselves in advance for the excesses of the ball. . . .

She is twelve years old when, during the course of one of these balls, she comes upon an unusual couple in the little room that was once the lodging of the old servant, long since dead, whose allotted task was fastening the pillows to the trees. The man disguised as a peasant, the woman in a cloud of muslin, as a bat. . . . The house feels as if it is rocking under waves of music, exploding with firecrackers, ringing with shouts of laughter. It is the first time she has passed unnoticed—her height, she is already tall, plus a simple black mask offer her an invisibility that intoxicates her. She encounters a knight raising the visor of his helmet to down a draft of champagne, a woman dressed as a toreador—Olga guesses that she is a woman from the contours of her body ("I'm grown up if I can guess that" she thinks, proudly). . . . In a drawing room there is a man stretched out on a divan, his shirt wide open, with a pale face that women are dabbing at with wet towels. In the room next door a table strewn with the ruins of dinner and one solitary guest, who has removed his wig and his mask and is eating, as if to say, "I don't care what anyone says. I'm tired, I'm hungry, and I'm eating!" Suddenly a motley group invades the room; there is an explosion of laughter, several hands pour different wines into his glass, pile his plate high with a mixture of foods. He objects, but his growls are stifled in his full mouth. The pranksters vanish, carrying off his wig. . . . This theft makes her jealous; she, too, would like to make a little mischief. Coming upon a young magician asleep, Li, she carries off her magic wand. A few minutes later the wand slips from her grasp and the sound of it falling interrupts the counterfeit peasant and the woman in muslin in their wild and tender wrestling match. The man lying back in the armchair opens his eyes wide, the upper part of his body rears up. The woman straddling his belly twists and turns so as not to topple over. . . . At the end of the corridor, in the hall with the dinner table: a servant takes a furtive swig from the glass of the man whose wig was stolen. . . . On the staircase the grandmother's portrait has been hung upside down, head downwards . . . the favorite trick of guests at these celebrations. She unhooks the portrait and turns it the right way up. At that moment the counterfeit peasant appears at the other end of the corridor. She rushes toward the din of a piano, hoping to melt into a crowd of dancers. But the pianist is alone. It is an outrageously Moorish, drunken Othello, swamping the room with a flood of bravura music and despair. The white keys are all stained with black. . . . Tiredness, the darkness, and the two glasses of champagne they gave her, without recognizing her face beneath the mask, make the ground in the garden unstable. The pearly foam of the apple trees invades the pathways, confusing her with the scented whiteness of their branches. Suddenly in the depths of these nocturnal thickets the galloping of a horse is heard. It draws closer, turning toward her, invisible, more and more threatening, seems to be pursuing her, ready to burst forth with the crash of broken branches. She presses herself against a tree trunk and at the same moment the horseman appears. It is an officer cadet who has come to the party with no thought of fancy dress; having quickly wearied of the wine-soaked merriment of the others, he has escaped and is now skimming through the garden and the sleeping fields. His black uniform sparkles with white petals. She realizes that he is the one she has been unconsciously searching for through all the rooms. . . .

Among the adults who speak to her next day she senses a slight hint of embarrassment both in their voices and in their eyes, that sometimes avoid her own, sometimes seem to be questioning her. For the first time in her life she enjoys their weakness. She grasps that their world is much less secure than it appears and that one can play on these insecurities. An unknown voice rings out inside her head: a mocking, aggressive voice that from now on takes it upon itself to seek out the shameful hidden corners of every thought, of every action; to stir the thick sediment of people's hearts. . . . When one of her cousins begins to play a melancholy polonaise in the evening this little voice pipes up: "And what if I told her that yesterday, in a room not ten yards from here, a woman dressed as a bat was writhing like one possessed astride the very man my poor cousin is hopelessly in love with . . ."

So the world is this exciting, cruel game. A game with inexhaustible permutations, with rules that one can change oneself during the course of play.

Three weeks later another celebration begins, as so often, with fireworks. Li officiates in her magician's cape, delighted with the applause and shouts that accompany each salvo. The merriment reaches its peak when a purple rocket fails to take off properly and propels a violent shower of sparks across the lawn, right up to the roots of the apple trees. Li joins in the general jubilation, her voice drowned in the guests' raucous chorus. It takes them several minutes to realize that her laughter is in fact a terrible sob of pain. The white gash that has ripped open her cheek, from chin to temple, is already filling with blood. . . . That night in the house, heavy with the silence of an aborted celebration, Olga ponders once more the uncertain and changing rules of the game they call life. Li is what the others call "a daughter of poor parents." According to all the storybooks, to common sense, and to the noble sentiments their childhood was reared on, Li deserved a wonderful compensation as a reward for her goodness and her modesty. And there she was atrociously wounded for life . . . So had they been right to turn the grandmother's portrait upside down? No doubt this wound is a nod and a wink addressed to them by life, by this real, complicated, hidden, provocative, pitiless, mocking life, that delights in thumbing its nose at decent sentiments.

Olga thinks she is getting to the heart of this life's logic: "If I hadn't dropped Li's magic wand in the doorway of the room where the peasant and the bat were embracing, the man wouldn't have sneered at her in front of everyone at the fireworks; he wouldn't have said, 'That magician sticks his nose in where he has no business and listens at doors.' Li wouldn't have heard that hurtful and unfair remark. Her hands would not have trembled. And the rocket would have gone up into the sky. . . . So everything depended on the caprice of that little stick of wood rolling on the floor!"

"Li wouldn't have been disfigured if that counterfeit peasant and the bat hadn't been yoked together by desire. . . ." Four years later in the spring of 1916 she says it again. Like the century, she is sixteen. Meanwhile her uncle has committed suicide, the estate has been sold, the old mansion razed to the ground, the garden destroyed. Where the house once stood all that is left is the rectangle of the foundations, covered in weeds. Little red beetles run along the worm-eaten timbers and across the granite flagstones colored with yellow lichen. And above it all in the springtime void of the sky the eye cannot help seeing again, as in a mirage, the vanished house, the windows that look so alive, the four columns of the facade, the wooden walls, blackened with time. Perplexed, she thinks she can recognize the arrangement of the rooms and the direction of the corridors in this transparent house. This great cube of air contains an unimaginable density of lives from long ago, a long sequence of generations: the chamber where her grandmother's coffin rests for three days; the noise of the parties, and that whole avalanche of words that were ephemeral but could inspire happiness or break hearts; all the nights of love; all the births; even that room, lost in the intersection of galleries and corridors—the one where a man in peasant costume gazes blearily at a woman whose panting gasps keep time with the rhythm of pleasure. And the bed on which a young girl lies, from whose face they will shortly remove the dressings already loosened by her impatient hand. . . .

The sight of this ethereal house crammed with so many existences makes her giddy. The walls are already melting into the sky, the windows fading into the blue—she has just time to see the tiny attic room where her grandparents' old servant lived, a cubbyhole that smelled of the resin from burnt wood, lit by a night-light flickering in front of the icon, where, whatever the weather, the narrow window always seemed to be looking out onto a snowy night. . . .

A young man of around twenty, her cousin, whose life used to be protected with the help of pillows tied to the trees, is already calling to her from the carriage, straightening up on his saddle, holding the reins. They are going back to St. Petersburg.

This cousin is one of the last remaining ghosts from those parties of long ago. Olga bumps into him occasionally at poetry evenings, in the restaurants where the artistic bohemia of the capital gather. In his poems he talks of the "the curse of princes" that affects him and gnaws at him. Only a small circle of initiates knows it is a reference to hemophilia. Those not in the know find his verses ridiculously overinflated and lachrymose. A different kind of verse is in fashion; Olga often declaims it like a stimulant before nights filled with rhythmic words, wine, sensuality, and cocaine:

> Pineapples in champagne! Pineapples in champagne!
> An unwonted savor, with sparkle and sting.
> I have donned a disguise: a Norwegian in Spain!
> For my pen is drunk and my heart's on the wing!

Indeed, she often has the impression that the costume balls have not come to an end at all and that currently the whole of Russia has succumbed to this craze for dressing up. You no longer know who is who. The great wind of liberty intoxicates them. You can kill a minister and find yourself acquitted. You can insult a policeman, spit in his face, and he will not stir. Apparently that poet rising to his feet at the back of the hall, a champagne flute in his hand, is a well-known revolutionary. And the man over there with his arm around the waist of a woman whose breasts are almost bare is a police informer. The singer just making a sign to the pianist is a conspirator in the plot against the Tsarina's monstrous favorite. And this very young woman here, with a strangely pale face, her eyes ringed with black, is the daughter of one of the most celebrated families in Russia. She has broken with her background, she is the muse of several poets, but has given herself to none of them on account of a mystical vow. . . .

Olga looks at herself in the long mirror that reflects both the room in the restaurant and the pale face with black rings around the eyes—her own. . . .

The ball goes on. The Tsarina's favorite is killed. The Tsar is overthrown. Assisted by his children, he cuts wood. At last the country seems to be responding to the dreams formulated in the old days at her uncle's house. Its onward march accelerates: outmoded traditions are smashed to smithereens, the head of the new government has to wear his arm in a sling after shaking hands with tens of thousands of enthusiastic fellow citizens. But soon the country's breathing becomes spasmodic: menacing groans can be heard. . . .

She joins in the ball with all the impatience of youth. She samples everything: decadence, futurism, workingmen's Sunday schools; she studies to be original in a world that is no longer surprised at anything. All around her debauchery is humdrum, insipid. One of the poets, before possessing his mistress, attaches bear's claws to his fingers. This will soon seem banal. . . . She explains to the men in love with her that she will only give herself to the one who will kill her and take her dead. This is more surprising than the bear's claws, because of her youth, perhaps, or her livid face with a look that is meant to be hellish; or else because of the seriousness with which she utters these idiocies. . . . Secretly she still thinks about that young horseman five years ago—galloping in the night through the white foam of the apple trees. She forbids herself to hope, but hopes all the same that her first love will have this freshness of snow. And the mocking and aggressive little voice lurking inside her never tires of sneering at this last island of sensibility in her heart. . . .

One day, vexed by the dullness of a landscape on her easel, she paints stripes across it savagely with a brush and a painter friend of hers speaks jokingly of "Stripeism." For several weeks she finds herself at the head of a new artistic movement. Until the same joker covers a portrait with curves and, in his turn, launches "Curvism.". . .

She thinks she has learned all the rules of the game called "life." Two years earlier Li was just starting at medical school. "So that's her compensation as a daughter of poor parents," Olga had thought with a smile and, knowing the rules of the game, began to wait for some ludicrous twist. It came with the war: Li abandoned her studies and, with a nurse's satchel on her shoulder, plunged into the mud of the trenches.

As for the young horseman all covered in petals from the apple trees, one autumn day she will learn of his death and will try to gauge whether her own indifference is real or simulated. So often all their emotions had been a fraud. . . . Irresolute, she will then start singing a German song, which, if there were any justice in heaven, should have brought the sky down on her head. The sky does not fall. Only a shower of freshly printed tracts thrown by someone from the roof. She will pick one up as she goes out. "Seizure of power. Peace Declared. Revolution," she will read distractedly. And she will heave a sigh: "Another one . . ." She will even smile: to learn that the war is over on the same day as learning of the death of that horseman of long ago will seem to her to conform perfectly to the pitiless mischief of life. The mocking voice within her will be roused and whisper, "It'll make a good masque for this evening—a dance before an open coffin!"

And she will weep all the same, for long hours, amazed herself at the abundance of her tears and the depth of feeling in them. But it will be too late.

Too late; for suddenly History seems to have had enough of their disguises and their pretensions to changing its course, accelerating its onward march. History or, quite simply, life lumbers into action like a great wild beast roused from a deep sleep and, in a monstrous pendulum swing of its mighty forces, begins to crush all these capricious, neurotic manikins embroiled in their sterile reflections. The People, whose name they had a habit of invoking between two glasses of champagne, between two stanzas, suddenly reveal themselves in the guise of a huge sailor from the Baltic, who breaks down their doors with the butt of his rifle; plunges his bayonet into their guts; rapes their wives; stifles the squeals of their children beneath his hobnailed boots. And walks out satisfied, enriched, smiling and proud, for he sniffs the wind of History. It is difficult not to fall under the spell of its elemental power. . . .

There are some who are beguiled and disguise themselves yet again, imitating the wind of History in their costume. Others flee, also in disguise. The head of the government removes his "People's friend" cap, slips into a nurse's dress, and escapes from the palace that has very nearly become his tomb. And the masquerade continues. Those who used to dress up as beggars at costume balls in the old days now beg, swathed in rags. Those who played at being ghosts or bats now hide in lofts, listening for the sound of hobnailed boots. Those who wore the executioner's hood now become executioners, or, more often, victims. . . . Later on, at the time of the exodus, Olga will learn that one of their footmen, now an important personage, has tortured and shot hundreds. "No doubt the very man," she conjectures, "who helped himself to a drink from a guest's glass. He wouldn't be able to pardon his masters for that. . . ." And the man she surprised coupling with a bat woman, the one who was so fond of talking about the People, will escape by disguising himself as a peasant and growing a long beard. . . .

History will far exceed their dreams. Its onward march will change from fast to furious. The mortal poisons of existence once evoked in their poems will now have the humdrum and bitter taste of hunger and continual petty terror, sticky with sweat. As for that equality, whose name was so often invoked on the terrace of the house at Ostrov, they will now taste it complete—in the endless tide of refugees, streaming from town to town, toward the south, toward the void of exile.

At one of these staging posts in a little unknown town, its streets riddled with chaotic rifle fire, she takes refuge in a great izba that astonishes her with the cleanliness and calm of its rooms, where one can hear the sleepy ticking of a clock and the quiet creak of footsteps on floorboards. Suddenly the door, held fast by a heavy hook, begins to rattle beneath violent jolting. The hook gives way. The figure that appears in the doorway looks like a woman of gigantic stature. On account of all the disparate garments it is wearing, in particular the fur coat, a woman's coat, unbuttoned, because too narrow across the shoulders. Beneath the coat several layers of blouses, one of them trimmed with lace. It is one of the soldiers who were shooting in the street a few minutes ago. . . . He catches her at the back of the house. His drunken eyes focus on a medallion under the collar he has just ripped with his hand. He tears it off with its little chain, stuffs it into his pocket, and freezes for a moment, as if undecided, looking at her with an offended air. She is astonished at the dull feebleness of the cry that her lungs manage to squeeze out. In a second her body is overwhelmed, split in two, pinned to the floor by a heavily writhing mass. For months she has heard the threats of the victorious soldiers. "We'll rip your guts out and hang you in them!" The picture conjured up by this one haunted her especially. . . . Now the burning pain in her loins seems almost derisory compared with the tortures she had feared. She suffers more from the acid stench of the copper cross that swings out from her violator's ginger chest hair and which she can feel dangling on her lips. And also from the bitter stench of the great dirty body. Despite this breath suffocating her she is suddenly aware of a rapid footstep and out of the corner of her eye she has time to glimpse a knee touching the ground. A revolver shot fills her head with muffled deafness, makes her screw up her eyes. The only sensation she is still aware of is the slow softening of the hardened flesh thrust into her belly. . . . And the thick trickle that begins to ooze onto her cheek from the soldier's temple. The enormous body becomes heavier still and finally releases her as it slips sideways, an inert mass. She takes refuge in another room. The sensation of a tensed member growing slack deep down within her imprints itself on her flesh. . . . As she passes back through the house she sees her blood-soaked footprints. Out in the yard a man, a real giant with the dark eyes of an Oriental, signals to her to wait. The shooting slowly becomes more distant. The man's clothes are little different from the trappings of the soldier he has just killed. He stares at her and almost smiles. "Prince Arbyelin," he murmurs, inclining his head before disappearing in the direction of the gunshots. She does not know if she has heard him. Her body is still reliving the death of the other man's flesh inside her. "That was your first love!" whispers a mocking voice in her thoughts. "That little bitch!" She suddenly finds this name for it and all at once feels aged. . . . Her pain is quickly dissipated by other pains. . . .

At Kiev, where she spends several weeks hidden in a basement filled with water up to her ankles, she learns of her cousin's death. After the reds have been driven out of the city, but only for a time, the relatives of the victims make their way to the place of execution. It is the courtyard of the former school. Up to the height of a man the walls are covered in a thick layer of dried blood, fragments of brain, shreds of skin with tufts of hair. Blood, black, stagnates in the gutter. . . . Later, when she is capable of thought again, the memory comes back to her of the poems that spoke of the "curse of princes." Now the hemophiliac's blood, the source of so many sorrowful verses, is mingled with the pulp of all these anonymous bloods in a gutter blocked with scraps of flesh.

At one moment she believes she has lost all feeling. . . . She passes through a succession of towns ravaged by fires, houses gutted by pillage, lampposts overloaded with hanged bodies (one day one of these corpses, already ancient, no doubt, falls and brushes her with the shreds of its arms). To be able still to hurt her, pain must now be particularly sharp—the fabric of her dress sticking to a wound and having to be ripped off. Or quite squalid—the maddening itch from fleas. Or quite stupid—waiting, among other women, for some torture to be devised by this puny man, dressed in a leather coat and hence a "commissar," who is suffering from toothache and examines the female prisoners with extra hatred until the moment when one of them offers him a little bottle of perfume (her last talisman of femininity) that eases the pain and affords them an unhoped-for reprieve.

She recognizes herself less and less as this starving creature covered in rags, with inflamed eyes. Seeing her own reflection in a broken shop window near the harbor, she greets it and asks the way to the embarkation quay. She walks barefoot, she no longer has anything to carry. This city on the coast of the Black Sea is the last outpost of freedom. They are already fighting in the suburbs. From time to time she has to walk around a dead body or hide behind a wall to avoid a hail of bullets. Standing in front of the shop window, and realizing her mistake, she experiences a brief stirring of consciousness, feels a strange twitching of her lips—a smile!—and tells herself that in this city at war the freedom they dreamed of for so long has been achieved. Totally. She could pick up the gun from that dead soldier lying beside the wall and kill the first person who came along. Or even rally the besieging army: her rags make her look like one of them. Or she could take shelter in an empty house and resist absurdly until the last cartridge. Or just walk into that theater, settle down in a plush-covered seat, and wait. Or finally, kill herself.

This moment of clear reasoning revives the fear, the suffering. And above all the instinct for survival. Panic-stricken, she loses her way at the intersections of roads, runs, retraces her footsteps, sees the dead soldier again—someone has already taken his rifle. Suddenly she hears notes of music. The ground floor of a deserted restaurant, the windows shattered, the doors torn off. Inside, a man dressed in a fur coat with frayed sleeves, a fur hat on his head, is playing the piano. The mouth of a ceramic stove is belching forth black smoke, covering both the room and the musician in black strands of soot. He is playing a tragic bravura air, from time to time wiping his cheeks, wet with tears. His swollen feet are bare: they slip on the pedals; the man grimaces and crashes his fingers down even more furiously. His face is almost black. "Othello!" a very old memory exclaims within her. She walks out and sees the harbor at the end of the road. She no longer hurries. Indifference and torpor return. As she goes up the gangplank she directs her gaze down into the dirty water between the granite of the quay and the boat. She feels herself to be of the same consistency as this cold, glaucous liquid—foul with oil, with flotsam, with dead fish. There is an immense temptation to lose herself in this substance so close to her, so as to suffer no more, no longer to have to unstick her eyelids with their accretions of dry, yellow crust.

And when her own shuddering becomes one with the painful heaving of the boat ambushed by a winter storm and she weeps from those tortured eyes, it will be neither because of the pains in her body nor because of the fear that draws prayers and cries from some of the other refugees. She is overwhelmed by the feeling that there is no one in the universe to whom she can address a prayer. Her whole being now is nothing more than her raw wounds and her skin infested with lice. And all her thoughts can only lead to this one conclusion: the world is evil. Evil is always more deceitful than man can imagine. Goodness is simply one of its tricks. "I'm suffering," she will groan, knowing that there is no one under heaven from whom she can hope for compassion. All she will see of heaven is the rectangle of cold, of salt breakers and howling squalls outside the door that the sailors fling open as they come running through. Her only heaven. As for this world—this is how she wanted it. So it has become.

And yet she will also weep at the moment when her neighbor, his face emaciated, his look deathly, hesitates for a second, and shares his bread with her. . . .

Later she will learn that the last ship left Russia a few hours after their sailing, carrying the very last refugees and the very last defenders of the city; among whom, when she gets to Constantinople, she will recognize a woman, armed and dressed as a soldier, with a deep scar across her cheek from chin to temple. Li . . .

Having reached Paris, after long detours across Europe lasting for several months, she finds the simplest things painfully affecting: a piece of scented soap that she often secretly inhales, feeling goose bumps on her skin with a tingling she had forgotten; the sweet scalding of the first mouthful of hot coffee in the morning calm of a bistro; language and gestures that are unthreatening; looks you do not have to scrutinize to guess if you are condemned or acquitted. Paris is like the neck of a funnel—into it immense Russia decants its human masses. It is impossible not to bump into people you have already encountered in the old life. She finds Li again. And a little later, the man who killed her violator and who had introduced himself before disappearing (as she thought, forever) as "Prince Arbyelin."

This new encounter is too perfect, too much like a storybook to be wasted. They sense that together as a couple, the destitute princess and the brave warrior in exile, they already belong to the dreams of these émigrés, who only survive thanks to dreams and memories. And it is without any hypocrisy that they both live out this dream for the others. She believes quite sincerely that she can never smile again, nor experience joy, nor permit herself to be happy after what she has lived through and seen. Above all, she contrives to convince herself that her life, to its very end (she is twenty-two in this year of 1922), will be a solemn and melancholy wake for the past.

Why then, one day, does she no longer believe this? They are in church, still in their roles of princess and exiled warrior; he tilts his head to hold back his tears; and she catches herself doubting the sincerity of their roles. . . . That day, as if he, too, had sensed a change, he eats with the hearty appetite of someone returning to life. . . .

One evening, some months later, she is surprised by the sight of a long feminine leg, her own, as she pulls on a silk stocking. Or rather by the vortex of petty and futile thoughts that fills her mind at that moment: are these stockings too dark? Will it be too hot in the restaurant where he is taking her, as it was yesterday over in Saint-Raphaël? He must be getting impatient, we're late, he's going to knock on the door again. . . . He knocks, scolds her. To defuse his anger she tells him to come in. He comes in, lifting his arms in theatrical indignation and his expression suddenly changes when he sees the soft, delicate whiteness between the stocking she is fastening and the curve of her stomach. . . . She feels the prickle of his mustache on this bare island of her body.

Much later she will try to understand how this new masquerade could have tempted them—and so easily. The contagion of the Roaring Twenties, the gaiety of a people who wanted to forget the war, the reawakening of the émigrés after the shock of exile. The first literary evenings; the revival of fashionable life in this Russian Paris;

there are even costumed balls! Yet the real reason, she will admit to herself reluctantly, was quite simply physical. It was the beauty and strength of her own leg, stockinged in gray silk; her body liberating itself from the last traces of suffering and claiming its due. And also this man, angry with himself over his moment of sentimental weakness, his tears in church, who one day casts aside his melancholy warrior's mask and becomes once more the bon vivant and daredevil he has always been.

Their life, a new version of the masquerades of the old days, will take its tempo now from the impatient hammering at the door when that silk stocking was being slowly drawn up her leg; from the spinning clatter of the roulette wheel; and from the mighty swaying of an immense eucalyptus tree in the rain, that very night outside their window.

And then one day there is the suicide: Khodorsky, whose great friend and accomplice Prince Arbyelin is, sells his childhood home and kills himself. "He drank too much . . . It was his nerves . . . ," the prince mutters, affecting disdain. But they are aware that this death has banished a whole chapter of their lives into the past. "The end of the Roaring Twenties . . ." is how she thinks about it later. The truth is that during those frivolous and fugitive years they have simply exhausted their roles. And if they now marry in the very year of Khodorsky's death, it is to give themselves the illusion of an uninterrupted love. They set up house in Paris in winter in an apartment where the light comes in through the windows as if through bottle glass. "A good day for hanging oneself," he declaims, in imitation of the hero of a well-known play; later he takes to repeating this phrase, each time with less irony, soon with aggressive bitterness.

The child is born in 1932, the year in which the Russian émigré Pavel Gorgulov kills the French President, Paul Doumer, with a revolver. The Russians pass on to one another the last words of the condemned man as he is dragged to the scaffold: "All power to the Green Troika!" They say he went mad long before his crime. Yes, the very same year. It is hard not to think about the crashing blade and the spurting blood. She thinks of them when she learns of the child's hemophilia (a tiny scratch that occurs during the birth gives rise to an interminable trickle of blood). She already knows the ingenious cruelty of life: the sound of the guillotine simply lends an artistic touch to the despair that engulfs her.

Despair rapidly becomes their way of life. And when, after six and a half years of this harrowing routine, her husband leaves her, she is secretly grateful to him. For some months she lives through a pain that is finally quite pure, undiluted by any words. In her tragic exaltation she even ends up by justifying his departure ("his betrayal," she had called it earlier): the child's illness made other people's happiness a crime. In all innocence, he himself had become their judge, a silent, daunting witness. Later, after settling in Villiers-la-Forêt, she will come to regret having left Paris, and having refused all help. . . .

Yet it is here, in this sleepy little place, where everyone knows the creak of the door in the only bakery in the lower town, here in the monotony of these long provincial days, that, for the first time since her childhood, she will have the feeling of no longer acting a part; of finally being herself; of returning at last, after a tortuous and futile detour, to the life that was destined for her.

IN THE EARLY TWENTIES the old brewery building, overgrown with weeds and long strands of hops, was the first haven for the small Russian community that had landed at Villiers-la-Forêt. The structure of redbrick, turned brown by more than a century of sun and rain, bore a distant resemblance to a fortress, with its rectangle of walls surrounding an inner courtyard and narrow windows, half loopholes, half fanlights. The proximity of the river that ran behind the building increased this impression of an isolated fortification.

The first arrivals embarked on the adaptation of this place—so little intended for human habitation—with the enthusiastic zeal of pioneers, the excessive confidence of colonists. The manufacturing rooms were divided into unusual apartments, all very long. The southern part of the brewery accommodated the residents of the future retirement home. In an area located above the main entrance, which opened onto the lower town, they installed the first sets of shelves for the library. The building rapidly filled up with occupants and during the first months they believed that this spot, set apart from the town, would witness the birth of some new form of human existence—fraternal, just, almost like a family. An old Russian dream . . .

As the years went by these first hopes were eroded and the old brewery simply became a dwelling place that was remote and lacking in comfort. People hastened to leave as soon as they had the means and settled either in the narrow streets of the lower town, or, better still, in the town hall district, or, ultimately, in Paris. These different departures charted a kind of hierarchy of personal success, and engendered jealousy and rivalry which were occasionally dispelled by a different kind of departure: death. This would bring everyone together around the coffin of an elderly resident who was about to bid good-bye to the redbrick building. For a time this made all the other removals seem inconsequential and very much the same.

In the end only one visible trace remained of that first great dream: the strange structure some twenty yards long, an annex running alongside the wall of the brewery that faced the river. In their ignorance of architecture, the émigrés hoped they could easily double the number of apartments by surrounding the whole building with a long lean-to that would only need a single wall. But the materials turned out to be too expensive; some of the occupants were poor payers, and in the spring the river rose and flooded the section already built. A kind of little dinghy, borne there by the current, appeared washed up against the door. The base of the building was plastered with mud. Now the émigrés understood why the original inhabitants of Villiers-la-Forêt had left unoccupied the broad stretch of waste land between the brewery and the river. . . .

The lean-to house remained unoccupied until the arrival of the Princess Arbyelina in 1939. It was she who cleaned it and fitted it out, planted flowers under the windows and a service tree beside the front steps. And during the years that followed she was never confronted by the rising of the waters.

The old brewery was looked down on because of that very tribal aspect which, in the eyes of the first arrivals, should have ensured its renown. It acquired two ironic nicknames, used interchangeably by the émigrés, which, in time, even the French adopted: "the Golden Horde" and "the Caravanserai." Only a few pieces of machinery, overlaid with several layers of plaster and paint, still recalled the building's original function. The steel bar that ran across the refectory ceiling in the retirement home. The great gear wheel mounted between the windows in one corridor. And, above all, the enormous pulley embedded in the wall of the library. They had not risked removing it from its supports, for fear of seeing a whole story collapse. Moreover, the occupants of the Caravanserai had long since ceased to notice these iron relics here and there thrusting out their useless beams or levers.

Living in that strange annex, Olga had the feeling of being very remote from the communal life of the Caravanserai. Tacked on to the back of the old brewery, her house had no connection with the inner courtyard that was the nerve center of this home for exiles. To go to the library each morning she was obliged to walk beside the wall parallel with the riverbank, and make her way around two corners of the building; even sometimes to make a detour along one of the winding alleys of the lower town, so as to avoid waterlogged areas and piles of rubble overgrown with nettles left over from the abandoned building works. Thus each time she came in by the main gateway she had the illusion of arriving from a long way off. Furthermore, at the time when she settled there, half the apartments, overcrowded in earlier days, were uninhabited. During the war this scattering of the Horde would increase. The only occupants who remained there were those who would never be wealthy enough to leave, like the old cavalry officer; or those who were not yet wealthy enough—like the young artist whose smock was caked with motley layers of paint. Then there were the residents of the retirement home, who did not leave because they were waiting to die there. And some owners of vegetable patches, who were waiting for the harvest. And finally there were some eccentrics who were waiting for nothing and who made no distinction between the Caravanserai, Paris, or Nice. Occasionally, through the library window Olga would see one of these dreamers stopping in the middle of the courtyard and for a long time studying the movement of the clouds.

In the late autumn of 1946 her house seemed even more remote than usual from both the Caravanserai and the town; alien to the world. The rains isolated it, transforming the track that led around the wall into a dotted line of tufts of grass. Then came the cold that began to blanket this ephemeral pathway in hoarfrost. The power cuts announced regularly by the newspapers became no more unusual than the flickering of candles at the dark windows of the Caravanserai.

The thoughts and fears that had so tortured her during the preceding months had now been transmuted into a silent dialogue imagined between herself and Li. She confided to her friend, who was very understanding, as our partners in these imaginary conversations always are, that when young she felt she was living not for the sake of living but to prove to somebody that she was free to change the course of her life on a simple whim. Whim! Yes, her whole youth had been corroded by this restlessness, this posturing frenzy, this lust for defiance, for provocation, for negation. A life mistaken, spoiled, led astray, badly begun . . . No doubt Li would find the right word for it.

These silent dialogues were nothing other than brief interludes within the fabric—at once dense and transparent—through which she viewed everything in this world: the life of her son. She finally accepted him in the guise of the adolescent who had appeared to her one September evening, so composed, so discreet he hardly seemed to be there. Sometimes the tissue of her thoughts, from which the boy was never absent, grew denser and she felt stifled: this was on those occasions, often unexpected, when his illness returned.

She had had the same feeling of suffocation during the latest consultation with the doctor. This dry and almost disagreeable man pleased her. With him she had no fear that the worst might be hidden from her. . . . This time there were discordant notes in the tenor of the rather clumsy words of encouragement he addressed to the boy. She thought she could detect the consciously adopted tone designed to restore the confidence of an elderly invalid. A patient, in fact, whose decline is being closely monitored and to whom the physician promises several more years, with the openhandedness of a benefactor.

Next day there was another power cut. She was delighted: in the dim light at the library the traces of anguish left on her face caused by her conversation with the doctor would be harder to discern. The readers departed. She remained for a long moment at the window, and darkness fell as she watched. In the dusk a little point of light advanced slowly across the vast inner courtyard of the Caravanserai. Some elderly resident, for sure, candle in hand, making a visit to a friend who lived in the opposite wing of the building. In the wind an eddy of dead leaves swirled in broad circles along the walls, drawing with it the whirling pages of a newspaper. In the middle of the courtyard the little light stopped. Another figure could be made out dimly, face to face with the candle carrier. Their heads bent over the flame shielded by a feeble, almost translucent hand. . . . This meeting in the autumn wind over that fragile flame, Olga told herself, was perhaps a faint echo of the dream cherished by the original occupants of the Caravanserai.

It was another day spent without light. . . . A Saturday. The week that had preceded it was punctuated with cold showers that glazed the dull air. During the final night this fluid glass had congealed. The earth covered in frozen footprints and ruts as hard as stone made walking painful. The readers hastened to go home while they could still dimly see where they were putting their feet in the courtyard that bristled with sharp little ridges of frozen earth. . . .

As Olga emerged from the Caravanserai, she noticed how few and far between the windows were where candles flickered; she mused on this strange fortress that emptied more and more each year. At length, feeling her way across the unevenness of the earth, she slowly embarked upon her regular journey. First along an alleyway in the lower town, then around the walls of the old brewery . . . Reaching the corner of her house, she sensed that an indefinable change had just taken place in nature. A timid softening, a dull, silent relaxation. Even the tonality of the air was different—filled with a hazy, mauve luminosity. At midday the wind had still been blinding her with needles of tears: now it had dropped. Beyond the willow branches the river had the consistency of ink. And, with an old familiar joy, Olga recognized that moment of expectation, when nature holds its breath, that in her childhood days would herald the swirling of snow. . . .

She saw it through the little open window below the bathroom ceiling. The snowflakes entered the warm penumbra and vanished in a brief iridescent glitter. The silence was such that you could hear the rustling of the candle placed on the great porous slabs of the floor. . . .

She was drinking tea, her gaze lost in the wavering orange halo around the wick, when someone knocked on the door. Surprised, but not really, by this late visit, she walked down the corridor carrying the candle, her steps keeping time with the flickering of the flame. It was eleven o'clock in the evening. Only a Russian could appear so late with no other reason than a desire to talk. Or a Frenchman, but then with an urgent, serious reason. At the last minute the idea occurred to her that it might be a prowler. She turned the key, calling out an automatic "Who's there?" and opened the door. The candle blew out. There was nobody. . . . She went out onto the steps and even took several paces along beside the wall, as if to assuage a slight pang of anxiety. Nobody. The snowflakes were drifting sleepily in the gray air, giving off a spellbinding, ashen light. The earth was already half white. This, more than anything, was what lit up the night. Under snow, the meadow seemed more vast, and at each breath she took this emptiness entered her chest with a chill that was piquant and bitter. And remembered from a very long time ago.

Without abandoning her reverie, she slowly drank the tea that was scarcely warm now, and went into her bedroom. The scent of the bark burning in the stove was intoxicating. She went to draw back the curtains and fill the room with the blue reflection of the snow. . . . But she moved too abruptly. One of the rings, a heavy bronze ring, fell onto the carpet. The room seemed to be cut into two halves, one bathed in milky whiteness, the other darker than usual. She pulled up a chair. Then thought she must first find the curtain ring. Bent down. Realized that without a candle she could not see clearly enough in this dark half of the room. . . . Suddenly she felt herself overtaken by a pleasant lassitude that confused her in the sequence of her movements: seek, light, climb on chair, replace. No, first light the candle . . . or pick up the curtain ring. . . . Her strength failed her. A rapid drowsiness was already making her eyelids heavy, relaxing her body. The pearly brilliance of the snow bewitched her. She moved away from the window. The edge of the bed rose up behind her, made her knees give way. She sat down. Staying awake was now demanding an increasingly concentrated effort. She still believed it was the snow, the aroma of the burning bark, the intensity of her memories that had plunged her into this fog of tiredness. She lay down, undid the belt of her dressing gown. These actions were carried out more and more slowly, like the final few steps of a figurine on a music box. She teetered on the slippery brink of sleep in the absolute certainty that at all costs she must make these few waking moments last. . . .

He came into the room when she was in the ultimate stage of consciousness. The stage when for the last time the drowning swimmer manages to return to the surface, to see the sun, the sky, his life, still so close . . .

He stopped at the silvery and black frontier that divided the room. Silvery like the snow outside the window, the bluish transparency on the door, the chair, the carpet. Black like the darkness that hovered around the bed. He took a step. Tricked by the snowy phosphorescence of the night, he put his foot on the hem of the curtain that had just slipped down. Another ring fell. Inaudible at first on the carpet, then suddenly beginning to roll on the bare floorboards with a deafening—paralyzing—clatter.

Several interminable seconds of nonlife went by. The boy frozen in the magnesium brilliance. The woman drawing all the darkness in the room around her body . . . The curtain ring, following its perfidious trajectory, embarked on a slow, clicking roll. Slowly the circles tightened around a center—around a silence that never seemed to come. In this instant of nonlife cadenced by the turning of the ring in ever decreasing circles, she had time to understand everything. Or rather to be blinded by a blazing connect-the-dots line: the movement of the young stranger surprised at the beginning of the autumn; the reptile; the oil on the door hinges . . . And even that ruined bridge, the steel girder with a boy advancing along it like a sleepwalker. . . . A shout would have made him fall. As now, in crossing this room . . .

The curtain ring became still. After another endless minute she saw a long, thin shadow detaching itself against the background of the window whitened by snow. The outline of this apparition was lost in the blue twilight. The branches covered in hoarfrost parted as it passed. The crystals swirled slowly, sprinkling their bodies, melting on their skin. She was experiencing all this on the far side of sleep.

THE CURTAINS WERE CAREFULLY DRAWN, the rings rearranged on the curtain rod. It was the first thing she saw on waking and the last thing she was able to note with any kind of calm. "He must have thought the unhooked curtain was his fault and . . ."

She threw back the blanket, got up, observed her body beneath the open flaps of her dressing gown as if she had never seen it before. Then turned back toward the bed. The blanket! Someone had thrown it over her bare feet. . . . Someone? She caught herself still hoping for a mistake, a misunderstanding, the mysterious intervention of a "someone." . . . The stove door was closed—although it had been left slightly open the night before. . . . The whole room was booby-trapped with eloquent objects, incriminating evidence of a presence that did not even have to be proved.

Behind the thick velvet of the curtains a sparkling day could be sensed. The folds of material, although dark, were bursting with warm light and were on the brink of yielding to its dazzling torrent from one minute to the next. Isolated in a dark, ominous silence, the bedroom was about to be flooded by the sun, gutted by sounds. . . . She went to the door and hesitated a long time with her hand on the handle. Beyond the door there could only be a blinding void, vibrant with a shrill, intolerable resonance.

She pushed at the handle. She was struck by the utter banality of the long corridor, its dreary look, the old coatrack, the familiar smell. At the far end the walls were lit up by the shafts of light streaming in from her son's bedroom. . . . She walked toward it, vacantly, wide-eyed, with an unthinking faith—that everything would be resolved, by magic, wordlessly, as soon as their eyes met.

There was nobody in this bedroom, all radiant with sunlight. Nobody and yet he was there—in the crayon serving as a bookmark, in the shirt on the back of a chair. . . . As usual. As yesterday, as in two days' time. The cheerful permanence of things terrified her. And when the tea began to brew in her cup, as it did every day, she walked rapidly out of the kitchen, seized her coat, and left the house.

For if she had simply continued with the petty ritual of habitual actions she would have been transformed into a monstrous being: the woman to whom *that* had happened. *That* was yesterday evening, last night. She understood it but still managed to avoid naming it: *that*.

Everything around her resonated. The rays of the sun, the glittering of the drops of melted snow trickling off the roof of the Caravanserai, the fragments of ice beneath her feet. And amid all this din a single thought ricocheted ceaselessly back and forth from one side of her brain to the other: to leave! At first this saving solution took her breath away by its simplicity. Yes, to leave! Bordeaux, Marseilles . . . She already saw herself settled in a train, running away from what had just happened to her. Then suddenly this absurd recollection: "Trains to run faster: Bordeaux . . . Marseilles. . . ." So it was the paragraph glimpsed in a newspaper that had suggested destinations for her escape. Yet how could she go away? Leaving the child with whom? The child?

The drumming resumed in her temples even more forcefully. Yes, she must go away but go away forestalling yesterday evening, foiling it, before *that* could be given its definitive name. She had a presentiment of a place where the night she had just lived through would no longer appear like a horror and a monstrosity. A place or rather a time that was simultaneously now and yesterday but also a very distant day yet to come. A time where everything would be reconciled, mended, would find its justification. For a brief moment she believed she was breathing the airy serenity of this prefigured time.

Reality returned with a jolt: a passerby kept asking her a question.

"Are you going away?" this woman repeated, surprised at receiving no reply.

It was one of the readers from the library.

"Are you going to Paris?"

"No, why?"

Olga glanced around her. She had set off up one of the streets the occupants of the Caravanserai used to take when going to the station.

"Oh, I see. I thought . . ."

"No, no, I was just going for a walk . . ."

She turned into a different street and at once bumped into a whole group of Russians. Then an old couple who lived on the ground floor of the Caravanserai. A few steps farther on, a resident of the old people's home. They all stopped, greeted her, studied her with particular interest, it seemed to her. She no longer knew how to avoid this cavalcade of smiling faces, softened by the glorious sunlight, by the festive brilliance of the snow. The next turning was a blind alley. The baker's was closed. She felt as if she were an animal that could be tracked more easily on the whitened earth. And that their words only seemed to be harmless; their eyes were scrutinizing her. What did they guess? How far could their curiosity reach? Making her way past the whole procession, she finally arrived at its source—the Orthodox chapel. So it was a festival. And their words had indeed been harmless and their eyes had seen through nothing. Plunging into the darkness punctuated with lights, she felt a pleasant relaxation in her body. The chapel was deserted. All she could hear was the invisible presence of an old woman behind a pillar, sighing as she cleaned the floor covered in traces of melted snow and sand. Olga took refuge in the furthermost part and stopped before an icon. She had no prayer to formulate. Simply the desire to curl up in a remote corner away from the light, like an animal that has just been wounded and, not yet feeling pain, is preparing for it to come flooding in. Absently she touched the cracked surface of the icon, stared at the dull, expressionless face of the child, then that of the mother, her astonished eyes with heavy, oriental lids. Suddenly a grotesque detail made her step back a pace: the Virgin in the icon had three arms! Yes, two hands were holding the child and the third, parting the folds of the gown, was poised in a sign of the cross. It was the famous Russian Virgin with three arms. . . .

She spent the afternoon strolling slowly amid the trees that grew behind the Caravanserai. As evening approached the snow stopped melting. The sun became embedded in the branches, turned red. Sounds were distilled in the air with the clarity of isolated notes of music. She was all alone—the only other footmarks on the white surface apart from her own were the arrowhead prints of birds and those of a child, a boy with red hair who was throwing stones onto the sheet of frozen water between the wood and the river. His family had left the Caravanserai the previous spring but with a kind of childish faithfulness the young redhead still returned to his old playground. The little stones he was throwing did not succeed in breaking the ice and sped across the pool from one end to the other with a melodious tinkling.

At times, in obedience to a sudden command, she stopped and tried to feel dread, terror, to shiver, to let herself be blinded by the monstrousness of what had happened. "It's monstrous, monstrous, monstrous . . . How? Why? I must die! Run away. Howl, howl, howl!" But this febrile litany rang out inside her as if as a sop to her conscience, without shaking the dull numbness of her mind. She tried to shatter the torpor, to feign, for want of experiencing them, the emotions she should have felt. But there were no emotions! A nameless nothingness . . .

And alongside this void, an ample and airy silence that reigned all around; the roughness of the bark that her hand touched, leaning against a tree trunk. And the bitter, piquant chill of the snow; and the imperceptibly changing lights on its surface. The pale blue glitter of the snow-clad land; the orange disk of the low sun in the network of the branches. And a woman, herself, who was going to spend these last hours of the day wandering in the snow, stopping from time to time, as now, pressing a hand flat against the bark of a tree, removing one foot from its shoe, her fingers searching for little fragments of ice caught between the leather and the stocking. On the sheet of frozen water the red-haired boy continues with his game. He breaks off when he notices the presence of a stranger—an intruder, an adult. He waits for her to go away. The noisy sliding of the little stones resumes. For a second she believes she can see what the child sees with acute intensity. The dark bottom beneath the ice, with plants and leaves trapped in the crystal of the brown water. Then his gaze is lost for a long time in the branches set on fire by the sunset, and in the sky. A forgetfulness so profound that the stones he has gathered begin to slip from his fingers and fall into the snow one by one. . . .

She held on to the memory of this gaze as she slowly returned home. And it was in a very calm voice that she called out to her son as she opened the door. . . . He was not there. He had come in for lunch, then gone out again. In his absence she sensed an excessive generosity on the part of fate that she must still be wary of. Her mind was aroused, anxious. And almost at once the shoes caught her eye. The ones she had bought him on the black market some months previously, after selling her wedding ring. Quite fine, elegant shoes, despite their worn leather. He dreamed (she knew he sometimes tried them on) of wearing them next spring.

Now this pair of shoes was transformed in her eyes into something indecent, ambiguous. . . . They were arranged near the wall in the position of a short, very lively and agile pace. The agility of a young male who senses that his presence is both alarming and exciting. Olga bent down, struggling against the repugnance that made her fingers shake, and picked up one of them. Then thrust her hand inside it. The reflex action of many years, feeling to check if there was a nail with a point that might cause bleeding . . .

She did not have time to finish her examination. The shoe escaped from her hands and fell. And at the same moment a cry choked in her throat: "He was inside me!"

And other cries, stifled by the murmuring of the blood in her temples, echoed back: "He was inside my body . . ." Now she understood why *that* had remained nameless. For to name it she would not have to speak of emotions but to utter those rough, ugly, uncouth words that came pouring in a glutinous flow into her throat: "He violated me. He had me when he wanted to. He undressed me, took me, dressed me again . . ."

The horror of these words was such that, panic-stricken, she tried to step back into that afternoon of silence and snow spent under the trees. She half opened the front door. A clear blue dusk was already coloring the meadow that sloped down to the river. . . . No, that afternoon of peace had never existed!

An illusion, a trompe l'oeil of happiness. Now she saw that in reality it had not been a dreamy stroll but a breathless, stumbling race. A mad round amid the dark tree trunks. She had run in circles, trying to escape. Then she had stopped to remove the snow from her shoes and had thought of the peace that death brings. A woman quite other than herself had been born: one who could spend a long time—an eternity—contemplating the low sun entangled in the branches; the slithering of stones cast onto the crystal of frozen water; the eyes of a child lost in the sky. . . .

Yes, it was in thrall to death that she had been able to glimpse the unspeakable happiness of that late afternoon in winter.

As it fell, the black shoe had positioned itself very nimbly beside the other, this time imitating a very small, mincing step. Olga told herself that of all the solutions that had arisen in her shattered mind since that morning—to run away, to explain herself, to say nothing—death was the most tempting, the easiest to accept, and the least real. For every day she must continue carrying out a myriad preventive actions similar to the search for nails lurking inside shoes.

She picked up the one that had fallen to finish examining it. . . . At that moment someone knocked on the door.

Without panic, her heart silent, still, she went to open it, already seeing her son's eyes. She walked along the corridor with a very regular, tense step, as if she were mounting the scaffold.

The appearance on the threshold of the boy with red hair, the little thrower of stones, seemed like a hallucination that must be accepted calmly. From the child's exaggeratedly serious expression it was abundantly clear that he had been sent as a messenger and that he was conscious of the gravity of his mission. He said what he had been asked to say in that mix of Russian phrases and French words common among children born at the Caravanserai. There was a mix-up too, between the seriousness of the circumstance and the nervous smile that stretched his lips. Too overcome, he confused the logical sequence: "Near the bridge . . . Hospital . . . Hurt himself . . . They're asking for you to come . . ."

She stared at the redhead's mouth as if this mouth had an existence of its own. And her stare ended up by frightening the child. "He didn't even cry!" he shouted and began to run, unable to bear a moment longer the violence with which those eyes were skinning his lips.

By the end of the week she was able to bring her son home. His convalescence was a time of silent reunion. Immobility and pain made him a child again. She felt more a mother than ever.

The night of the first snowfall—that *night*—formed a vast country of deafness in her mind, that she learned to avoid thinking about and from which only a few sparse fragments came to her. They resembled the strings of air bubbles that are released from time to time by stagnant water. She realized, for example, why that *night* had taken place on the eve of a Sunday; just like the other one, when she had fallen asleep in the book room. Yes, a Sunday, when an abnormally long sleep could easily take on the appearance of sleeping in. . . . She also recalled that one of the rare games this taciturn child loved to play at the age of seven or eight consisted of ringing the front doorbell and then hiding, to create the mystery of a missing visitor. Within this prank, she told herself, there was an element, no doubt, of that wait for the return of his father, whose "long trip" never came to an end. . . .

These memories disturbed her but they did not last. Any more than the fleeting reflex of revulsion she had on seeing her son's leg, this pale leg from which the plaster had just been removed. The knee and especially the foot were still swollen, and the little row of toes had a childish and strangely equivocal prettiness on this swollen and grayish flesh, on this big man's foot. . . . The doctor palpated the foot with sure and precise gestures, reminiscent of those of a craftsman handling a piece of wood. Dry and far from talkative, he seemed to take a certain delight in the terseness of his own comments, from which there was no appeal. "We shall have to operate to straighten the knee," he explained in a tone designed to avoid all sentimentality. "But we'll do it later, when he's had some rest . . ." The same evening she reread for the thousandth time the pages especially devoted, as it seemed to her, to this very case, to that very day in the life of her son. Reading these books, she often had the absurd impression that their authors knew her child and could foresee the course of his illness. This illusion was singularly powerful that evening, in the lines that she recited mentally, recognizing them from memory from the shape of the paragraphs:

> If the leg is more or less flexed on the thigh this only permits walking on the ball of the foot, which is painful and tiring. The muscles of the lower limb will atrophy. . . .

That night before going to sleep she called to mind, but in an intensely physical way, the infinite complexity of the years she had lived through, a jumble, without beginning or end, without any logic. The memory of the child was woven into this tangled web, like an exposed vein, burning. She pictured again the pale adolescent in the doctor's office, putting on his clothes with abrupt haste. She saw his fragile wrists and, when he looked up, the tiny bluish vessels beneath his eyes. . . . She was unable to stay in bed, went to the window, and with closed eyelids, her forehead pressed against the window, told herself that such was the logic of this painful and chaotic life. And in the spring the boy would be fifteen, if there was a spring for him. . . .

Then one December evening she noticed the light trace of white powder on the fine film that always formed on her infusion. Astonished by her own calmness, she poured away the liquid, washed the little copper vessel, placed it on the drain board. And, feeling herself observed by all the objects, by the walls, went into her bedroom.

THE VITALITY WAS ALL IN THE ARCHES of the eyebrows, in the tense line of the mouth. Only this partial image, like a sketch for a death mask—her face—could be seen, lying profiled on the pillow. The body had vanished, swathed in the icy folds of the sheets. And deep down in this absence, buried in its numb whiteness, her heartbeats were like the grating of damp matches.

What she could see was limited to what was reflected in the long mirror facing the bed. It was tinged with the ruddy glow throbbing in the stove behind its half-open door. In the sleeping depths of the mirror the round enamel face of the clock's great dial stood out clearly. And the hands, traveling backward, marked off this strange reflected time in reverse. She considered the passing of the minutes from back to front with slight irritation. And she was surprised still to be able to think, or to be irritated. She suddenly wanted to understand the logic of this inside-out dial: if it showed a quarter to one in the morning in the mirror, then what in reality . . . ? Her mind plunged with relief into this mathematical glissade. But it turned out to be difficult to guess the time from the position of the hands in the mirror. All at once she felt tormented by one of those whims sometimes imposed by pointless impulses, half caprice, half superstition. It became impossible for her not to turn around, not to look at the dial. She began prying her head up from the pillow. . . . And at that same instant she saw, still in the dark reflection of the mirror, that a long section of shadow between the door and the jamb was slowly growing broader. . . .

Her head froze, slightly raised, trapped by her whim of curiosity. She closed her eyes and with infinite slowness began to lower her cheek down toward the hollow left in the pillow. Little by little. Her neck stiffened, supporting a lead weight. Her temple probed the distance still left to travel. This distance seemed vertiginous, as if her head were sinking into a bottomless void. Yet her face already felt hot, as it sensed the warmth of the pillow close at hand, and even recognized the texture of the fabric. And through closed eyelids she sensed that a living presence had appeared in the open doorway and was slowly slipping into the room, modifying its volume, the familiar relationships between objects, and even, one might have said, the regular sound of the clock.

The bedroom was filled with the viscous silence of nocturnal rooms where a slow coupling is taking place; or, indeed, a murder; or even the meticulous work needed to eradicate the traces of a murder. It was the numbness of a room, where in the depths of the night bodies are going through the motions of an erotic, or criminal, dumb show.

When her temple finally touched the pillow her eyelashes blinked involuntarily. And this was her last clear perception during the whole night: at the end of the room the long, dark overcoat opened on a naked body, a white body, slim. It did not look like any other body; it did not look like a body at all; it did not look like anything she had ever seen in her life. . . .

Her eyelids were closed again, as if in death. Her face, half buried in the burning down of the pillow. Her body nonexistent. Outside her there was nothing but the purple darkness into which the whole bedroom dissolved, that merged into the darkness outside the windows.

It was in this sanguine ink that suddenly the outline, at once burning and frozen, of a shoulder manifested itself, then that of a woman's breast. And the point of the breast—firm, taut. Another sinuous curve was swiftly felt, that of the arm and a moment later that of the hip. It was neither a sensation nor a caress. It could have been a raindrop making this fleeting trace along her skin. . . .

The line suddenly broke off. There was a rapid movement of air, a whirlwind crossing the bedroom. A slight creak of the door closing told her that she was hearing again. Against her skin, under her skin, she now felt the carnal sketch of an unknown body, an outline poignant in its unfinished beauty.

She fell asleep when the windows were already beginning to turn pale. She woke up again at once. And explained to herself very calmly—only a momentary plunge into despair took her breath away—why he had fled. He must have noticed an unaccustomed tautness in her sleeping body, in its too perfect lethargy. . . . He had snatched up his coat and rushed to the door. And with his hand on the handle he had lived through that momentary but appalling dilemma known to all criminals: to flee or to return to cover your tracks at the risk of being done for. He had gone back toward the bed, had covered up the inert body with a blanket, had straightened out the slippers that he had kicked aside in his flight. . . .

Criminal . . . She repeated it ceaselessly during that sleepless night. Criminal was the silence she had kept. Her acceptance. Her resignation. Criminal too, the nakedness of the youth, concealed beneath a man's long overcoat. Criminal that whole night . . .

And yet there was something false about those menacing syllables. Something "too clever," she thought. Crime, perversion, monstrousness, sin . . . She caught herself seeking out ever more punishing words. But the words merely seemed as if written on the page of a book. Typographical symbols devoid of life.

In the morning she noticed that this time the curtains were open (during the first night they had remained drawn). The day was gray and windy (that other awakening had been to sunlight). . . . She sensed that these parallels concealed a fearsome truth that would be revealed to her at any minute now. A physical, corporeal truth that gripped the muscles of her stomach, rose up to her heart and closed over it, like a hand around a bunch of grapes in the tangle of leaves.

The truth that the words repeated throughout the night did not suffice to tell.

There were no longer any words but these things that offered themselves to her gaze with their mystery, with a mysterious smile almost. The cold smile of one who already knows the secret. The curtains; the lamp with its great orange shade lording it on the bedside shelf; the well-worn slippers, comfortable to her feet but suddenly unfamiliar; the door handle . . . struck by an inspiration, she opened the wardrobe, rummaged among several garments on their coat hangers, took out the black dress, her only remaining elegant outfit. Its pleats, its neckline trimmed with silk braid . . . The dress, too, was silently telling a secret that was about to burst forth. . . .

She went out into the corridor, this time with no fear. And as all the objects seemed to want to confide in her, the big cardboard box on top of the old closet caught her eye. For years now, when dusting or repainting the walls, she had wondered what it could contain and had then forgotten about it until she came to clean again. . . . She pulled up a stool, drew the box toward her, opened it. The thing it contained turned out to be strangely solitary, like a relic at the heart of a shrine. It was a plaster cast, no doubt one of the first of those she had made for her son, something he had learned to fashion for himself while still very young. This one was of such a small size that at first glance she did not know if the plaster had been shaped around a leg or an arm. Of course, it was a child's leg and she recognized the touching delicacy of its shape. . . . She put the cast back in the box and closed it; then unable to curb her desire, seized the plaster mold again, pressed it to her cheek, her lips. And it was then that the secret rang out: "Incest!"

The word shattered into a number of memories, each one earlier than the last. They reverberated in the night of the first snow and even before that night. During the night when the sleeping draft had not worked. And even earlier, when for the first time she had surprised that young stranger beside the kitchen range. And even further back than that in her memories. That old overcoat of her husband's on the youth's naked body. The previous winter she had darned it and, seeing it on her son's shoulders, had had to make a rapid, strenuous effort not to think about her husband's body. . . . And her unique evening dress. And the unique opportunity for wearing it—the evenings when L.M. took her to the theater. She would arrive at Li's house and entrust the boy to her and begin to make herself ready. When she went out, dressed, with her hair up and perfumed, her neck and shoulders very pale, the boy observed her with an insistent and hostile look. That made her laugh. She embraced him, enveloping him in her perfume, ruffling his hair and tickling his ear with her warm voice, imitating a lover's voice, which is, in its turn, an imitation of the voice we use in speaking to children. . . . And there were also the slippers. As quite a young child he had put them on one day for fun when she was still in bed and gone out into the corridor making the soles clatter on the floor. She had protested feebly; he had not obeyed her. She had been overwhelmed by an acute pleasure, that of feeling herself tenderly dominated, of not knowing how to or wanting to resist. . . .

Pushing the box back onto the top of the closet she climbed down from the stool. Now it had all been said. There was nothing else to understand. She knew everything, even *that*: the word "incest" had already resounded within her but in such cavernous depths of her mind that, surfacing into speech, it had been transmuted into "crime," "monstrousness," "horror." Like those deep sea fish which, drawn to the surface, explode or transform themselves into an unrecognizable lump of flesh.

Even the rhythmic spasm that her final discovery had provoked in her was from now on familiar to her. The hand that arose in the pit of her stomach, pressed on her lungs, taking her breath away; gripped her heart, a bunch of grapes that the hand either squeezed or released, at every thought, then suddenly crushed until there was a red hot throbbing in her temples.

She knew equally that all the means of salvation she had imagined in fact only added up to one. To break the curse of those nights she must both flee and remain; explain herself and above all say nothing; change her life and continue as if nothing had happened; both die and live while forbidding herself all thought of death.

"During the first night the curtains were drawn, during the second, open," she recalled for no reason. Yes, the reason for it was her headlong flight forward, proof that she was already living the life where one could neither live nor die.

It was with the feeling of embarking on this new life, a step at a time, that Olga drank her tea, left a note for her son, and went out, as she did every Sunday morning. She walked through the streets of the lower town, gray streets, their pavements strewn with tiny granules of snow. Without admitting it to herself she was hoping for a sign, a jolt in this provincial calm that might have attested to the irremediable yet utterly mundane deformation of her life. A woman who lived at the Caravanserai appeared at the end of the street, drew level with her, and, after greeting her, asked,"Are you going to Paris?"

"No, I was going for a walk . . ."

Olga waited for the street to become empty again, then turned toward the station.

In the train, watching the dismal fields and the little towns devoid of life floating past, her heart like a crushed bunch of grapes, she repeated several times, "Enough said. Impossible to live. Impossible to die . . ."

The train stopped for a few minutes in a little station beyond which there arose the sad, dull houses of a village similar to Villiers-la-Forêt but rendered even more inanimate by this cold, windy day. The only thing that attracted her eye was a window squeezed into the recess of a tiny yard. All around was the network of the alleyways, the naive jumble of doors, roofs, overhanging top stories: and then this window, lit by the feeble light of one bulb, with its Sunday-morning calm. . . .

A sudden intuition struck Olga; she turned away. So somewhere in this world there could be a place where what she had to live through could be lived! A life beyond "Enough said." A secret life, inaccessible to others. Like the one hidden behind the window that a distracted passenger on a train had just noticed.

As she was emerging from the Metro in Paris she felt the tiredness and the nervous exhaustion of the past weeks catching up with her. The steps of the staircase suddenly gave way under her feet; she clung to the rail. And with half-closed eyes she heard a plaintive, almost childish voice within her begging, "Please make Li understand! If only she can guess everything and tell me what to do. If I can just have a moment of peace. . . ." As she resumed her journey she recognized in this tone close to tears the old familiar voice of the "little bitch."

"When we were at school before the revolution, you remember the plank the headmistress made them tie to the backs of the girls with stooping shoulders, so they held themselves straight. You could tell them a mile off, the poor crucified things, with their shoulders square and their backs straight. . . . And then one fine day no more planks! The newspapers talked about liberty and emancipation. . . ."

She was trying to explain to Li the feeling that had been an unconscious element in all her thoughts since adolescence. The feeling that one day life had lost all its rectitude, correctness, regularity. One day a strange whim had crept into their lives in Russia, into the whole country. Suddenly they had been seized with the desire to prove that this rectitude was no more than a chimera, a shopkeeper's prejudice. And that one could live disregarding it, or, better still, thumbing one's nose at it. Furthermore, life itself seemed to confirm this: a Siberian peasant appointed and dismissed ministers; he "purified" (as he called these couplings) the Tsarina's ladies-in-waiting and even, according to malicious tongues, the Tsarina herself—all of them being in thrall to his inexhaustible carnal drive. Newspapers portrayed the Tsar as an enormous oval pair of buttocks surmounted by a crown. Killing a policeman became an exploit in the name of liberty. . . . And then one day they had stopped strapping planks to the backs of stooping schoolgirls.

In explaining this Olga suddenly believed she could understand herself. Yes, once the planks had been removed everything in the country collapsed. In her memory it was the recollection of a purely physical slackening. For a time to be twisted and ungainly had become quite the fashion. . . . In the very spring when their backs had been liberated she had taken part in a masked ball for the first time. Walking down a corridor (the portrait of her grandmother had been hung upside down) she had come upon a man and a woman coupling in an armchair. And like millions and millions of people at that time she had discovered that a certain order of things was cracking apart, on the brink of crumbling, or indeed that there was no order, no rectitude, merely servile custom binding them (like the plank at your back) to laws that were said to be natural. . . . Later she found herself listening to the poet who fixed bear's claws to his fingers. Another poet claimed he drank champagne from the skull of his suicidal beloved. And then there was that patron of the arts who commissioned an icon portraying a huge naked succubus. . . .

And for a few days each of these caprices, like a drug, offered an intoxicating sense of liberation; but stronger and stronger doses were soon needed, more and more bizarre combinations. They all of them aspired to the ultimate caprice, the one that would have liberated them from the last trappings of this world. She herself had had this feeling one evening in St. Petersburg, returning from a party with a man who pretended to believe what she was telling him in extravagant and funereal tones. She said she was only willing to give herself to a man who would agree to kill her afterward. Or was it before? Obsessed with her playacting she herself forgot the original version. This man, the painter who had just invented "Stripeism," was confident that this seventeen-year-old girl would soon be his umpteenth mistress. And he had no intention of killing her, either afterward or (especially not) before. But he was playacting and hardly noticing that he was playacting. As for her, by dint of thinking and talking about "the curse that had blighted her blood," she had ended up believing that it was to her future lover that she would pass it on and not to her child. . . .

* * *

After a moment Olga sensed that Li was listening to her with slight apprehension—the fear of someone who already foresees a confession that may well catch them off guard, invest the friend's familiar face with unknown, disturbing features. And even undermine an old friendship. At intervals she began adding her own comments to the story with a vigor and a passion that each time struck a wrong note. She waxed indignant about the torture that used to be inflicted on pupils straightened out with the plank; mocked the couple surprised in an armchair. . . . And when Olga talked about the depraved life in the capital of her youth, Li had begun to murmur, as if apologizing,"Oh, but you see, I never really saw much of that life. In the trenches what we saw mostly was death. . . ."

From the kitchen came the whistle of the kettle. Their tentative conversation broke off. Left alone for a few minutes, Olga felt relieved. She had lost hope of any miracle of understanding. . . . And yet she seemed to sense that Li, also alone for a moment, was timidly preparing the way for an unutterable confession of her own. And when she came in carrying two cups and an old teapot with a chipped spout on a tray, when she set about arranging the tray and pouring the tea with an exaggeratedly concerned air, and fussing unnecessarily about each little detail ("Wait, I'll get you another spoon . . ."), Olga understood that behind these words a serious statement, hard to articulate, was already forming.

"You know what I was saying just now about the trenches and soldiers," said Li, while her hands continued to hover around the tray. "Well, I lived among them for three years. So I know what I'm talking about. They were mostly young. And I noticed that some of them—but they were very rare—died without believing in death. And at the moment when they died we didn't believe in it either, at least not right away. . . ."

Her voice faded and, almost in a whisper, turning her eyes away, she breathed, "But for you, it's not the same. There's a child. Your child. . . . I'm sorry, I'm being stupid . . ."

And not knowing how to break the spell of silence brought on by her words, she disappeared into the next room and returned with a bundle of newspapers in her arms.

"You'll say that I'm not being objective," she announced in an almost cheerful tone, wanting to make a fresh start after the previous sentence. "But, you see, in the field of science and . . . medicine" (her voice slid once more toward a fear of being hurtful) "the Russians, well, the Soviets, are very advanced. Listen to what I read yesterday, and it wasn't in *Pravda* but in *Le Figaro:* 'A Russian scientist, Professor A. A. Isotor, has made the sensational discovery that the radius of the earth measures eight hundred meters more than was previously believed and that the earth itself is apparently not spherical but elliptical. . . .' I just thought that perhaps with your son, you could . . . , well, take him there, if only for an examination . . . , for a week or two . . ."

Olga could not help smiling. And to avoid passing over this suggestion yet again in silence she asked, "So when do you think you'll be leaving?"

"I think everything will be ready by the end of April. The last snows will have melted in Russia and I'll be able to go there by road. . . ."

"The last snows . . . in Russia . . ." These words sank into Olga's memory and resurfaced occasionally during the return journey. Each time the echo of them brought with it a brief moment of daydreaming. Then the hardness of dry and final words shattered its snowy aura. Final was the certainty of never being able to tell even her closest friend what had happened to her. The very worst thing that Li could imagine was the deterioration of the child's illness. But *that!* No, for a person with a healthy mind it was inconceivable. . . . As it was for all these passengers sitting around her in the train. She felt a transparent wall rising up between her and them, a glass dome transforming her, with her desperate desire to confide, into a fish in an aquarium. For an instant it seemed to her that even if she had uttered a long wail of misery none of her neighbors would have turned their heads.

"The last snows . . . in Russia." She tried to hold on to the sound of the words in her mind, to make it last. And to say (to Li, or to someone else) what was out of bounds to words. "You see, I talked to you about my youth to justify myself. Everything was disintegrating, going off the rails, and our lives were a reflection of those sick early years of the century. We strove to resemble them. And so instead of living we played at leading unnatural, capricious lives. We were under the impression that alongside us, the normal life that we despised, because it was too rectilinear, continued in parallel and that we could always come back to it when we had had enough of our games. But one day I saw that my two lives had grown too far apart and that I must now follow to the end the one I had chosen for fun, in the defiance of youth. And I have lived this ill-chosen life, with my eyes fixed on the other one. And what is happening to me today—you've guessed, haven't you, without my explaining it to you, you've guessed everything and you haven't turned away from me—Yes, everything in the life I am leading now that is monstrous, criminal, odious, is in the very nature of this unnatural life . . . Tell me very simply what I must do. Tell me my face gives nothing away, nor the expression in my eyes, nor my voice. Do you think one day I may be able to look at those trees, those rails, that sky the way I did before?"

It was dark when she reached Villiers-la-Forêt. As she was removing her shoes in the hall she noticed that the pair of men's shoes had moved. "He must have tried them on again, looking forward to wearing them in the spring . . ." She pictured this very young man, slim, with dark hair, a pair of well polished shoes on his feet, preening himself in front of the mirror in her absence. . . .

"All this is what madness must look like," she told herself, and went into her bedroom.

Two weeks later, one December evening, everything was repeated with infallible, fanatical precision: the hint of white powder on the surface of the infusion; the slightly mechanical stiffness of her hand as it poured away the liquid and washed the little copper saucepan. And in her bedroom, the familiar clock face reflected in the mirror, telling the time backward. . . .

A slight tremor almost betrayed her. The response of her flesh—neck, shoulder, breast—to the burning touch of the icy fingers lightly stroking it had been too violent. She felt no connection with this female body. And in the purple void beyond her eyelids there stretched an unknown body. A body with the scent of hoarfrost brought in among the folds of a man's long overcoat. . . . Her brief tremor and a repressed "Oh!" had risked revealing that she was not asleep. The fingers paused in their caress, then came to life again. She became yet more absent. Under the touch of the fingers that were slowly growing warmer, she discovered the delicacy of her collarbone and the dense weight of her breast as it held the caress. She lay on one side, her face half buried in the pillow. An ideal pose, she thought, for her pretense of sleeping, and one that allowed her not to be a part of what was happening to this woman's body as it was caressed. But suddenly the fingers pressed more firmly on her shoulder, then her hip, as if to turn her over. She felt feverishly present in this body once more; imprisoned in it. And, once placed on her back, she was too exposed, could no longer lie. . . .

The fingers squeezing her shoulder relaxed their grip. A dry creak could be heard at the other end of the room. Without opening her eyes she recognized the sound. A burning log, as it collapsed, had pushed against the door of the stove. Between her eyelashes she made out the image in the mirror. A naked youth, crouching beside the stove, was gathering up small sticks, burnt out or still glowing, and tossing them into the embers . . .

In the morning when he came into the kitchen she noticed a discreet dressing on one of his fingers. "Have you cut your hand?" she asked him without thinking, as she would have done in the old days.

"No," he replied simply. "No . . ."

It took her some time to realize that after that morning their paths were crossing less and less often.

Several nights followed, calm nights, spent with her eyes open, only rarely punctuated with brief oblivious intervals of sleep. Her days, on the other hand, flew past in a state of distraught weariness, which was intruded on by the faces of the residents of the Caravanserai and the readers at the library. Eyes unbearable in their insistence; lips coming too close; words articulated with a slow, wet sucking sound that distracted her attention and left their meaning unclear. She would reel back and turn aside; then start talking to cover up her awkwardness. Her own voice deafened her, as if it were resonating somewhere behind her. And an obsessive thought, like a frayed thread being vainly thrust into the eye of a needle, revolved in her drowsy mind: "What if I made no more infusions in the evening? He would understand everything. . . . No, I must continue but drink them in my room. No, I can't. He'll guess. . . ."

The following evening she took the little saucepan into her bedroom. And a few minutes later, glancing through a half-open door, glimpsed a shadow flitting down the corridor and slipping into the kitchen. Or perhaps she just thought she glimpsed it? She was no longer entirely sure of what she saw. The next morning she did not find the little vessel on her bedside table. "So I didn't bring it," she noted, dulled by sleep; but then suddenly realized that the business with the cup went back to the night before, or even the night before that. In her memory the days overlapped, then disintegrated, revealing a glimpse of an opaque matter, without hours, without sounds.

And when one evening she again saw the fine white dust on the surface of the infusion, this did not seem like a repetition but rather the continuation of the action interrupted several days earlier, the night when the sparks from the firewood had burst out of the stove. And so, the icy fingers continued their pressure on her shoulder, on her hip. Her body tipped slowly onto her back. . . . And her tiredness, her exhaustion were such that she did not have to feign sleep. For the moment she felt dead. In place of the confused thoughts, the feverish words that for weeks had echoed in her mind day and night, a heavy, regular sound took her over entirely—like the sound of the wind in the tall treetops in a forest in winter. . . .

All at once this deathly calm was broken. Despite her closed eyes she saw, saw the room, the bed, their two bodies. Her fleeting death was at an end. A movement, a slight stiffening, she did not quite know what, must have betrayed her. She heard the rustling of footsteps, had time to glimpse a candle flame, a long flame spread out horizontally, sucked in by the darkness of the corridor.

It was this candle that allowed her to keep madness at bay. She would spend the morning explaining to herself in a quite measured way that on account of the power cuts everyone was reduced to using candles and that one must be wary of fires, especially in families with young children and that . . . She was afraid of deviating for a moment from the protective logic of these trivialities.

Over several days she would carry on her body the sensation of a supple and timid weight.

And then there would be a night when, without having drunk the infusion dusted with white crystals, she would fall asleep, no longer able to withstand the mountain of lost sleep weighing down her eyelids. She would fall asleep at the very moment when a candle flame appeared in the slow gliding of the door. And would wake a moment later, alone, in the dark. With a sick person's alertness she would smell the odor of the wick and the breath of cold, of ice, of night, that the long overcoat carried in its folds. And she would guess that the gaze that had just been resting on her had sensed the torment of her sleeping body and that his nocturnal visit had only lasted for a moment of brief, silent compassion.

THE DAY AFTER THAT NIGHT she surprised herself in front of the mirror—a face tugged this way and that by grimaces and on her lips a long breathless whisper: "Tarantella, tarantella, tarantula, ta-ra, ta-ra, tarantas. . . ." There was no possibility of stopping, for immediately other words, perfectly reasonable phrases, with all the infallible logic that often characterizes the arguments of the insane, began to hiss within her. Yes, the very same phrases whose good sense had seemed to be her salvation several days earlier. Now their intonation, obtuse and imperturbable, terrified her.

"He came bringing a candle. It's dangerous. What's dangerous? That he came . . . That coat. He puts it on so he can quickly cover his naked body if I wake suddenly. If I woke up he could say that the French door was open and he came to close it. No doubt he's already thought of all the possible answers. . . . He has only touched my body, a woman's body that intrigues him. Yes, that's how it must be said. He has caressed a woman's body. If I could become that nameless woman. Better still faceless. An accident? A face covered in bandages, invisible. And the body asleep, not responsible . . . When all is said and done what has happened so far is harmless. . . . I live in hope that it will remain harmless. So I accept it; I'm becoming used to it; I have nothing against what happens next, on condition that it does not go beyond a certain limit. What limit?"

She began reciting her "tarantula—tarantella," again, even more feverishly, her eyes half closed, her head animated by little quivers. At all costs she must not let the thought that was forming be born. . . .

In response to this incoherent prayer there was a sudden knocking at the front door. No, in truth, the knocking had been audible for some time now and it was the noise of it that had sparked off the "tarantella-tarantula." For, hearing someone knocking, she had to stifle the inadmissible thought: "What if it were someone who . . . ta-ra, ta-ra . . . someone coming to . . . tarantella, tarantella . . . coming to say that . . . shut up . . . tarantella . . . tarantula . . . the child . . . shut up . . . tara, tara . . . that the child has . . . shut up . . . the face under the bandages . . . ta-ra, ta-ra . . . my face, mine, mine, mine . . . tarantella-ta-ra-ta . . . Certainly not he . . . and if it is he . . . months in hospital . . . no . . . no . . . You're hoping for an accident . . . Shut up . . . ta-ra, ta-ra . . ."

She opened the door. In the telegram the postman held out to her she read that someone was informing her of their return to Paris. Left alone, she did not immediately succeed in matching to this someone the initials "L.M." and told herself with stupefaction that to other people these letters signified "her friend" or "her lover." . . . She knew that after a long absence L.M. would send telegrams—a way of skipping a few stages in a reunion, limiting the period of reproaches, excuses, coldness, and forgiveness eventually granted. "Mountains of work. Will be in Paris Saturday," he wrote this time. Behind these words she heard a tone of voice that sought to forestall all objections.

"How strange it is," she thought. "So that's still going on. In their lives. Down there . . ."

She understood that from now on "down there" started outside her own front door.

She knew what was going to happen. He would leave the car beneath the row of plane trees near the station, make his way down into the lower town, taking little deserted streets, and would cheerfully proclaim to her that not a single resident of the Caravanserai had seen him. In the hall, after kissing her, he would run his fingers over the top of the chest of drawers, over that corner sawed off so many years ago. And he would inquire after the health of her son with a very labored air of involvement. They would go off to Paris. While driving he would talk a lot, but would fail to hide his slight lack of self-assurance, his nervousness—the awkward uncertainty of a man confronting the woman who has to accept the scraps of life that he grants her. . . . He would talk more copiously still during part of the night, reassured by her affection, by the absence of reproaches, by the constancy of this woman's body which, after a long separation, would be faultlessly adept at resurrecting the delicate erotic memory of the slightest words and caresses. . . . In the morning she would be the first to leave the hotel, citing one of her usual pretexts (a visit to a friend, shopping . . .), and he, while offering to take her back to Villiers-la-Forêt, would not manage to suppress a note of grateful relief in his voice. . . .

She took a wry pleasure in anticipating how the little scenarios of their reunion would unfold. He came in, kissed her, touched the corner of the chest of drawers, then, lowering his voice, promised to send her the address of "an excellent practitioner, almost a friend, though sadly I've rather lost touch with him." In the car he talked about the camps he had visited in Germany; about the ice on the road that made driving difficult; about their compatriots returning to Russia; about the price of meat. He sensed that he was talking too much, resented the woman's silence, became irritated and allowed a brittle tone to enter his words, that seemed to be saying, "There's no point in sulking. I can't offer you any other way of life. Take it or leave it."

But if she was silent, it was not at all out of resentment. It was almost with admiration that she noted the solidity of this world of routine. The "practitioner," this phantom who materialized every time during the first few minutes of their meetings, like an obligatory form of politeness. This nervousness that she could banish by brushing her hand against his at the wheel. The aggressive nervousness that was instantly transformed into voluble, apologetic affection. . . . In the morning this solidity made her smile. "I could come back with you, you know . . ." he said, leaving that slight hesitation at the end of his sentence, where she hastened to insert her habitual refusal.

As she left the hotel she thought that for him the obligation to take her back would have been as painful as it is for a man to have to offer caresses in the aftermath of lovemaking. . . . Out in the street she took a couple of turnings at random, went into a café, sat down by the window, and hardly a minute later saw him walking past on the sidewalk. The man who had just kissed her and spoken a few words of farewell . . . He passed the café, almost brushing against the corner, but did not notice her. She saw him consulting his watch and pulling a face in mild irritation. A little farther on he stopped; before getting into the car he scraped the soles of his shoes, which were covered in dirty snow, against the edge of the sidewalk.

"A man came yesterday to a muddy and mournful little town," she noted, observing his actions, "and brought a woman to Paris, whose body he hugged, whose breasts he squeezed, whose belly he crushed for several hours. And now he is carefully cleaning his shoes while this woman watches him in a cold street, with houses that look as if they were patched together from gray and black. A man who, during the night, while he was waiting for the next upsurge of desire, kept talking about thousands of corpses dug up in mass graves in Germany. He said he wanted to write a collection of poems on this theme but that 'the subject matter' was 'resistant.' He spoke with anxious excitement, clearly in order to compensate with words for the slow return of his desire . . ."

She broke off, already feeling herself drawn toward a descent into madness that was all too close. No, it was better to remain in . . . she almost thought "their world." The world in which they called "love" what had just passed between the man scraping his shoes and the woman watching him through a café window. . . .

She did not go to see Li, precisely because she was afraid that the latter, convinced of the intensity of this "love," might question her about the man who had just left.

In spite of everything, that night in Paris was a great comfort to her. Their meeting was just like the previous ones, so there was nothing about her that gave away to other people what she was living through in her house in Villiers-la-Forêt. . . .

It was only on the day after her return that she dared to admit to herself the real reason for the secretly beneficial effect of that night in Paris: at no time had any gesture, any caress, any pleasure received or given reminded her of what it was that henceforth bound them to each other, herself and her son.

Four

BUT FOR HER FEAR of appearing ridiculous in her own eyes she would have schooled herself before Christmas Eve to be more natural in the gestures, smiles, and words she would need during their meal together. But her lips trembled slightly when repeating the words she had just addressed to her son, asking him to go and find some branches in the wood behind the Caravanserai. She had spoken with such artificial casualness it seemed to her that he had acquiesced and gone out before she had even finished her sentence. And now, over and over, she was silently reshaping the words that, by their self-conscious tone, must have given away what was inadmissible. . . . From time to time she got up, readjusted the tablecloth on the kitchen table, made slight changes to the place settings, the plates, the little basket with very thin slices of bread. Then, going out into the corridor, she looked at herself in the mirror between the front door and the chest of drawers. Her black dress, the one she used to wear to go to the theater, struck her as too tight-fitting, the neckline too plunging. She removed the belt, put it on again, removed it again. Then covered her shoulders with a shawl. Going back into the kitchen she felt the lid of the pan on the range. "Everything's going to be cold now. What on earth's keeping you?" She was relieved to hear herself addressing this question to her son. Her words seemed to be rediscovering their innocence. . . .

The end of the year had arrived too suddenly. She had almost forgotten about the winter festive season. Generally, several families at the Caravanserai gathered in the refectory at the retirement home for a joint celebration, children and elderly residents together. But since last winter more families, like the red-haired boy's, had moved out; and two of the old people, including Xenia, had died. That evening all that could be heard along the bare corridors of the unlit building was the discreet clicking of locks, as one resident or another half opened the door and listened for a long time, hoping to recognize the sounds of people at dinner. . . .

Several times she had to trim the wicks of the two candles that were beginning to flicker and throw out little strands of soot. The lid of the pan was scarcely warm. "What on earth's keeping you? I'll have to reheat everything now," she repeated, but her voice seemed tense again and already tinged with anxiety. The cold was rapidly invading the kitchen now that the fire had gone out. She gathered up some wood shavings, then a handful of black dust, from the coal that was long since used up, and threw it all into the depths of the range. She washed her hands and, unable to bear it any longer, went into the hall, opened the door. The clear, icy night took her breath away. She wanted to call out, changed her mind, closed the door. And, walking back along the corridor, stopped, undecided, in her bedroom. The reflection of her black dress in the mirror slyly awakened a tender and obscure memory. . . .

The front door banged, footsteps rang out on the floor, and from the kitchen there came the hollow rattle of a bucket. A shout, quite unaccustomed in the boy's mouth, a shout that was simultaneously joyful and commanding, seemed to seek her out through the house: "Mom, can you help me? It's very urgent! Otherwise they're going to die . . ."

She ran along the corridor, took her coat off the hook, and, without asking for explanations, followed her son, who was already leaping down off the front steps.

He led her in the darkness to the bottom of a great snow-covered meadow at the edge of the wood. He ran in among the first of the trees, from time to time disappearing behind a trunk, turning to see if she was coming after him. She followed close on his heels, as if in a strange dream, blinded by the moon every now and then when it pierced through the network of branches.

They found themselves beside a broad sheet of water, the pool that sometimes formed a small loop in the river, sometimes, when it rained less, shrank into a tiny pond, filled with weed. The pool the red-haired boy was playing beside, she remembered, on the day of the first snow . . .

"Look!" Her son's voice was muted now, speaking like one afraid to cause an echo in some terrible or holy place. "Another night of frost and they would all be dead. . . ."

The surface of the pond was covered in ice; a single breach, smaller than a footprint, gave a glimpse of the black, open water. And the dark, glazed surface was streaked with incessant movements, a brief, frenetic shuddering, followed by a slow, drowsy rotation. Sometimes, in the watery reflection of the moon, there was a glint of scales; one could make out the shape of fins, the silvery patches of gills . . . .

They began the rescue with excessive haste, as if these few fish trapped by the cold had only minutes to live. She watched her son plunging his hand into the icy water up to the elbow, and lifting out the slippery bodies, numbed by the lack of air and hardly struggling anymore. He released them into the bucket she held out to him and, lying down on the snow again, resumed his fishing. To ease his task she cleared the water of slivers of ice, pulled out skeins of weed, and occasionally helped him roll up the soaking sleeves of his jacket. Their hurried efforts merged everything into a feverish whole, the gestures, the crunch of snow under their feet, the glittering of the moon broken up on the black surface of the open water, the creaking of the ice, the trickle of the dripping water, their terse exchanges, like orders given on board ship in the midst of a storm. In this flurry their eyes met from time to time for a fraction of a second—and they were surprised at how much the silence of these exchanged looks was detached from their haste. . . . She noticed that her son's right hand had several grazes on the knuckles. But there was so much ice and so much cold water around that the blood had scarcely made the skin pink and had stopped flowing. Perhaps for the first time since the boy's birth, she could contemplate his bleeding without anxiety and said nothing to him. . . .

He released the fish, one by one, coming as close as possible to the icy river bank. Their bodies shuddered for a moment in his hand, then their quivering lives blended with the dark current, the cold, dense weight of which was palpable. After that he emptied the bucket, pouring out the rest of the water with several tufts of weed and lumps of ice. The tinkling of the last drops had a rare resonance, a purity that etched the outlines of the trees and rekindled the reflection of the moon in a frozen puddle. They looked at one another mutely: two ghosts with their faces silvered by the moon, their clothes in disarray; two motionless figures in the night on the bank of a smooth, impenetrable stream. . . . A scrap of wind suddenly brought with it an imperceptible whisper of life, a faint mixture of shouts and music. She turned her gaze in the direction of the upper town.

"They're having a party down there," he said, as if in a daydream and without taking his eyes off the water that glittered at his feet.

"Down there," she repeated to herself as she walked beside him. "Down there . . ." So he, too, was conscious of living somewhere else.

In the course of that night on the riverbank he must have cut his knee without being aware of it in the flurry of the rescue. Next day a blood-filled swelling formed and grew rapidly larger. In the evening his temperature went up abruptly. On several previous occasions the doctor who was based in the upper town had refused to come. There was no longer a proper road between Villiers-la-Forêt and the Caravanserai, now swathed in darkness. She herself took a good quarter of an hour simply to make her way around the building and reach the main gateway. The footpath that followed the wall had disappeared; in certain places the squalls had sculpted long snowdrifts that barred the way.

She knocked at the house of the "doctor-just-between-ourselves." He opened it at once, although it was past midnight, as if he were expecting her visit. As he walked along with her, he kept up a conversation with professional sagacity about "the harshest winter for a hundred years." All the time he was operating, as on previous occasions, he gave vent to little whispering laughs. It was as if he did not believe what he was being told and had his own opinion on the boy's illness. "It's nothing at all, really nothing at all," he repeated, without interrupting his chuckles. And, just as before, he accompanied his actions with patter, like a fairground magician. "Now then. First of all, all nice and neat, we dra-a-a-in off all the fluid, like so-o-o-o! And now a mag-ni-fi-cent saline dressing. . . ." Before leaving he leaned his face toward the boy and, still in the style of an illusionist, proclaimed, "And tomorrow you'll be back on your feet, all right? Like a real trooper." As he went out he said again, but this time in his normal voice, "Naturally, all this is just between ourselves."

Next day the boy got up. . . . She noticed that it was only at these moments of unexpected and unhoped-for recovery that she prayed. The rest of the time her inner vows took the form of a continuous babble of words that she was scarcely aware of anymore. Her rare conscious prayers, on the other hand, included violent threats to the one they were addressed to and demanded a complete turnaround in her son's life, an impossible rehabilitation that must be possible because it was her son. And so that evening, with her face pressed into her hands, her lips dry with the whispering of silent words, she implored, insisted on a miracle. . . . Later on, during the night, now calmer, she realized with bitter sadness that this miracle was linked to that strange personage, the "doctor-just-between-ourselves" who had opened his door to her, wearing an old, neatly pressed tuxedo, with a bow tie beneath his Adam's apple, just as if at midnight, in the dark and icy fortress of the Caravanserai, he were preparing to go to a party. "A poor madman, like all the rest of us here," she thought. The words of her feverish prayer came back to her now as a weary echo. Listening to them, she reluctantly admitted to herself that her secret hope was at least to delay the arrival of the next relapse, the next hemorrhage. Just to win a few days' respite, during which she could live with the illusion of a successful miracle, without feeling too ashamed of her weakness.

It was during those days, one evening, that he appeared in her room again. . . .

The last week of the year was always a very singular time in the lives of the inhabitants of the Caravanserai. The days that came after Christmas and New Year's Day seemed suddenly to backtrack, for the Russian Christmas and New Year came two weeks later than the French celebrations and created the illusion of a fresh end to the year. This delay gave rise to an astonishing confusion in time; to a parenthesis that could not be found in any calendar; to a delight, often unconscious, at not being a part of the life that resumed its sad rhythm in January.

In that winter of 1947 those two lost weeks between the holidays, in the last days of the Russian December, seemed to the émigrés even more empty, even more detached from the ordinary life of Villiers-la-Forêt, than usual. On the ground floor occupied by the retirement home, in a small hall next to the refectory, they had brought in a Christmas tree, as they did every year. But this time there was nothing festive about the presence of the tree in this bleak, cold building: it felt more as if the forest were invading an abandoned house. One evening as she was leaving the library, Olga came upon a man twirling softly in front of the tree in the darkness. Hearing her footsteps, he fled. She realized that he had been waltzing all alone by the light of a candle fixed lopsidedly to one of the branches. She had an impulse to blow it out but did nothing, thinking that the man might perhaps be waiting for her to go before resuming his solitary twirling. . . .

One day, on a particularly cold morning, she went into the lower town in search of bread. As she left the Caravanserai she noticed that her own footprints on the smooth surface of the snow were the very first of the day. The bakery was closed; she had to go all the way up to the one located in the upper town, next to the church. She tried several times to button up the collar of her coat, but her numb fingers no longer obeyed her, and the wind came streaming in at her unbuttoned collar, up her sleeves. Speaking to the baker's wife, she suddenly felt dumb, her frozen lips articulating with great difficulty. The woman listened to her with the exaggerated and scornful patience people have for stammerers, then held out a round loaf to her. Olga did not dare to say that she had asked for something else. And all through the day at the corners of her mouth she retained that painful sensation of congealed words.

That night, for several eternal seconds, he slept pressed against the inert woman's body—against herself.

This, too, was one of those days lost between two calendars, a day of pale colors, hazy in the cold and the wind, a long twilight that lasted from dawn until dusk. . . . As the night began she saw him appearing once more on the threshold of her room. She molded herself almost effortlessly into the temporary death that made her body limp. He lifted her arm carefully, to rearrange it, and it fell back with the soft heaviness of sleep. This death only required one thing of her: to feel totally removed from the stealthy rearrangement imposed on her body; from the caresses, barely perceptible and always seemingly amazed at themselves; from the whole slow and timid enchantment of gestures and held breaths. Yes, to distance herself from her body, to be intensely dead within it . . .

An infinitely remote sound, the chimes of a clock lost in the night, reached her in her death, woke her. Her eyelashes quivered, creating a fine, iridescent chink. She saw. A candle placed on the floor in a narrow china mug, the fierce flickering of the flames behind the stove door . . . And these two naked beings that she contemplated with a gaze still removed, external, like someone observing them from outside, through the window. The body of a woman lying on her back, tall, beautiful, in perfect repose. And, like a bowstring suddenly slackened, the body of a youth, fragile and very pale, stretched out on its side, the head tilted back, the mouth half open. He was asleep. . . .

During the few moments that this sleep lasted, she had the time to grasp everything. Or rather all that she would sense next morning and reflect on in the course of the days that followed, all already foreseen, was condensed in her eyes, still dazzled by their ability to remain wide open. She understood the tiredness beyond human endurance of this young body, the exhaustion accumulated over weeks, months. This brief, trancelike swoon after countless nights of wakefulness. Thanks to this momentary collapse, she believed she could plumb the abyss he bore within himself, without ever letting anything show. He had fallen asleep as children do, in midgesture, in midword. . . . The distant striking of the hours fell silent. Now there was just the tinkling of crystals against the window, gusts of invisible air coming warm from the fire and cold from the window, and the subtle scent of burning wood. And these two naked bodies. Located beyond words, outside all judgment. The mind could brush against them, situate their whiteness in the shadows, in the silence, in the penetrating aroma from the fire; but shattered against the threshold beyond which it could articulate nothing more.

From very far away, a few seconds after the first chimes, came a response: the same twelve strokes, now stilled, now heightened by the wind. She quickly closed her eyes again. He got up so swiftly that he gave the impression of flying as he crossed the room, snatched up the coat and the candle, and pulled open the door. . . .

His sleep had lasted for as long as the interval between midnight striking and its echo on a New Year's Eve that existed only in the old calendar.

ON THE DAY AFTER that phantom New Year's Eve the morning began for her well before daybreak, still in the confused sleepiness of the night, with its long smoky flame flickering on the stub of a melted candle. Padding about, she came and went in the bedroom, opened boxes filled with letters and old papers, sifted through them, and threw most of them into a plywood chest beside the stove where everything accumulated that could be used to stoke the fire. The empty space that was gradually cleared on top of the closet, hitherto piled high with these cardboard boxes, afforded her a vague but real delight. The feeling you have before an impending journey or moving house . . .

She heard her son opening the front door and walking down the wooden steps—some slivers of ice between the planks creaked under his feet. Hidden by the curtain, she watched him all along the footpath as he followed it. Who was he?

A youth clad in an overcoat too broad and still too long for him. Was he her son who would greet the occupants of the Caravanserai he encountered, as well as some French people he knew in the upper town, receiving their greetings in the most natural way in the world? Or was he that unrecognizable young being in a fleeting moment of sleep spent beside a woman's body at night in this room, as it flickered and swayed in the light of a candle placed on the ground?

When her eyes had got used to the rhythm of this figure's tread as he walked beside the wall, she noticed that at each step his foot, his heel seemed to be stamping on the frozen footpath in anger. She just managed to suppress the thought that was already spreading like acid: "He's limping . . ." The words cut off. Now she remembered that in the night, when observing this fragile body stretched out beside her own, she had noticed a blue and yellow mark around the knee, the trace of the last hematoma. . . . As a gust of wind blew open the panels of his coat his silhouette broadened and disappeared around the corner of the building. Again she imagined all the faces the boy's eyes would encounter on the road and in the town. They bore a strange resemblance to the outraged and disdainful ones that she pictured one day condemning the life they led as this odd couple. It was then that she murmured harshly, while intending something other than these half-irrational words, "To hell with them all, with their chimes and their bakeries! They'll never understand . . ."

The next day the postman did not deliver the newspapers subscribed to by the library at the Caravanserai. Some of the rare readers, who were still braving the cold and the snow-covered paths, spoke of a journalists' strike, or a printers' strike, nobody knew exactly what. The postman repeated his explanation three or four more times and in the end they stopped noticing the absence of news. . . . The train that went to Paris every morning suffered several delays as a result of snowfalls and one fine day (it was said that ice had warped the joints on the track) it stayed immobilized all day. Henceforth the capital and the outside world seemed improbable places. Power cuts plunged even the upper town into darkness from six o'clock in the evening. As for the fortress, the old brewery, the people of Villiers took to wondering if it was still inhabited.

The library often remained deserted. Nor was anyone ever seen in the courtyard that was strewn with the humps of snowdrifts. Entrenched in their homes, the occupants spent these brief twilit days on the alert for the slightest sounds in the corridors, and trying to interpret them, picturing one another shivering as they kept watch under a blanket or with a shoulder pressed against the stone of a meagerly heated stove. And if they did appear in the library it was only to leave again almost at once, without even telling their usual stories, simply embellishing this information, culled from a newspaper a week old: "The coldest winter for eighty years . . . For a hundred years . . . For a hundred and twenty years. . . ."

During these lifeless days her thoughts often returned to that boy clad in a heavy man's overcoat, stamping with his foot on the frozen earth as he walked, as if in a gesture of childish anger. "He had no childhood," she said to herself. None of the simple joys the world owes a child. A garden around the family house, visits to grandparents . . . And more besides . . . None of all that. Pain. Anxious anticipation of further pain. An uneasy respite that would only last long enough to allow hope to be born and disappear.

One day she tried to rescue what could still be recovered from that void, insignificant scraps; a smile here, a moment of relief there. There was so little. Almost nothing. This memory perhaps: a cold, sunny day, a recollection from one of those winters lost in the first years of the impoverished childhood that she had not noticed passing . . . He is five or six and is seeing snow for the first time in his life. He runs toward her, making the dead leaves strewn with crystals crackle under his feet, and he shows her a fragment of ice with several blades of grass and a tiny flower head imprisoned in its moist transparency. She is on the brink of going into raptures, or embarking on scientific explanations. But some intuition holds back her words. They remain side by side, silent, watching the slow melting of the beauty and the release of the stalks, which, once outside the ice, become limp, and lose their magic.

She was lost so deeply in this moment of time past that it took her an instant for her eyes to focus on the winter dusk and the footpath running beside the wall of the Caravanserai. She was on her way back from the library. In one place she was obliged to press firmly against the wall, almost to flatten herself against its rough surface, in order to scramble over a big pile of snow. She accomplished this sequence of intricate maneuvers slowly and mechanically, already feeling she was somewhere else. . . . In a long summer's evening several years before. The light of a hot, hazy sunset. The walls of the Caravanserai are warm and, as they were every summer, garlanded with hops. She is sitting on her wooden front steps, motionless, daydreaming, watching the footsteps of the child, this seven-year-old boy as he walks along the riverbank, stoops, rummages in the sand. Then comes over to her, radiant. "Look at this shape!" It is a fragment of limestone containing the broad, hollow spiral, studded with iridescent spangles, of an ammonite. The hollow is reminiscent of something and the similarity is disturbing. "It looks like a plaster cast for my knee," murmurs the child. She catches his eye, feels at a loss, and feigns gaiety: "Yes, but you know, your plaster cast . . ." The child interrupts her. Pressing his ear to the imprint of the shell, he is listening: "You can hear the sound of the sea. . . . it's a sea that's not there anymore. . . ." He holds out his treasure to her. She puts it to her ear, listens. What can be heard is the still of the evening, the cry of a bird, the carefully held in breathing of the child. . . .

This blossoming of moments from long ago lasted until nightfall. Almost unaware she pushed open the door, took off her coat, went to light the range and make the tea. . . . But alongside this activity these fragments of the past were unfolding, always quite humble and, it could have been said, useless, allowing her to dwell in their luminous time. She went up to the table, picked up her cup, the teapot. . . . (A spring day, still in Paris in that dark apartment where the only ray of sunlight that ever comes in is at the end of the afternoon, reflected from the windows of the house across the street. The apartment where there is already a feeling of an imminent departure. The wan sunlight sidles onto the table and irradiates a bouquet of wild cherry blossom. Pausing on the threshold, she comes upon the child, his face buried in the white clusters, whispering in imitation of several voices, first pleading in tone, then passionate. She takes a step backward and the creak of a floorboard gives her away. The child raises his head. For a long time they look at each other in silence. . . .) She came to herself in the middle of the kitchen, unable to think what to do with the cup and the teapot she was still holding, as if they were objects whose use was unknown. . . .

Later in the evening she realized she had made an annoying omission, put her coat on again, went out onto the front steps, and cut notches all over the thick layer of ice on them with the help of an old ax. Then she walked back up the little footpath that ran beside the wall and slashed the slippery slope on the incline at the most dangerous spot. . . .

Before she went to sleep there were several more luminous lapses into the past. And once, as she emerged and saw again in a flash all these images that her memory had secretly retained, she had this thought, which was so obvious it dazzled her: "So, I've forgotten nothing, I haven't missed anything at all . . ." Sleep was already numbing her mind. All she could grasp was that, without knowing it, she had preserved what was essential in this childhood, the part that was silent, true, unique.

. . . Next morning she would remember that the previous evening, lost in her reverie, she had drunk the infusion without examining its surface. She would guess that he had entered her room and come upon her, relaxed in unfeigned sleep.

IT WAS ON THAT MORNING, a winter morning, violet with cold, that for her time lost its rhythm of hours, days, and weeks.

She saw the young figure in the long overcoat passing beneath the window, pictured the slippery, frozen footpath he must follow, ran outside and cupped her hands to her mouth. Too late. He was already climbing the little steep, icy section—with that slightly brutal agility adolescents have, as their growing strength affirms itself. Having conquered it, he quickened his pace and turned the corner around the Caravanserai. . . .

The limpid silence that reigned all about gradually seeped into her. The branch beside the steps was quivering where the boy had brushed against it and shedding a light veil of hoarfrost crystals that made rainbows in the air. Her mind was empty, but with her whole being she felt that she could have stood there on the steps forever, looking out at the snow-covered meadow sloping down toward the river; at this slow powder of crystals falling from a branch stirred by already imperceptible vibrations. Yes, stood there in the sun-drenched sleepiness of a morning that belonged to no year, to no era, to no country. That did not even belong to her life but to quite another life, in which contemplating glittering snowflakes in silence, in the absence of all thought, was becoming essential . . .

She looked at other branches, higher up, reaching toward the pale blue of the sky, then at those of the woodland beyond the walls of the Caravanserai. The sun, still low, softened their black, angular lines with a purple-tinged glow. It seemed to her that she had never felt so mysteriously close to these trees, their bark, their bare branches. Nor so intensely exposed beneath the sky, so intensely herself, facing this immense, patient expectation . . .

The glittering specks of the hoarfrost still meandered in the icy air. The calm seemed infinite. And yet within this silent radiance it was as if you could hear a faint, continuous tinkling—sounds beyond hearing echoed one another with faultless purity and precision. The air faintly pink; the dark tracery of the branches; the dancing of the crystals; the fortress of the Caravanserai still in the blue shadow of the night; the sunlight lightly touching the snow among the trees . . . This ethereal equilibrium of lights and silences was alive, guarded its own transparency, was not going anywhere. Motionless on the little wooden steps, she was a part of it and felt herself to be strangely necessary to all that surrounded her. . . .

The figure that appeared at the other end of the footpath was that of the postman. He brought a telegram signed "L.M.," offering a choice of two dates for their next meeting. She went indoors and read the few impersonal words a second time. The dates seemed to her as fantastic as the months of the French revolutionary calendar—all those *"nivôses"* and *"pluviôses,"* very evocative, but from a completely different era. Paris, a gray morning; a man scraping the soles of his shoes on the edge of the sidewalk before getting into his car . . . "So all of that is still going on somewhere," she told herself, feeling as if she were recalling a life she had abandoned ten years before. The man was still walking about in that busy, humid Paris that smelled of the smoky warmth of cafés, the sweatiness of the Metro. He went to his editorial offices, argued, gesticulated, talked on the telephone, and every evening made his typewriter vibrate with the dry and nervous drumming of his fingers. Then he looked in his calendar and chose these two dates that were still free and sent a telegram. . . .

When she went out again a few minutes later to go to the Caravanserai, the luminosity of the air, the shadows, the branches, the sky, the smell of the cold had imperceptibly reshaped the equilibrium that had linked them a moment ago. She felt this change very intimately. As if she were taking part in the transition from one tonality to another, physically, within her own body.

In the immobility of that winter weather there was one day when, precisely because of these tonalities, she sensed that her son would come to her. . . .

That night the wind howled noisily in the chimney, making the fire blaze in the stove. Sometimes the flames died back, cowed; sometimes they swelled and thrust fine blue tongues out through the chink of the cast iron door. Then suddenly the absence of noise would be deafening, as if the house, snatched up by a squall, were already floating through the night, far from the earth in a soundless, black transparency. The flickering of the candle grew still, and fixed the shadows on the walls of the bedroom. The fire was silent. The scent of burning wood gave contours to the darkness that were invisible but could be perceived if you closed your eyes and inhaled deeply.

Thus it was, her eyes half closed, her breathing intoxicated, that she abandoned herself to this fresh moment of silence. . . . A minute earlier, seeing the sections of a thick branch stacked beside the stove, she had said to herself that this meager firewood would be just enough to give her the illusion, at the start of the night, of going to sleep in a house that was inhabited. She had shivered, picturing herself waking up, well before dawn, in a room smelling of dead, icy smoke. . . . But now even this branch and the fragments of mossy bark scattered on the floor gave off an indefinable happiness. There was, she felt, an unknown joy in the roughness of this bark, in the scented acidity of the smoke, in the thunderous rage of the wind, and in this silence as perfect as the shape of the motionless candle flame. . . . She crouched down, put a part of the branch in the fire, and arranged the rest of the wood carefully beside the stove. A scrap of bark could have cracked beneath the foot of someone walking in the dark. . . .

She knew he would come that night. Everything proclaimed it.

In the kitchen she saw a slight trace of white on the brown surface of the infusion, emptied it into the sink, and went out. Coming back into her bedroom she hesitated for a second, then thrust another scrap of the branch into the depths of the stove.

It was his going, always abrupt, as if running away, that broke the night. The moment was shattered. Taking fright, the body vanished beneath the flaps of the overcoat; the feet, in a ballet of lightning movements, avoided the floorboards booby-trapped with creaks. . . . He stopped on the threshold of the room, returned toward the stove with the same tightrope walker's nimbleness, seized the last piece of the branch, almost threw it into the embers, then decided not to, put the wood down, glanced at the bed, crossed the room, and vanished behind the door as it cautiously slid to.

She waited for a long while without any notion of hours or minutes. Then got up, put the rest of the wood in among the barely flickering flames, and got back into bed. Her reverie, that veered between vigil and dream, lasted through the revival, then the dying of the fire. The whole night was condensed into the unique sensation that hasty visit had left her with; the chilled young body, with warmth flooding into it, first the fingers, a little later the lips, the arm that lay for a moment across her shoulder, her breast. . . . The memory of it, still fresh, could be inhaled, like the scent of the fire, like the gusts of icy air that spilled into the room with each squall.

She had to get up again in the dark. The cold was becoming unbearable. It was as if it were lurking in her clothes; they felt stiff and seemed shrunken. The rough sides of the stove no longer retained a spark of life. . . . Outside the wind had died down, or rather it had risen far above the earth and was driving the clouds along at an unusual height in a rapid, spellbinding flight. From time to time their billowing was swollen with a milky pallor, the moon appeared, then a star, both immediately hidden again. In this shifting gloom she crossed the meadow, a creaking carapace of hardened snow. She found nothing. Everything that could be burned had long since been gathered up by the inhabitants of the Caravanserai. . . . She went toward the wood and after a long, vain trawl, wrenched a twisted branch out of the snow—derisory when she pictured the flames that would only last a few minutes on these little sticks. She straightened up, her head buzzing, her eyes confused with the effort. The vision forming in her eyes was wholly inward: a house tacked on to the wall of a somber, half inhabited building, a winter night, infinite isolation; and in the very depths of this solitude, a room, the silent life of a fire. And this couple, a woman sunk in a sleep more unshakable than a lethargy and a youth with slow movements and a dazzled look, himself surprised by the magic of his crime . . . A mother and her son.

"So I'm mad," she said to herself with calm resignation, studying the pieces of the branch she had just broken up. Her gaze strayed between the dark trunks around her, into the thickets burdened with snow, and then soared up toward the tops of the trees. She saw that over its whole nocturnal expanse the sky had cleared. The last clouds, in a wispy procession, seemed to be streaming vertically away from the earth, as if attracted by the moon, and disappearing into its faintly iridescent halo.

It was then, with her gaze focused on that ascending flight, that she pictured the whole earth, the globe, the world peopled by men. Yes, all those men talking, smiling, weeping, embracing one another, praying to their gods, killing millions of their fellows, and, just as if nothing had happened, continuing to love one another, pray, and hope, before crossing through the fine layer of earth that separated all that ferment from the immobility of the dead.

The words she heard herself whispering surprised her less than the little cloud of her breath shining in a moonbeam: "They are the ones living in complete madness. They, down there, on their globe . . ." She stooped and began to pick up the pieces of the broken branch. . . . Beyond the last trees in the wood she saw the house: the moon appeared around the wall of the Caravanserai, shone down on the snow-covered front steps, and turned one of the windows blue. She still saw it from that distant perspective, toppling down from the vertical flight of the clouds. Still saw the planet as a whole and on the dark, nocturnal side of it a long dwelling, leaned up against a wall. And that couple forgotten by the world. A woman and a youth. A mother and her son . . . A slight cloud arose from her lips once more. The murmur of her words melted into the frozen air. . . . A strange couple. A youth who will die. His last winter, perhaps. Last spring. He thinks about it. And the woman's body that he loves, the first body in his life. And the last . . .

The faint cloudiness about her lips from these words was dispersed. Now there was only the blue of the moonlight on the snow-covered steps. And a trace of snow, too, on that branch above the footpath. The footprints beneath the trees, her own, those of another. The silence. The night when he had come, stayed, and left. A night so agonizingly alive, so close to death.

That was precisely how it must be, she now understood: the woman; the youth; their unspeakable intimacy in the house poised on the brink of a winter's night, on the brink of a void, quite foreign to the globe that seethed with human lives, hasty and cruel. She experienced it as a supreme truth. A truth made manifest through the bluish translucency on the steps, through the trembling of a constellation just above the wall of the Caravanserai, through her solitude under this sky. Nobody in the world, in the universe, knew she was standing there, her body limpid with cold, her eyes wide open. . . . She understood that, if expressed in words, this truth would signify madness. But this was a moment when words were being transformed into white vapor and their only message was their brief gleaming in the stellar light. . . .

She planned to burn her trophies in the kitchen range to make some tea and at the same time to wait for the dawn, when looking for firewood would be easier. She could not believe her eyes when she saw all the branches stacked together beside the range. There were still some drops of melted snow glistening on the bark. . . . She remembered the glance he had directed at the dying fire in the stove as he fled the room. So, an hour or two before her he had been wandering about in the darkness among the trees. The footprints she had seen in the snow were his. . . . What amazed her most was knowing that they had both looked at the same night sky, seen the same mists escaping from their mouths. Some unfathomable minutes apart.

She did not write a fresh letter to L.M. but sent him the old one, that laborious letter breaking things off. She even forgot to correct the date on it.

THE LIFE SHE LIVED NOW was no longer divided into days or hours, nor into coming and going; nor into actions; nor into fears; nor into expectations; nor into causes and their effects. There was suddenly a particular light (like the calm pallor above an abandoned railroad track that she had been obliged to follow, one afternoon of milder weather); her eyes took in everything, discerning all the nuances in the air (the silvery tint of the fields, the unexpected gold of the sun shining on the rooftops of the already distant town); and she experienced this light, these subtle colorations of the air as profound events in her life.

It was to avoid her usual path, now awash under the porous snow of the thaw, that on her way home that day she had walked around the station and approached the Caravanserai from the opposite direction. A train went by; she continued on her way, stepping from one tie to the next, listening for a long time to the fading vibration of the rails. Then the track branched into two. This one, the old one, that in days gone by used to serve the brewery, soon ended in a buffer stop. . . . In the distance the roofs of the town clustered about the church were bathed in a golden radiance that shone through a fleeting rift in the clouds. Over here, beside the buffer stop, it was almost dark. Leaning her elbows on the barrier, she remained stock still for a moment, her gaze lost in the expanse of the fields, which in this pale light had the softness of suede. The patch of sunlight on the town faded. . . . She was alone at the end of this forgotten track. She felt secretly at one with the misty distances, and close to this bare shrub that grew between the rails. The rain began to fall, merging her still further with the low sky and the soft snow that gave off a vivid, heady coolness. . . .

That evening there was another moment that absorbed her into its profound harmony. The rain continued to pour down heavily, but its torrents were arrested by the return of the cold that put an end to a day and a half of mild weather. The earth hardened and the streams of water seemed to freeze in midflight. They crashed against the ground, against the layer of ice on the fields, against the roof, in the branches of the trees—and the night rang with an infinite variety of ceaseless tinklings. This crystalline cascade drowned all other sounds, crushed any shadow of a thought with its glass beads, permeated her body with its delicate flow.

She could hardly hear the crackling of the fire any longer above this headache-inducing din. Only the tallest flames that rose above the tangle of the wood could pierce through the incessant roar of the icy torrent. Its deafening rattle had the fluidity of rain, while the ferocity of its noise kept her awake. And the flames surged up in that nocturnal bedroom besieged by an icy downpour, now on this side of sleep, now in her dreams, amid countless warm, supple, aromatic spurts of resin. . . .

When he came in, shielding the candle with his hand, his footsteps, his movements, the whiteness of his body that she could sense without lifting her eyelids, all these things hovered between the two nights, sometimes deep in her dream, then suddenly breaking the boundary of it with an incredibly vibrant caress. The hesitant hand seemed to be making its way between long rivulets of sound to enfold her breast, to find peace upon it, while they awaited an ebb tide back into the dream. There, where their bodies would be nothing but the same endless wave, a shadow with the scent of snow, the flickering amber of fire.

He remained in her without moving, his breath suspended, his body weightless. A motionless flight above a sleeping lake . . . She could still feel the weight of him in her groin, in her belly when he was no longer there, as she slowly returned across the tides of fire and crystal and again found herself in a room surrounded by a rainy winter's night.

. . . In the morning the treads of the front steps rang out underfoot like glass. She walked down them and made her way across the upside-down sky, a looking glass colored pink by the day's dawning. The trees, the windows of the house, the wall of the Caravanserai were all reflected in it with the clarity of an engraving. The bushes laden with thousands of frozen drops of water looked like strange crystal candelabra abandoned here and there in the snow. She took several steps and lost her balance but had time to realize that she was going to fall and anticipated her tumble by letting herself slide. Half stretched out, she pressed against the ground to raise herself and suddenly encountered her own face reflected in the ice, so calm and so distant that, once on her feet, she turned back with an unconscious urge to see that calm expression in the same place again. . . .

There was a day when everything swirled in a hypnotic flurry of snowflakes. The roofs of the town, the Caravanserai, the willows along the riverbank—everything disappeared piece by piece, as if delicately coated in white with a paintbrush. . . .

Then another day when the color was extraordinary. A pale violet, very faint, scarcely mauve out in the whiteness of the fields; denser, dark blue beneath the wall and in the alleys of the lower town; and more vibrant, almost palpable in a broad, plum colored sweep above the horizon . . .

And another day, when in the evening she was intoxicated by suddenly discovering the various scents given off by the branches thrown down beside the stove—a whole forest, with different essences, some acid, some heady, with the coolness of the frost that emitted shrill whistles in the flames as it melted. The aroma of moss, of wet bark, of the life asleep in all the trees.

Each of these moments carried within itself a mystery ready to be revealed, ripe to be experienced, but which was still hidden, making their abundance painful, like some mountain landscapes that are too beautiful, too awesome, for our lungs, which begin to struggle for air. . . .

On the day of the dancing blizzard the long overcoat he took off when he came into the room was white with snowflakes. His hair as well. She felt several drops of melted snow trickling onto her breast. . . . On the day of the amazing violet light they ran into each other in the upper town, he returning from school, she with her shopping bag. There was no embarrassment, no forced words. In that mauve, blue, and violet light everything became at once unreal and natural: the street, an inhabitant of the Caravanserai greeting them, the two of them together. They walked along, looked at each other from time to time, recognized each other as people recognize each other in dreams, with a clairvoyance sharpened by reality, but in a fantastic setting. At one moment, as she crossed a long strip of bare ice beside the bombed-out pharmacy, she leaned on his arm. . . .

And it was thanks to him that she discovered the different scents of the flesh of trees. One night, as he left the room, he crouched down and touched one of the branches drying beside the stove. She repeated this gesture an hour later as she put more wood on the fire. And also out of curiosity. A mossy shape reminded her of a moth. She touched it, as he had just done, and suddenly inhaled a complex mixture of scents. Kneeling there with her eyes closed, she smelled their elusive range. She sensed the coolness of a body, of the body that, before joining her (she knew it now), had been impregnated with cold in a frenzied coming and going on the frozen slope between the house and the river. He had just left her and his presence was slowly awakening within her, in her groin, in her belly, and mingling with the slightly bitter or acid tastes of the branches, with the perfumed warmth of the fire, with the silence. And what she was living through became so full then, so painfully close to the revelation of a mystery, that she opened the French door, filled her hands with snow, and buried her face in it, as if in an ether mask.

★ ★ ★

This elation was broken some nights later when once again he remained in her for long, still minutes. It was at that moment that the dilated suspense at the base of her belly trapped her. For a fraction of a second she felt it like a caress and for a moment lost the regularity of breathing she had taught herself. On previous nights this suspense had represented an ordeal that must be passed through in a transient death of all her senses, skimming silently over the void. This time it was a caress, a dense, titillating gust that snaked upward toward her chest and exploded in her throat. . . . Two other nights the same spasm was repeated, the same flaring up of the air she was breathing. Her surprise diminished and during the third night it became a kind of inadmissible anticipation that prepared her breathing and shaped her body. . . . She no longer had to die in order to give herself to him.

By midday the broad halo around the pale sun was already visible—a sign of great frosts. The air rang out with sharp, dry rustling. At nightfall the windows were covered with hoarfrost patterns. . . . That evening she examined the infusion, threw it away, went to her room and stopped for a moment, holding the candle, to contemplate the fragile beauty of the curlicues of ice: chiseled stems, crystalline corollas. . . .

That night he got up in such haste that she stiffened, believing she must have unconsciously given herself away. A little light filtered between her lashes. She saw him standing between the door and the window, his body tensely arched, his head and shoulders thrown back, his eyes tightly shut. . . . No longer hiding in sleep, she watched him, her breath held in pity, in distress. He was pounding the base of his belly with his hands; which were closed, as if over a prey, and shook with rapid tremors. Now his uplifted face, with the same grimace of brutal pain, expressed a kind of prayer, a supplication addressed to someone whom only his own closed eyes could see. His mouth, gasping, swallowed air with a rictus that laid bare his teeth. His hands, crossing over one another, tensed more violently, a convulsion and then another ran through his body—he looked like a butterfly beating against a windowpane. . . . But already, slowly, the muscles were relaxing. A clarity of repose softened his features, then, very quickly gave way to bitterness, weariness. With a clumsy gait, as if he needed to learn how to walk all over again, he went to pick up his long overcoat, took out a handkerchief, applied it to his stomach, crumpled it, put it away. . . .

It was as he was going out that he tripped, stumbled, and rocked back on his heels. As he sought to steady himself, he placed the flat of his hand against the window for a moment. This light touch was enough. He straightened himself up and left the room. In the darkness she thought she could hear his young heart, arrested by fear, starting to beat again. . . .

She got up often that night. Put wood on the fire, went back to bed again. No word, not even the beginnings of a thought, interrupted the silence that reigned within her. The visions that exploded silently before her eyes were inaccessible to words. She saw again the young face with its tortured and blissful rictus, the eyes closed but dazzled with light. The body assaulted by violent spurts of pleasure. But above all the knee that remained bent back, though the body was tensed like an arrow, a knee bulkier than the other, an interruption in the pure white line of his nakedness.

No, it would have been impossible to put that into words. This fusion of love with death lent itself only to mute fascination, to absolute incomprehension, more penetrating than any thought. . . . She got up, thrust a fragment of wood into the embers, and noticed the phosphorescence of the hoarfrost on the dark window. The suppleness of her own movements astonished her. There was something almost joyful in the agility with which her body stood up, crouched beside the stove, skimmed across the room in a few steps. Without trying to put it into words, she sensed that a new bond was being formed between her own life and this death so close, so freighted with love. . . .

That night she could still see no more in this bond than the quite physical simplicity with which, on the days that followed, she would learn how to hold within her groin this young body assaulted by waves of pleasure. He would no longer be the butterfly beating against a windowpane. He would not flee. He would remain in her until the end, until the bitterness, that would spread like the shadow of a loving hand across his face, now at peace.

In the morning the window covered in hoarfrost was ablaze with a thousand sparks of sunlight and resembled a fault in granular quartz. The rekindled fire appeared pale in these red rays that split the facets of the ice. No sound, not one birdcall, came from outside. The peace and the cold of that winter's Sunday surrounded their house just as an immense snow-covered pine forest would have done.

She spent several long minutes at the frozen window all streaked with sun. Her gaze distractedly picked out the stems and fronds that the ice had woven on the glass. . . . Suddenly amid this capricious tapestry she noticed an astonishing contour. A hand! Yes, the print he had left the previous evening when he leaned lightly on the glass to stop himself falling. The outline of his fingers that the night had covered in delicate tendrils of frost. She brought her face closer, intending to study this crystalline design in more detail. A cold breath intoxicated her. All she had experienced since the fall was mysteriously concentrated in that chill, a single sensation of pain and joy beyond her strength. Everything, the past night, even those days buried in periods of her life she no longer ever thought about, everything returned in a single inspiration. A draft that inhaled all those nights that could not be spoken of. A gust that also breathed in the snowy scent of the immense forest surrounding their house, a forest that did not exist, but whose wintry calm was already entering her breast, dilating it still more, to infinity . . .

She regained consciousness several seconds later. Got up, feeling a strange heaviness in her movements, saw reflected in the mirror a long scratch filling with blood that traced a fine curve from her cheekbone to the corner of her mouth. Taking confused, dull steps, she stood a small round table upright that had been knocked over, picked up a little ceramic vase that had lost its handle but was not broken. . . . While she did this she was living intensely elsewhere. She was walking into a great wooden mansion, a great silent house surrounded by snow-laden trees. She walked along corridors, whose walls were crowded with portraits that followed her with suspicious looks; and slipped into a tiny room tucked away on the top floor. . . . There at a narrow window decorated with hoarfrost patterns she forgets herself for a long time. She, the growing girl, who is elated to the point of giddiness by these crystal flowers and fronds. Bringing her lips close to the windowpane she blows lightly. Through the little melted hole she sees a forest burdened with snow as far as the eye can see. . . .

Without detaching her eyes from that moment, she wiped the blood from her cheek; chopped some wood; prepared the meal and later spoke to the people at the library; lived other nights and other days. Her gaze forever focused on the endless forest in the snow. She no longer remembered having lived any other way.

Five

THE DOCTOR, AS EVER, said little, but after long weeks of solitude these few sentences seemed to her like an elaborate, almost overwhelming speech. Nor was she listening to him properly. It was an old habit of hers: the doctor's observations caused pages to appear in her memory with the description of the illness, the symptoms, and the treatments, pages she knew right down to the very arrangement of paragraphs. The doctor spoke as he wrote out the prescription, breaking off to reread it, and it was into these pauses that fragments of the pages learned by heart would insert themselves: ". . . the softened bone began to cavitate; small pockets of dead tissue formed cysts. The bony extremities became deformed, and adopted unaccustomed postures. The joint gave rise to a progressive chronic disability. . . ."

There was nothing new to her either in what she was hearing or in the trains of thought unfolding in her mind. She could not stop herself following through these prognoses to the limit; first picturing the worst case, then the cure; the two extremes, despair and a miracle. All parents of sick children, she already knew, came to terms with their distress in this way.

The lamp on the desk flickered. In a brief moment of darkness she saw the pale ghost, her son, still half undressed, tugging at the inside-out sleeve of his shirt. And outside the window waves of drifting snow clung to the panes. . . . The light returned, the doctor finished writing and, in his voice that always sounded as if he were irritated by incomprehension, reached his conclusion: they would have to think of an operation. "This summer, so as not to make him miss his academic year," he added in a less dry tone, turning toward the boy. . . . The lamp went out again, they spent several moments in silence, gradually growing accustomed to the soporific blue of the night-light above the door. In the corridor cries could be heard and the drumming of footsteps.

This wait in the darkness was salutary. All morning Paris had assaulted them with too many words, too many objects, too much gesticulation. And even in this office she had suffered from the same excess: sheets of paper, files; pens, the paper knife; the doctor's voice that had to be decoded; his apparently indifferent glances, in which, nevertheless, she saw herself perceived as a woman obliged to please. . . . The minutes they spent in the half light eradicated the brutal superabundance of sensations. They could hear flurries of snow being hurled against the windowpanes, and somewhere in the depths of the city the muffled hoot of a siren. . . . The doctor grumbled and struck a match. The light of an oil lamp shone. They said good-bye but he chose to accompany them to the exit; that wait in the darkness had brought them closer together. . . . As he walked beside her in the ill-lit corridor, he felt obliged to speak and uttered a sentence that was clearly meaningless but which crucified her. It was one of those very French turns of phrase that mislead foreigners with their disconcerting thoughtlessness. "At this stage in the game, you know," he sighed, "it's best to take each day as it comes." There was a note of melancholy, almost of tenderness in his voice. He abandoned the caution reflected in his customary tone, dry and feigning irritation. "In which case," he added, in an already neutral voice, as he opened the door for them, "sufficient unto the day is the evil thereof." He must have sensed himself that his remark was double-edged.

The whole of Paris was plunged in darkness. Only the car headlights cut through the whirling clouds of snow. They crossed the Seine on a ghostly bridge, whose gigantic steel curves seemed to sway in time with the surging of the snow squalls. In one street, hemmed in between blind houses, a small gathering was gesticulating around a woman who lay on the trodden snow. A little farther on, a bus was unable to get started, the acid air flayed the nostrils and blocked the throat; then a fresh gust of wind swept them clean. It was at this point, trying to escape the asphyxiating cacophony of the cars, that she mistook the road. Instead of emerging onto the avenue that would have led them straight to Li's house, they came upon a monotonous, endless wall. Should they go right? Left? What she wanted most of all was to turn her back on the squalls. From the other side of the enclosure repulsive, sickly sweet effluvia wafted over; in calmer weather, no doubt, these stagnated within the walls of the abattoir. . . . They walked along, often slipping, catching hold of each other's arms. She raised her brow into the snow, as if to drive out the sentence that was absurdly matching the rhythm of her footsteps: "At-this-stage-in-the-game-at-this-stage-in-the-game. . . ."

Suddenly in the darkness lashed with squalls a cry arose quite inhuman in its power, a bellow torn from the entrails of an animal, a maddened and tragic call. She shivered, quickened her step, stumbled. He grasped her elbow, supported her as she almost fell. Their faces came so close that she could see the slight trembling of his lips and heard his voice despite the wind's fury: "Don't be afraid . . ."

She gazed into his eyes and asked, in total unawareness, simply echoing his voice, "Afraid of what . . . ?"

"Of anything," he replied and they continued walking.

Li went off to sleep in her studio, leaving them in the tiny sitting room crammed not only with furniture but also, a recent addition, cardboard boxes and cases, in preparation for her departure.

They were alone: she, bedded down on the little sofa, whose curve she had to mold herself to in order to sleep; he on the armchairs pushed together, squeezed between the piano and the table. . . . They could not sleep and both sensed this, sensed the discreet wakefulness of the other in the darkness. . . . Finally she recognized breathing that was no longer careful of the other's presence, the inimitable syncopated, touching music of a sleeper's respiration. She turned over onto her back, prepared for long sleepless hours, happy, even, with the strangeness of this place, where conjuring up the impressions that had assailed her could pass for an insomniac's game. . . . By reaching out her arm she could have touched the armchairs in which her son was asleep. This dark apartment in a great dark, deserted city; the two of them, so near to each other, with this unique, unspeakable, monstrous bond between them . . . The night began to ring in her ears. She moved, reached out with her hand, grasped a box of matches, held the flame close to her watch. It was half past four in the morning. She got up and put on her clothes; this action already felt like a welcome prelude to their escape. The water in the tiny bathroom was icy, like in an abandoned house; the minor domestic disorder in the kitchen also heralded preparations for departure. She opened the door at the back that looked onto the little yard. The snowstorm had abated. The last flakes drifted down slowly, attracted by the light of the candle. The snow was smooth, virgin, even the birds had not yet had time to star it with their footprints. In their garments of white the walls, cornices, and chimney pots had a fluid, downy beauty. . . .

She sensed that someone was coming, then heard his footsteps. She turned, and met his gaze; they understood it was pointless to exchange ritual questions. He stood beside her and watched the spinning of the snowflakes, detaching themselves from the gray sky and falling slowly toward the candle flame. . . . They were already in flight as they drank a cup of quickly cooled tea, nibbled some bread, and wrote a note of thanks to Li. They both sensed, without putting it into words, that they had to be gone from the city in advance of the light, in advance of the crowds in the streets, in advance of the trampled snow. . . . And when they collapsed, breathless, onto the seat of an empty car, in the first train of the morning; when she saw the young face opposite her in the twilight, his eyes closing, already weighed down with sleep, she understood, without wanting to understand, that this escape, this empty train, swaying as it clattered drowsily along, these windows blinded with snowflakes, the two of them with their deep abyss and even his still childlike hands, quivering slightly as he started to dream—all this was another life, the very first moments of which she was just discovering.

From now on it seemed to her that other people could understand her, though not because of the words she spoke. An object, she felt, a gesture, a scent would suffice. Back in January, during that lost time between the old and the new calendars, she had given the nurse at the retirement home a gray angora openwork shawl. The young woman had come to the library looking for accounts of the war, hoping, she said, to find in them some information about the place where her lover had died. Beneath the worn fabric of her woolen dress the shivering of her thin body was perceptible; and on her lips and in her eyes the fierce struggle between pride at having lived through such a beautiful and tragic love affair and humiliating fear at being suspected of lying. . . . She had gone away, with the shawl around her shoulders, quite perplexed, not knowing what to make of this gift; and at that moment Olga had had a dizzying insight into this woman's life: the evenings in a poorly heated room, the tiny scrap of comfort the gray wool might bring to her body. . . .

One day, after their return from Paris, she interrupted the old swordsman who had launched into his usual tale of fighting. She spoke very softly, as if to herself, of a carnival night long ago, in a great mansion at the edge of a forest; of a garden, all foaming with apple blossom. And of the young horseman who had suddenly appeared before a girl overcome with giddiness. It seemed to her that this man who for years had tirelessly been waving his arm about in imitation of saber fighting, this cutter-off of heads, was no different from that young horseman long ago in the midst of the garden at night. And that she needed to say to him very simply, "Forget the wars and the blood. I know you are haunted by the look of a man you killed. The eyes of a man who can already feel the blade cutting into his neck. And that to escape him you are forever calling out your 's-s-shlim' and laughing and frightening other people with your laughter. Forget. For in your own youth there must have been a night, meadows with cool grass, a garden white with flowers that you rode through on your horse. . . ." The only words she actually uttered were: "night," "apple blossom," "white petals in the horse's mane . . ." It seemed to her that the face of the man listening to her was freed of its grimaces, became simple and serious. He never performed his swordsman act in front of her again.

From now on she perceived herself as being much closer to other people. Closer to the fields, to the nights, the trees, the clouds, the skies these people carried within them, that formed a silent language in which they could understand her without words. One day, with a joy that stung her brow as if peppered with grapeshot, she had this crazy hope: perhaps even what she was living through could one day be admitted?

Among the new messages, whose increasingly clear resonance she was now receiving, there was a night when all one could hear was the drowsy rhythm of rare, heavy drops trickling down from the mass of soft snow on the roof, splashing in a melodious cascade, close to the steps and under the windows. Her body, for several nights past, had learned to give itself, while seeming still, to avoid the brutal break, to preserve the slow settling of bodies that have taken pleasure. . . . That night she found the rhythm of that silent separation. When his body was exhausted she felt his temple laid, for a moment, against her lips. A vein was throbbing, crazily. As she gave this involuntary kiss she sensed the pulsations gradually calming down. . . .

Another occasion for her to speak to the being whose understanding she already hoped for came on that evening of the thaw. She made a mistake when examining the infusion, no doubt confusing the pollen of the macerated flowers with traces of the powder. He did not come. . . . She waited for a long time, beyond what was already an unlikely hour, then, to break the spell of this waiting and to find sleep again, she got up, dressed, went out onto the steps.

The night was clear. The air was softer; scents, long imprisoned by the cold, were flowing readily, like the slightly bitter aroma of damp bark. The snow had been undermined by a multitude of invisible tricklings, still covert, that filled the night with an incessant peal of water drops. She felt she was moving forward across an endless musical instrument, snapping several strings at each sacrilegious step. . . .

She stopped halfway between the house and the river, no longer wanting to disturb the melodious trembling of the slowly subsiding snows. Tilting her head back, she plunged in among the stars for a long time. A silent, unflagging wind descended from these nocturnal depths. She staggered, suddenly exalted, her eyes looked around for support. The shadow of the wood, the dark reflection of the water, the dim fields on the opposite bank. The sky from which spilled the powerful and constant wind. All this lived, breathed, and seemed to see her, to be focusing some kind of infinite gaze upon her. A gaze that understood everything but did not judge. It was there, facing her, about her, within her. Everything was said by this immense wordless, motionless presence. . . . The wind was still blowing from the summit of the sky, from its dark reaches scarcely marked with the buoys of stars. She was responding to the eyes staring at her, impassive eyes, but whose absolute compassion she sensed. . . .

She went home with the feeling of descending slowly from a very great height. Moving forward, she sought unconsciously to tread in the footprints left from her outward journey, so as not to snap any more strings. Up on the steps she cast a glance behind her: on the stretch of snow a string of footprints led out into the night with no return. And when she looked up a powerful gust of wind, falling vertically, struck her eyelids.

ONE EVENING SHE NOTICED that the great pile of snow that had accumulated behind the wall of their house had shrunk into a grayish sponge around which the glistening, naked clay of the earth lay uncovered. Confused feelings gripped her: this exhaustion of the cold was quite natural, quite expected, but at the same time heavy with hidden menace. Was the winter (their winter!) now going to be woven imperceptibly back into the indifferent round of the seasons? This very normality seemed at once salutary and fraught with vague dangers. . . . A few days later when she was clipping together the newspapers that the postman had once more started delivering to the Caravanserai after several months of eclipse, she came upon this headline: RHINE ICE DYNAMITED TO OPEN WAY FOR SHIPPING DELAYED BY UNPRECEDENTED FROSTS. Strangely, her heart missed a beat and she heard a little silent cry: "But why all this hurry?"

Then there was the night of all-enveloping fog, smelling of the sea. . . . With closed eyes she gave herself, happy, unthinking, liberated even by her blindness, by the uselessness of words, by the abandon she no longer had to feign. . . . It was this forgetfulness that must have given her away. She sighed, or rather took a breath like a child about to cry. He detached himself from her body and fled. She went through a long moment of nonlife before understanding the real reason for his flight.

It was a continuous sound, growing louder, more fluid. It was gradually permeating the muffled heaviness of the fog. . . . At the first light of dawn, when she opened the window, she saw the meadow flooded, the willows standing in the middle of a lake, the water rippling gently a few yards away from the front steps. . . .

By evening the entire Caravanserai had become an island and their house a little promontory above the calm, misty expanse of the waters.

It was the "doctor-just-between-ourselves," wearing long rubber boots, who brought them bread on the second day of the flood. Then the water rose several inches more and even this equipment became inadequate. People forgot them as they waited for the sun to return and the waters to fall.

The days were misty and mild, seeming not so much to exist now as to be a return to a far distant past when even pain was obliterated. At night all one could hear was the soothing lapping of the water on the front steps. And that night, when he came into her room, the cries of a flock of birds—no doubt migrants exhausted by their flight that had found no place to land and were alighting on the roof of the Caravanserai . . . It was beneath the rising tide of these innumerable cries that she surrendered her body to him again, her body which imperceptibly, from one night to the next, had won a secret freedom, inaccessible in aroused love. Her body that, in a death that was profoundly alive, responded to caresses and fashioned desire. A sleeping lover's body. Born in the depths of a dream that the boy could relive indefinitely.

When she opened the door in the morning she alarmed a dozen birds that had settled on the roof. They emitted indignant cries and began to circle over the dull mirror of the waters. Over the inverted sky that began at the top of the front steps, in which their silent, white wings could be seen slipping along . . .

Several days and nights were swamped in this misty calm, the drowsy idleness of the waters. Finally, one evening when it was still light, she noticed that the reflections of the clouds on the flooded meadow had moved farther from the house. A strip of bruised land emerged, bristling with stalks and clumps of grass, like the dorsal fin of an immense fish. This terra firma saturated with moisture surrounded the house and ran along the wall of the Caravanserai. . . . Through the window she saw her son, a shopping bag on his shoulder, walking away slowly, sounding out with his feet the uncertain dotted line of this first footpath. An hour later he returned, laden. His shape was reflected in the waters now ablaze with the sunset. She hesitated, then went to greet him on the steps. They stayed there for a time, both of them, without looking at each other, motionless before the now tranquil expanse.

That evening, or perhaps it was the next, a thought struck her with the painfulness and beauty of its truth. If what they were living through could be called love, then it was an absolute love, for it was fashioned from a prohibition inviolable yet violated, a love visible only in the sight of God, because monstrously inconceivable to mankind, a love experienced as the everlasting first moment of another life. . . .

For months her thoughts had spilled into the unthinkable and had become meaningless. Their return now disturbed her. She would have liked to go on living in the transparent and silent simplicity of the senses. Yes, to go back to the scent of the fire, to the powdery hoarfrost tumbling through the air from a snowy branch . . . But already a new link of chain was latching on to her mind: "For the boy this may be his first and last love. And for me? It is also my first and last love; for no one has ever loved me like this, with such a passionate fear of causing me harm. No one will ever love me like this again . . ." The truth of these words was born of lightness but, once uttered, became disturbing.

That night anxiety returned in the guise of a strange noise: it was as if someone were walking along in the water beside the house with careful steps, attempting, through the somnambulistic slowness of their pace, to minimize the little telltale splashes.

Next morning a bleak wind was blowing with inhuman, menacing power. It tore at a number of long, dry strands of hops on the walls of the Caravanserai, brandishing them in its rainy squalls like a monstrous topknot of snakes. As she went into the building through the porch, she heard the sound of an unusual tumult, the slamming of shutters in one of the empty apartments, but, in particular, a slow, distant, metallic creaking, like the noise of rusty hinges. Along the corridor that led to the main library hall this creaking increased in volume, becoming a ponderous, rhythmical crashing. The sounds of voices, on the other hand, became fainter and fainter, then faded away; and it was amid a crowd of dumbfounded spectators that this scene met her eyes.

High up near the ceiling the huge gearwheel for the pulley, mounted on girders fixed into the wall, was revolving with a mesmerizing slowness. Had the wind dislodged some locking wedge in the machinery, stopped for long decades? Or had the electrician who came to repair a breakdown in the current the previous day made a mistake over the cable? A cleaner had noticed the wheel moving that morning and alerted the others. . . . Now the gearwheel was continuing to rotate steadily and inexorably in its blind power. The chain that ran around it could be seen traveling down, inch by inch, through a hole in the floor that had been hidden by a square of plywood. And, having disappeared, it rose again from the depths of the cellar. . . . Suddenly, with a brief grinding, the plywood gave way, and there, welded to the chain, a bucket covered in rust and slime could be seen surging up, slowly bringing to the surface what must once have been water from a deep well that supplied the brewery. . . . A bitter, earthy smell, an odor, it seemed, of flesh and death, invaded the room. Another bucket appeared, then another and yet another. The first one was already at the top of the chain and tipped, spilling out its viscous liquid where once, no doubt, there was a large vessel. The odor became more pungent, with its sweetish base of grain rotting in the bowels of the earth, with its disturbing, wild savor of fermentation. The subterranean mud from a fresh bucket was already decanting itself over its tilting rim. . . . As if suddenly roused from sleep, a man rushed into the corridor to switch off the current.

THERE WAS AN ABUNDANCE OF LIGHT, almost too much for eyes accustomed to the fog; an abundance of sparkling sky; an abundance of damp, glistening watercolor tones. The meadow that the river had gradually uncovered as it receded looked like a broad russet-and-yellow pelt, all ruffled, drying in the sun.

She perceived this surge of light with the sensibility of an invalid. Each ray of sun, each new color was simultaneously a joy and a torture. One day she told herself she must dig the ground in the narrow bed beneath the windows and plant the first flowers. Her heart stood still: she had a vision of herself the previous autumn on a fine September evening, pulling up the dead stalks at that same spot. . . . On another occasion, returning late from the Caravanserai, she went down as far as the little expanse of water at the bottom of the meadow. The moon was shining on it and in the distance the tiny pond looked as if it were frozen. She went up to it and touched the surface with the sole of her shoe. Lazy rings rippled across the moon's liquid gold. As on that unimaginable Christmas night when they had broken the ice and rescued the fish . . .

Each evening was imperceptibly gaining a few more moments of light. And that evening it was particularly noticeable, for a narrow ray of coppery sunlight came streaming in obliquely at the kitchen window; from now on it was going to return, less unexpectedly and a little wider, each day.

It was by this already springlike light that she noticed a fine white film on the brown flowers of the infusion. She emptied it automatically on returning from the bathroom; went into the bedroom and froze, stunned. The bedroom, too, was bathed in light and had nothing nocturnal about it. And yet he could come in from one minute to the next!

She quickly drew the curtains (they were too narrow and always left a gap), threw some fragments of wood into the stove (they had stopped having fires more than a week before), and decided to put a lamp on her bedside table, the heavy lamp with the silk shade that generally stood on the shelves. Once switched on, it reduced the brilliance of the sun that was tangled in the branches of the willows and seemed determined not to set. . . .

It was one of those clumsy and vague gestures that are made in the act of love. A hand suddenly forgetting how to move in the real world. She felt this hand, these cool, gentle fingers, touching her shoulder, folding round her breast. . . .

Then the hand flitted away, describing a hesitant circle, unnecessarily broad (was he trying to move the lampshade that was too big, too close; to switch off the light?). With her eyes closed she sensed the movement and a second later came the noise. The start of the noise . . .

What happened was so swift and so irremediable that several hours later and even some days later she went on living in that instant just before the noise. She would come to the Caravanserai, meet the residents, and listen to them, but in the innermost part of herself the same scene continued to unfold; it could not end, once it ended life would have become impossible.

. . . From beneath her closed eyelids she was aware of a hand flitting about, as clumsy as a nocturnal bird obliged to fly in broad daylight. Feeling its way in the void, the hand knocked against the lampshade. . . . The start of the noise came from the grinding of the lamp's china base against the wood of the little bedside table. Through her eyelashes she sensed the beginnings of a fall. Her reflex—china, breakage, cut hand, blood—forestalled all thought. She stretched out her arm. Realized immediately. Froze. The lamp fell. He tore himself away from this woman's body that had suddenly come to life, hurled himself from the room.

An elderly resident was talking to her about how the days were warm now but the nights still chilly. She agreed, echoing the trivial remarks made to her, but her own life was condensed into the vision of those few gestures: a hand reaches out aimlessly into the half light; a lampshade tilts; an arm is flung out; freezes. . . .

And the scene explodes under the violent lighting of horror: a youth mired in a woman's groin. A mother and her son . . .

HER MIND'S EYE REMAINED IMPRISONED in that room, in the endless repetition of a suspended gesture. And also in that terrifying reflection in the mirror: a woman lying on her back, her knees apart, her belly offered, one arm outstretched, petrified.

And when she glanced outside, the flood tide of spring blinded her with its headlong joy. Everything in the world was changing before one's eyes—the trees, still bare the day before, became covered with the bluish veil of the first leaves; the tall stem of a wild plant thrust up toward the sun between the planks of the front steps; people emerged from their snug dens at the Caravanserai as if at a prearranged signal. The throng of them oppressed her. They were incredibly numerous and noisy, full of familiarity and a coarse appetite for life. Their remarks (she had the impression that they always shouted when they addressed one another) left her perplexed. In the library hall one day they were commenting enthusiastically on the announcement that the bridge would be rebuilt. They acclaimed the new bridge as if a new era in their lives were promised. "A direct road link with Paris!" bellowed an old army officer who went to Paris once a year. They were also rubbing their hands over the decision of the authorities to "clear the scrub from both banks." She was stunned to realize that by scrub they meant the woodland behind the Caravanserai. She intervened, trying to say that the trees there, even those that were too old or stunted, had a magic on icy mornings, or at night, covered in hoarfrost. . . . But her words made no impact, as if spoken in a totally different conversation.

The days had become so warm that the residents often left their windows open, which was how, one day when she was walking around the building, she involuntarily overheard a remark. Without difficulty she recognized the voice of the nurse; not her usual voice, however, she sounded almost gleeful.

"And this shawl," she was saying. "She presents it to me like a queen giving it to her servant. A lot of use it'll be to me in this hot weather, that's for sure. . . ."

Another voice, that of the director, was acquiescing less distinctly. . . . Olga quickened her step for fear of being seen; dumbfounded and appalled, with an unconscious murmur on her lips: "But it's not true! I gave her that shawl in the depths of winter. . . ." Then she calmed down, recalling the nurse's animated and excited voice, and told herself that, strangely enough, people can readily derive immediate and much more varied satisfaction from malice and evil than from good. . . .

Some days later as she closed the library door she heard a hissing cry at the end of the corridor: "S-s-shlim! S-s-shlim!"

Everything blinded her, numbed her, jostled her in this world of light and noise. Numbing too was the opinion of the "doctor-just-between-ourselves" whom she met one day in the town. He spoke boldly, smiling and staring at her without concealing his curiosity. According to him ("in the first place" he said, crooking his little finger) her son's condition was not that serious; furthermore, all French doctors (he crooked the fourth finger) were scaremongers; but, above all (the middle finger and an emphatic smile), one must not lose one's joie de vivre. His tone astonished her. She glimpsed a fleeting meaning in these encouraging words. He was dressed with an elegance that struck her as aggressive and almost deranged in this modest street (his bow tie, the tight-fitting suit over a squat body, his pointed black shoes). But everything seemed aggressive and strange to her now in this renewed life. And, after all, he did have a habit of joking, even when operating.

Her son changed greatly. His existence as a self-effacing adolescent was transformed into a conspicuous absence, a manifest state of siege, which she would not have dared to break in any case. . . . One evening he was in the kitchen when she came home from the Caravanserai. In the kitchen . . . He must have known what that signified for the two of them. He heard her footfall on the front steps and made such a frenzied headlong dash to his room, flew down the long corridor with such desperate speed, that in the movement of air created by his flight she seemed to sense a breath from the deep abyss he carried within him.

THIS ABYSS OPENED UP in the middle of a hot day in May, almost like high summer. . . .

Even the first days of May were incredible. The month arrived suddenly, while she felt she was still in February or, at most, March; it was burning hot and the residents of the Caravanserai, who only the day before had been speaking of an unprecedented winter, now began quoting from the newspapers that promised "an early, scorching summer. . . ."

More incredible still was the obsessive, tortured watch she found herself keeping behind the branches of the willow trees, near the ruined bridge. There she waited, her eyes bruised by what she saw through the swaying branches. On one of the steel girders, several yards from the bank, stood three young bodies in bathing suits. One by one they plunged into the water, diving in among concrete blocks bristling with their rusty armature. . . . She recognized the figure of her son by the violent aura of fragility that emanated from this very pale, slim body, so different from the other two—sturdy, reddened by the sun, with rather short, curved legs, bodies that already prefigured ordinary, male stockiness. When he swayed slightly on the beam before diving he looked like a tall plaster statue, tilting dangerously and falling. "He's the most handsome!" clamored the voice within her that she could no longer control. At that moment she saw him heaving himself up onto a higher girder. His companions seemed to be hesitating, then deciding against. He stood all alone, above their heads. She saw his face, indifferent and almost sad; his arms held behind him, like a bird's wings; and suddenly his knee, disproportionately swollen, shining in the harsh light, like a ball of ivory. Without thinking she waved her hand, on the brink of calling to him. . . .

But her cry froze on her lips. On the bank, near the half ruined pillar, stood a group of very young girls who were going through a complete performance, switching from squeals of admiration after a dive to somewhat disdainful indifference—which was even more provocative to the three divers.

He pushed off from the girder, bending his knees briefly, turned a somersault in the air, split the waters, and vanished into darkness—she had screwed up her eyelids tight. The young female audience applauded when they saw him surfacing. He did not so much as glance at them and went to climb up the derelict shell once more. This time he climbed a little bit higher, standing with his feet on a narrow ledge. The mood in the small group changed to one that children display spontaneously when a game becomes too dangerous. There were a few cries of merriment, but it was clearly put on; then they exchanged uneasy looks, wrongfooted, as they watched his climb, his stillness before the plunge, his flight. . . .

When he reappeared on the surface their voices were almost frightened and discordant, as if they had discovered the existence of a secret, insane reason behind his courage.

He climbed up once more, swayed for a moment on the top girder (one of the girls shouted out a shrill "No!" and sobbed), then regained his balance, opened his arms, flew.

She opened her eyes, became aware of the twigs brushing against her face, the sun causing the smell of hot mud to hover above the glittering water. Her son was alone down there, sitting on a concrete slab. Already dressed, he was lacing up his shoes (that pair he had dreamed of wearing when spring came . . .). The little group of colorful dresses and his two companions were far away. They were walking along the bank: the boys throwing stones, trying to skim them over the water; their girlfriends shouting as they counted, arguing. Moods change quickly when you're young, observed a voice within her head that she was not listening to. . . . He smoothed down his hair, tucked his shirt into his trousers, threw a glance in the direction of the young people as they walked away, then set off toward the Caravanserai. . . . She did not stir, both hoping and fearing that he might turn and see her and that then by magic, all would be resolved and filled with light, would become simple, like the swaying of these long leaves in front of her eyelashes. . . . But he walked on, his head bowed, without looking behind him. He limped; he seemed used to walking like this.

That night she saw his silhouette once more standing up on the steel shelf before diving. At this stage she found the recollection still heart-stopping but bearable; beneath his fine skin she thought she could detect the pulsing of his heart. He hurled himself from the girder, flew, and in that instant his body became perfect—a shaft of light amid the blackened concrete and the rust. . . .

One by one she pictured the faces of the adolescent girls who had egged on the divers. Those long plunges into a rectangle of water surrounded by ironwork were for the benefit of one of them. (And it was she, perhaps, who had let out a hysterical cry.) Or perhaps it was for the one who, on the contrary, displayed the most complete indifference to the spectacle. The caprices of these youthful attractions are always unpredictable. With all its sentimental banality, this thought suddenly made her feel better, releasing the tension in her body which, since the scene on the riverbank, had been reduced to a stifling, clammy spasm. "Yes, it's the age he's at," she thought, buoyed along by this inner relaxation. "His age and the fine spring weather." She recalled the brightly colored dresses and the naive, innocent cut of them, the stroll beside the water. . . . And nature's sweet daily progress toward the joy and idleness of summer. Her son was simply being drawn into the wholly seasonal tide of first loves, and late sunsets. Important too, was the cheerful assurance the doctor-just-between-ourselves had given her: everything was not all that serious. A momentary vision flashed before her eyes, the ghost of a dream—

one of those little dresses walking beside the painfully recognizable figure of her son. . . .

With a start she broke free from this reverie, got up, and switched on the lamp whose base had been stuck together again with strips of paper. The lamp. The bed. The dark, cold stove. The curtains with the narrow strip of night. And in her mind's eye that couple, two young people in love on a summer's evening . . . The discord was agonizing. All that had happened in that room during the winter nights was accepted and acceptable, pardonable and pardoned on this one condition: that afterward there would be nothing, a void, a bottomless nothingness . . . death. But now this springtime, the summer evening stroll she had pictured, that seemed so likely; this puppy love so stupidly natural and legitimate; all this naive and sunny healthiness of life was banishing their winter into the realms of the unspeakable. In his eyes, after all, what could this room be to him now?

Her thoughts flitted among a thousand things, seeking the solace of a memory, the ghost of a day; but the summer sun hounded her, hounded her on the riverbank, toward sounds, toward voices. "How easy it is," she said to herself with sudden bitterness. "A little cotton print dress, a little coquetry, and presto, he's ready to do anything for you. . . ." She stopped herself, this jealousy seemed too absurd. And, above all: "No, no, he didn't give a hoot for any of their dresses. . . . He was diving to . . . to . . ."

To kill himself . . . She could not check the racing of her thoughts—accurate, trivial, serious, futile, essential. . . . She needed to hit upon some idea that was logical and perfectly obvious; one that would offer her a respite. "Wait, wait. The bridge. Yes, the bridge . . . Well, the bridge was not as high as all that. The topmost girder was probably only six feet above the water. . . ."

Then a surprising visual change took place. The giddy height she had observed in terror during those suicidal dives subsided in her memory, and was now scarcely as tall as a human figure. She no longer knew if she had really seen that girder poised, as it had seemed to her, high against the sky. Indeed, she was now sure that it had all been almost harmless sport, a few perfectly safe dives. She remembered the young spectators on the bank. She thought she could clearly see one of them holding hands with her son and coming back to the Caravanserai with him. . . .

"No! He came home alone!" a very precise memory objected within her. But already the vision of the two young people on a path beside the river seemed to her to have been actually, certainly, observed, indelibly fixed in her mind. She was astonished to realize that it was enough to picture a face or a place for them to become quite naturally transformed into things experienced.

Dazed, she attempted to find some clear, indisputable reality amid the chaos of her thoughts. By an inexplicable caprice of memory this turned out to be the face of the nurse at the retirement home. The unhappy woman who took pleasure in making fun of the gift she had received, the shawl she had accepted one winter's evening. . . . Now her face was tinged with a repentant softness, her lips trembled as she uttered words of apology. And once again this repentance seemed . . . no! quite simply it was completely authentic. Yes, the encounter had occurred several days previously.

For a moment she succeeded in thinking of nothing, still sitting on the edge of the bed, leaning forward slightly, her eyes half closed, expressionless. That was how she saw herself in the mirror facing the bed. A naked woman, motionless, in the middle of a spring night. This precise mirror image calmed her. She turned her head toward the window, her double in the glass did the same. Smoothed the blanket. The other one repeated her gesture with precision. It was then that the lamp caught her eye. . . .

The scene that had since then been played out a thousand times in her memory once more embarked on its sequence of actions: a hand knocks the lampshade; an arm tries to stop it falling; that instinctive, blind lunge; his escape; and the reflection in the mirror that shows a woman lying there, more inert than a corpse. . . . She observed this woman and noticed a new expression on her face that appeared to be more and more accentuated: a mixture of tenderness, sensuality, immodesty, and lasciviousness. Her knees remained wide apart, her belly lay exposed between long, supple thighs. . . .

She tapped on the switch, as if swatting an insect that refuses to die. But in the darkness everything became even more real. Now there was the young face buried in the hollow of the naked woman's shoulder, the lips drowning in her breast. . . . And now the woman's body was arching, closing about the other one, guiding it. . . .

She stood at the French door and, without being aware of it, repeated over and over again in a feverish whisper, "No, it was never like that . . . never . . . never . . . never like that. . . ." But to the slow, stubborn flow of memories her mind had just added the woman's arms embracing the fragile form of a boy; a moaning that she no longer concealed; and their newfound courage, for both of them knew that her sleeping was only pretense. . . .

For several hours weariness interrupted the growth of this incurable tumor that was slowly swelling in her memory.

In the morning imagined reality, false, but terrifying in its truth, continued to gain ground, but calmly now, as if in a country definitively conquered. . . . In the afternoon there were a lot of people in the library. At one moment she turned away and began drawing the curtains across the windows. "Too much sun!" she murmured, trying to keep her face hidden in the dusty folds for as long as possible. . . . In a room lit by the flames flickering out of a stove she had just seen a woman slowly combing the thick flow of her hair, standing at a French door open onto a snowy night, out of which an almost warm breath of air was blowing. Her head was tilted, her gaze lost in the reflection in the windowpane, watching the movements of a youth who came into the room, stopped, and gazed at her in silence. . . . She knew, she could not deny that had happened to her. She simply did not want other people to guess it by peering into her eyes.

The evening was light and long. She was in the kitchen, mechanically tearing up a letter (one of the many letters from L.M. that she no longer even read), when the front door banged with unusual haste. She did not stir, her back turned, so as to let him slip by without her seeing him. But he came in and she heard his voice, which, while striving for calm, had a childish ring to it: "Mom, I think I've just done something stupid. Could you call the . . . what's his name . . . the doctor-just-between-ourselves?"

She turned. He lifted the hand that he had been pressing against his left temple. A pocket of blood bulged over his left eyebrow; already he could not open the eye.

FOR THE SECOND TIME RUNNING she was up all night in the boy's room. At an uncertain hour, when the sky was still very dark, objects began to break free of the ties that normally held them. This made their presence more and more inexplicable. She had brought the lamp in here to have more light in case of need. Now that explanation no longer sufficed. The lamp stood beside the bed where the boy slept. Switched off and almost frightening in its silent idleness, no longer linked with brightness, but with dark, indecipherable visions . . . And the doctor-just-between-ourselves? He had stayed, for his help might be needed urgently. But . . . No, nothing . . . He had installed himself in the book room, in no way embarrassed about this nocturnal sojourn in their house. He had filled the little cubbyhole with his cigar smoke and was now reading or dozing. And from time to time came to the patient's bedside. Each time she gave a start, his arrival was so silken: for greater comfort he was in his stocking feet. He took visible pleasure in seeing her tremble. He smiled but at once adopted a firm and reassuring air, felt the swelling that by now almost entirely covered the boy's left eye, and went away again. . . . At one moment in the darkness she thought she could see this man in his socks lurking at the end of the corridor, watching. She was very much afraid but then immediately woke up.

Her eyes resting on the boy's deformed face struggled constantly against growing accustomed to it: not to accept this puffy mask, to wipe it clean with the intensity of her look. She turned the compresses on the swollen brow, lifted the blanket and wiped away the trickles of sweat on his chest, in the hollow between his collarbones, on his neck. And each time she touched him, simply and almost without thinking, it woke the seething nocturnal visions within her, drew her toward a winter's night, toward a carnal encounter that was increasingly frenzied, increasingly real. . . . Even the town outside the dark window, shimmering in a beam of light, was also an improbable ghost town, with its gigantic ruin of the wrecked bridge and the station from which, for several days now, no trains had departed. "Rail strike," she repeated mentally, and the words murmured above this body on fire betokened a wide-eyed, intelligent madness. . . . She looked at the thermometer (one hundred and four degrees, fever, as an hour earlier), switched off the lamp, closed her eyes.

When he became delirious in a headlong, seething hiss, she failed to wrest herself from sleep immediately. Listening to him, she believed she was still in a painful and confused dream. Little by little his gasping words formed into a confession that only delirium could have brought to the level of his lips. She did not so much hear but—with each painful whisper—saw a place materializing that it took her only a moment to recognize. . . .

. . . It was a little ground floor apartment crammed with a jumble of furniture. A woman, youthful again, in her long black dress. A boy watching the woman's final preparations. She puts on the earrings that cast iridescent gleams onto her neck and her bare shoulders. The bell rings at the front door, she kisses the boy, who is already bedded down on the armchairs pushed together as a makeshift bed, and goes to open it. Mingling with the warm, piquant perfume she gives off as she passes, he can smell the damp odor of the street and the strong, invasive scent of the intruder's eau de cologne. . . .

The sick boy's voice petered out in a series of brief, sibilant groans. She changed the compresses. The swelling of dark, shining blood had extended toward his temple. The right eye opened for a moment but did not focus on anything, flitted onto the lamp, onto the hand that was applying the icy cloth to his brow. Almost at once the delirium started again. Eventually she could even grasp the words that were being swallowed up in the hissing spasms of the fever.

. . . It was still the woman in evening dress getting ready to go to the theater and waiting for the man who was supposed to come and fetch her. This time she and her son are sitting at table drinking tea. Half an hour later, as she puts on her earrings in front of a mirror she suddenly feels pleasantly weary. She sits down on the little sofa and even decides to lie down for a few moments while awaiting her companion's arrival. Sleep overtakes her before the end of this thought. . . .

She changed the compresses, already burning hot, shook the thermometer, inserted it with care. The whispering still emanating from his dry lips had become indistinct.

And suddenly he began to cry out in an almost conscious voice. In his cry the woman in the black dress suddenly found herself half naked, laid out in sinister beauty, for she was dead! Dead, dead, dead . . .

He repeated the word "dead," choking violently, shaking his disfigured head and scratching at the blanket with his fingernails.

Dumbfounded, powerless, she knew she should get up, run to the book room, wake the doctor. But then he would have heard this all too clear delirium! And guessed everything!

The cries ceased abruptly and a second later the doctor-just-between-ourselves opened the door. "Ah, he's found his voice, our young man." He grunted and yawned elaborately.

An hour later he operated. He had flung back the curtains with energetic abruptness, admitting a still pale dawn, unhoped for in that room that seemed doomed to darkness. . . . He made incisions, removed blood clots, swabbed. And gave a commentary on his actions in an almost tender voice, all the time using Russian diminutives, even for the scalpel, the swabs, the saline. She felt as if she were watching a game, and participating in it when from time to time she passed him a bottle, a syringe. . . .

When he left he kissed her hand and promised to come back at noon and even to stay and "browse" (a wink) in the little book room if need be. . . .

She spent the afternoon sometimes in the boy's room, sometimes, when he slept, sitting on the front steps that were all overgrown with wild plants. What the night had revealed to her was unfolding now in a clear and definitive sequence of scenes. . . .

. . . It had been in the spring of the previous year, possibly exactly a year before. Generally, when she went to Paris with her son, L.M. invited her out to the theater. Or at least, when he invited her, she came to Paris, left the boy at Li's, and came back to collect him in the morning. On that occasion Li had been away and the boy was to spend the night on his own. It was hard to guess how deeply he detested those theater evenings; those nights (when, in theory, his mother came home after the play); and the man who rang the doorbell. . . . Li used to take sleeping drafts—the little sachet that made her vague when she woke up.

"What if you took two of them?" he asked one day.

"Oh, I shouldn't wake up till noon."

"Three?"

"I should sleep like a dead woman."

That evening he emptied three sachets into the cup of tea that the young woman in her black dress was about to drink. . . . An hour afterward he lived through long, frightening, and delicious minutes. The doorbell rang impatiently, furiously; he even heard several oaths, then a drumming on the shutters. The woman lay stretched out on the sofa, her impassive and remote beauty untroubled. There was a squeal of tires as they pulled away outside the window, soon lost in the other sounds of cars in the street. . . . There he was in that little sitting room lit only by a table lamp, a room cluttered with curios, books, and icons . . . And in the middle of it this woman, this stranger whom he found it impossible to recognize as his mother. Her face was disturbingly youthful; a little capricious crease that he had never noticed before gave a slight upward lift to the corners of her mouth. The curve of her body expressed a strange expectancy.

And apart from the fine haze of perfume he detected quite a new, carnal scent about her, more a ghost than a scent, that filled him with wonder and almost hurt his lungs. . . . He did not yet know how to assess the deepness of her slumber. Ready to take flight at the first flicker of her eyelashes, he stretched out his arm, touched her hand that lay on her stomach, then her shoulder. Then, emboldened, telling himself that, if need be, he would have a good excuse for waking her, he touched the delicate hollow hinted at between her breasts, the beginnings of which were revealed by her décolletage. He had always been fascinated by this spot on a woman's body. She did not stir. . . . Already uneasy, he brought his ear close to the sleeping woman's face. And could hear no breathing. He remembered Li's words: "I should sleep like a dead woman!" Dead! He jumped up in a panic, thought of running to the kitchen to fetch water, then changed his mind. He had seen or read somewhere that doctors put their ear to the patient's chest and even massage it in order to restore breathing. With trembling fingers he unfastened two hooks on the crossed flaps of the décolletage, laid bare a shoulder, then a breast, pressed his ear to it. . . . Finally stood up with a singing in his ears, his breathing irregular. And gazed at her endlessly, this woman unrecognizable beneath her light makeup, with her hair piled high, her black velvet dress, and, above all, her nakedness. This woman who should have belonged to another and who now remained with him, so deliciously accessible to his eyes, to his caress. . . .

"It was a year ago," she thought, calling to mind a dazzling halo of days, of skies seen since then. . . . On the footpath that led across the meadow from the Caravanserai a man appeared. She recognized the doctor-just-between-ourselves approaching with his bag. For the second night.

It rained that night. After the heat of the previous weeks the air seemed cold, autumnal. She remained in an armchair beside the bed until morning. The fever had abated. The wound was no longer bleeding. He slept peacefully and only woke once, in the middle of the night. They looked at each other for a long moment without speaking. Then he screwed up his eyes tightly, as if under the effect of a sudden scalding. She saw his eyelashes gleaming with tiny sparks and hastened to switch off the lamp.

The cool, gray days at the beginning of June marked the habitual lassitude of spring, breathless after a riot of blooming and the heat of May. The foliage was already heavy, dense and dark, like the end of summer. The meadow that sloped down to the river was once more covered with tall grasses, tinged with white here and there by the silvery down of dandelions gone to seed. And steady, quiet rainfall interrupted the mists that hung in the air, as on October mornings.

She liked the calming effect of this brief foretaste of the fall. Since that night of the delirium she knew everything from start to finish about that year of her life. Now, amid the haze of a temporary fall, it seemed as if she had come through, as if she were timidly resuming the interrupted course of her days.

One evening, when walking around the Caravanserai, she noticed that the bushes growing beneath the walls and beside the track were all pearly with white clusters. The dusk air also had this snowy tinge. . . . The night was so chilly she had to light the fire. And did not sleep. Winter nights arose in her mind's eye one after another, beyond words in their hard beauty, with the trembling chasms of their skies, with that same scent of burning bark, a mere detail but which opened up an unfathomable cavalcade of hours. It was the first time she had returned to it. This return still had a bruising intensity. Yet her memory was already initiating her into the mysterious science of entering into that other life.

During these few autumnal days in mid-June, days of her son's convalescence, there flickered within her once more the crazy hope: that someone would listen to her, would understand her, understand, above all, that what she had lived through belonged to a life quite other than her own. So far this someone had no face, only a soul, vast and silent.

THE SUMMER RETURNED with unprecedented storms and a blazing sun that the citizens of Villiers-la-Forêt welcomed as dazzling evidence of the "first real vacation of peacetime" that was the talk of the papers. And even the little community of the Caravanserai sniffed this new air and gathered in the library, animatedly discussing the articles about the Tour de France 47, the first since the war; the new Paris Peace Conference; and especially the headline that proclaimed: FRANCE FINALLY TURNS THE CORNER. . . .

In spite of herself, or rather with secret complicity, she succumbed to this seasonal excitement. One day she caught herself studying the photos in a newspaper accompanying a long feature, "Where to Spend your Vacation," with envious admiration. A family (the parents and their two children) were cycling along a country road. She could not tear herself away from it. She liked everything about these vacationers: their family togetherness; their provisions well wrapped up on their carriers; the quiet road; and the gentle, orderly countryside. She suddenly longed to lose herself, like them, in the happy banality of these summer days, to have their French common sense, "so wonderfully French," she thought. Then she remembered her hope of finding a soul in whom she could confide, to whom she could speak about the depths of despair she had known. That seemed grotesque to her now. She must forget. Yes, forget! For these much-vaunted depths were in fact nothing more than moments of uneasy tenderness that no mother and no son can escape. Quite simply, they had gone a little further than others had done in this forbidden temptation. Besides, there had only been, all in all, eight or perhaps ten nights when . . .

She felt strong now, because she had decided not to remember. She must become a bit more stupid, be confident, talk about vacations. And it was as if she wanted to punish, wound, and destroy a being silently present within her that she forced herself to read the text of the article: "This year many foreign visitors—English, Scandinavians, Americans—plan to sample the delights of France. We owe a warm welcome to these visitors when they come to the places where for two years soldiers from their own countries fought for the liberation of Europe. . . ."

This summery and agreeably simple world accepted her. She gave herself over to it, its joys and its gossip, with the fervor of a convert. Each new day seemed to justify her. The readers seemed happy to see her taking part in their discussions, just as in the old days.

At the end of the month she took her son to Paris. The doctor ("the French doctor" they called him, so as not to confuse him with the doctor-just-between-ourselves) examined the boy, arranged for him to be admitted to his ward, and told them the date of the operation. "The crooked leg will be straightened out under general anesthesia," she read again that same evening in the pages she could recite by heart; their technical language reassured her. She could already picture her son walking normally in a life that had become ordinary again. . . .

After the operation, the date of which, so much dreaded in advance, arrived with surprising ease, the boy was to remain in the hospital for a number of days. And even her almost daily trips to Paris became a real apprenticeship for her in the blissful triviality of life.

Always in a hurry to get back to the Caravanserai, to the library, she had no time to see Li. It was only on July 14, thanks to the public holiday, that she could visit the photographer's little apartment. . . .

The evening was unbearably oppressive with the smell that dusty streets have just before a storm, with a hazy, purple sky and the turmoil of leaves in brief gusts of wind. Li was still in her studio in the cellar, busy with the last clients of the day. And indeed it was only the studio that retained an air of habitability. In the main rooms the furniture had been replaced by pyramids of cardboard boxes of all shapes and sizes. On the bare walls there were countless dark punctures—left by the hooks on which pictures, photos, and icons had hung. . . .

She waited for a moment in the miniature courtyard, surrounded by windows on several floors. They were all open, to capture every tiniest breath of cool air on that stifling evening. You could hear the sizzling of oil in a frying pan, the gurgling of water running away, the clatter of crockery, scraps of conversation, snatches of music. An aroma, compounded of roofs cooling after the heat of the day, laundry, and burned fat, hung in the darkness above the paved square of ground. She was just about to go down into the studio when suddenly she noticed, in the shadiest corner of the yard, the shrub that was struggling to grow against the wall, beneath the drainpipe. And to flower invisibly, out of sight of all those noisy windows. She went up to it and buried her face in the clusters of flowers with which it was studded. The scent was subtle. A freshness of snow . . . The feeling that she could enter, linger, and merge into this cold breath made her giddy. For a moment she thought she was walking through a snow-covered forest in winter, on a morning barely silvered by the dawn, in the midst of trees, sleeping but secretly aware of her presence. She was not alone. She had a companion on this slow stroll. An infinite peace filled the space that lay between their two souls . . .

Li called her from the studio doorway. She was leaving for Russia in ten days. All she had left to do was to pack up the last of her panels: a sailor with incredibly broad shoulders presenting a bunch of flowers to a wasp-waisted young thing and, on the other one, a naked man and woman squeezed in among a crowd in tuxedos and evening gowns.

★ ★ ★

Two days later, coming back from Paris, she ran into the doctor-just-between-ourselves. He behaved as if he just happened to be in the road that led out into the square in front of the station. She would have believed him if she had not glanced through the window of the coach a few seconds before the train stopped. She recognized this man in a brown suit. The speed with which he moved as he left the shade of a plane tree, where he had been sheltering from the sun, gave him away. The train was slowing down and through the windowpane she saw him watching the station exit then slightly adjusting his shirt collar. . . .

They walked back together. Listening to him she thought that, had she not glanced through that coach window, his words would have had quite another meaning. And that he himself, the man walking beside her, chatting, animated and jovial, would have been somebody else. Yes, he would still have been the "doctor-just-between-ourselves," self-effacing and obliging. Now she was aware of the suppressed energy in him, with which he had emerged out of the shadows. And also the easy smoothness that had colored his feigned surprise: "My goodness, it's you! What fair wind has brought you my way?" Now she was seeing things she had never noticed before: his heavy and strangely unpleasant-looking cuff links, the backs of his very broad hands, covered in hairs on which little drops of sweat glistened. . . . But, in particular, his brown, oily eyes, with which he gave her swift sidelong glances that seemed, as they slid away, to hold her prisoner in their reflection. Yes, he walked without looking at her but she felt she was held, snared beneath his eyelids.

She had no recollection of inviting him to take tea with her. And yet there he was, seated opposite her in the kitchen that still glowed with the sunset; and he was talking, only breaking off to take a little sip for form's sake. She got up from time to time, chased a bee, set about pretending to listen to him but in reality was noticing, despite herself, fresh, absurd, and mysteriously important details: his square, yellowish fingernails; his forehead that filled with wrinkles when he gave a theatrical sigh, wrinkles that went right up to his bald pate and made it less shiny. . . . It was one of those odd moments when you sense the imminent approach of some gesture, drawing inexorably closer.

As he was leaving he stopped in the hall and kissed her hand. Or rather, without bowing, he raised her hand and pressed it for a long time to his lips. When she made a movement of impatience he caught her by the waist with unexpected agility. She drew back to avoid his face. But to her surprise he did not go for her mouth. He remained still for a moment, forcing her into this precariously off-center posture, and supporting the weight of her body arched against his palm. Clumsily she pulled herself free from him and collided with the door frame. And her shout of "Go away!" was mingled with a brief cry of pain and her hand rubbing her bruised elbow. Facing her, he smiled, massive, sure of himself. But the voice that emerged from this mass was strangely shrill, stammering, like those sentences that have been long prepared but which, when the time comes, emerge quite convoluted and breathless: "I'll come again tomorrow . . . Maybe we could first . . . Well, I know a little restaurant . . ."

That night her focus switched restlessly between several very different personages. The elderly gentleman who had come out from the Caravanserai several times, often at nightfall in the snow, to care for an ailing boy . . . The man in the brown suit who came walking toward her without noticing her and suddenly uttered a cry of joy . . . The man who took little sips of tea and spoke of the solitude "we must confront together". . . And that other man, again, who confessed that for years he had wanted to speak to her. And as he said it, his cuff links and his hairy wrists seemed to belong to someone else. She found it impossible to reassemble all these men into one, this aging male with his smooth, tanned, bald head, who had seized her waist, already taking delight in her submissive body.

On her return from Paris the next day she studied with concern the trees at the edge of the station square. Nobody. On the door of her house there was a little rectangle of paper. "I called for tea, I will be back for dinner." It was in deciphering the signature that she recognized the element that was common to all the men who had troubled her in the night. As if this commonplace, mildly ridiculous name, that she had known but forgotten—yes, as if simply seeing it written down, "Sergei Golets," had created a generic term for all these characters.

He was the man who had fathomed her secret (she did not know how, nor to what extent). The madness of her secret. Her madness . . . Yes, he was someone who treated her as he would have treated a simpleminded person who can be exploited.

It was already almost nine o'clock in the evening. She walked along beside the house with hurried steps, plunged in under the trees of the wood. You could cross it in five minutes, but the maze of footpaths created the illusion of a refuge. The ground was dappled with long copper rays, slowly turning pale. Darkness was gradually spilling into the shady corners. The moonlight turned the glades into lakes, into streams of a somnolent blue. The repeated cry of a bird rang out with the sound of icicles snapping. She had the sudden idea that it might be possible to stay there, not to leave these moments in time, to travel back through them. . . . Then, remembering the madness a man had just detected in her, she hastened to return.

As she pressed the switch she thought that Golets might notice the light and come. . . . At the same moment she heard the steady, almost nonchalant rapping at the door. She switched off the light, then at once switched it on again, annoyed by her own cowardice, went to the hall but decided not to open up and to say nothing. He knocked again and remarked without raising his voice, sensing that she was close at hand, "I know you're there. Open the door. . . . I have a message for you." There was a jarring note of barely disguised mockery in his voice. "Yes, he talks as if to a feebleminded woman," she thought again. She went back into the kitchen and suddenly heard the snapping of a stem: he was walking along beside the wall, treading on the flowers in the darkness. She remembered that the French door in her bedroom had been left ajar. Hardly had the thought occurred when it became reality: at the end of the corridor the ancient hinges emitted a long musical creak. She rushed to the other end of the apartment, switched on the light, just had time to focus her eyes on the familiar and woeful interior: the lamp with the patched-up china base, the stove, the bed, the wardrobe with a mirror. . . .

And amid all these objects, with their patina of familiarity, a man putting his head through the gap where the French door was ajar, just like one of those volatile interiors in a bad dream.

"Just two words . . . Yesterday I forgot to tell you. . . ." He smiled, hypnotizing her with his fixed stare, and made his way into the room with brief, swift advances, while seeming to be motionless every time she was on the point of rebuking him.

She felt desperately distant from this scene. The words that rang out in her head and then burst forth from her lips seemed to emanate from somebody else: "Go away! Get out! Quickly!" Ineffectual commands that had not affected the distracted look on her own face nor produced any effect on the man who did not move and yet kept coming closer. She, too, was absent from her body and the man knew it: infancy, drunkenness, and madness all disarm the body in this way and it becomes an easy prey.

"I didn't tell you yesterday," he began, with the excitement of one who sees his strategy coming to fruition. "I love you. I have loved you for years. . . . No, let me . . ."

She swung her hand clumsily. He intercepted her slap and kissed her hand passionately, then grasped her waist, caught her dispossessed body off balance and thrust it toward the bed. She saw a round face, gleaming with sweat, and heard herself shouting out a completely illogical remark: "Let me go! Your neck is hideous!"

It was these absurd, half-choking words that stopped him in his tracks. The man straightened up, let her go, and felt his neck. "What did you say? What's the matter with my neck?"

His skin was shaved too close, red, and covered in tiny swellings. He took a step toward the mirror, realized that this movement was ridiculous, lost countenance.

"Go away!" she said in a weary voice. "I beg you . . ."

She went to the French door, drew back the curtain, and flung it open. He obeyed her, murmuring with a vexed sneer, "All right, all right . . . But all the same you won't refuse me the pleasure of an excursion with you? Tomorrow afternoon . . ." He went out, turned, and waited for her reply. She shook her head and tugged at the handle. The cuff link glittered—he was quick enough to block the door.

"One last word," he called, his lips unable to achieve a reconciliation between smiling and twitching with rage. "The very last, I assure you. Now this glass door you are crushing my arm with"—she let go of the handle—"this French door, which is somewhat too wide for these curtains, or rather the curtains are too narrow, if you prefer . . ."

She was seized by a profound internal shuddering that rose rapidly in her stomach and up to her chest and constricted the muscles of her throat. The man was about to blurt out something irreparable, she had a precise, blinding intuition of it. She had sensed it unconsciously, ever since his maneuvering began, and it was this presentiment that had left her disarmed in confronting him.

". . . These curtains, that really are too narrow you see, are not wholly unknown to me. I have this strange habit, you see: I like to go for a walk late in the evening before going to bed. You know how it is, when you live alone. . . . And then, I'm very observant . . ."

She should have interrupted him, stopped him on the brink of the next sentence. . . . She should have let him have his way just now, accepted his kisses, given herself to him, for what he was about to say was a thousand times more monstrous. But the air was becoming heavy, like damp cotton wool, hindering gestures, stifling the voice.

"Especially with the frosts last winter, I was often worried: you have a . . . mm . . . sick child in this shack; one never knows. One evening when I was passing very close by, almost beneath your windows, I glanced your way; the curtains were drawn but they are, as I've said, too narrow. . . . So I looked in and . . .

". . . And I saw you, you and your son, naked, in an act of love."

No! He did not say it. She thought he was going to and the sentence immediately became real, inseparable from what had gone before. Perhaps he did then speak of their nakedness as well, of the carnal strangeness of the couple they made. . . . She no longer knew.

"So at all events, no doubt you will understand my astonishment . . . I've seen worse things in my time . . . I'm no choirboy myself, far from it. But even so! Fortunately I'm not a gossip, otherwise, you know what the wagging tongues are like at the Caravanserai and elsewhere. . . .

". . . And when I offered you my . . . friendship, it was so as to be able to talk to you more freely about all this, you understand, in intimacy. And to give you the possibility of living a normal life as a woman, with a man who would enable you to enjoy . . ."

No! He did not speak those last words, but even so, they were real, and inescapable, for she had imagined them.

In fact, he was no longer there. She was alone, sitting on the bed, facing the mirror. He had gone, bidding her a good night and proposing that they should take a trip in a boat the next day. She had agreed, nodding several times.

That night she found herself wandering for some time in an endless, shadowy apartment, exploring its labyrinthine passages before going to lie down on a bed. Her son came in, just as she had seen him on the afternoon when he was diving—naked, his body wet, making the sheets damp and cooling them deliciously. She felt this coolness against her breast, in her thighs. He kissed her; his lips tasted of the stems and leaves of water plants. Their freedom was such that their bodies moved as if underwater, their gestures marvelously weightless. It was when she found herself on her knees, dominated by him, that she noticed that the armchair turned toward the wall in the corner of this unknown room had someone in it. . . . She could only see the arm on the armrest—a heavy cuff link glittered in the half-darkness. And the more violent their sensual enjoyment became, the more the profile of the seated man detached itself from the back of the chair. She was on the brink of recognizing him when at last, with a cry, still choked with pleasure, she wrested herself from sleep. An object was digging into her shoulder. She switched on the light and from within the folds of the tangled sheets she plucked out a cuff link.

With a final effort at sane reasoning she formulated this eerie and incongruous thought and rejoiced in its absurdity: "There was no dragon!" That was it, she needed to speak of improbable things that had no chance of becoming real. No dragon! An unknown apartment, that man in the armchair, perhaps. But no dragon. Like that she would finally manage to distinguish the true from the false. . . .

This exercise seemed to calm her. A respite of several minutes during which she got up, went into the book room, took down a fat encyclopedic volume, leafed through it with a clumsy, nervous hand. And quickly hit upon the engraving: "A boa constrictor attacking an antelope." The glistening body, covered in arabesques, was strangling its victim. "The dragon . . . ," she whispered and recalled that, in the vast apartment she had just left, she had forgotten to switch off the lamp on the bedside table.

THE SOUNDS COMING THROUGH the heat haze were blurred, liquid. The cries of children paddling at the edge of the river, the lowing of a herd. . . . And the lazy plashing of oars. To push the boat clear from the low, muddy bank just now he had had to take off his shoes, roll up his pants, and step into the water. Now she could see the broad, hardened soles of his feet. And on his forehead the smear of clay he had left when wiping away drops of sweat. For her this brown streak was a particularly odd source of distress in this world of sunlight and apathy. She could not say to him, "You've made a mark on your face," still less could she dip her fingers into the water and wash his brow for him. . . .

That would have been quite unthinkable. The man sitting facing her, his bare heels wedged against the timbers of the boat, was an utterly strange being: a man who desired her and who was taking her out in a boat on a stifling July day, fulfilling a ritual that was a prelude to the night, when he would violate her as much as he desired, as of right, without any resistance on her part. Before their boat trip, as they walked through the upper town, he had invited her into the shooting gallery. He had not missed a single target; as he walked out he had looked at her with the air of a child expecting praise. . . . This was the very man who had materialized in a labyrinthine apartment in the armchair facing the wall, the man spying on them with a smile of connivance. She recalled the great bed, the sheets with their scent of the river, yes, precisely the same smell as this tepid water rippling beneath the low sides of the dinghy. Under this watchful gaze she and the boy, whose body was still wet, had tried to mask their love. Yes, they were searching in all innocence for some object lost among the folds of the devastated bed. But while going through the motions of this search they were embracing, exchanging kisses, giving themselves to each other. . . .

She forced herself to listen. Golets had just spoken to her. Doubtless it was his "We really must make hay while the sun shines: because you never know," that he kept repeating every five minutes. The smear of clay on his forehead was drawing out into a long, sinuous trickle. "If only I could ask him: that apartment, that simulated search in a disordered bed—were they real?" said a hopeless voice within her. It was the "little bitch," she recognized it almost joyfully, for these words were the only ones that still linked her to this day, to this man's conversation, to life. . . . She leaned forward, thrust her hand into the water. She was going to wash away the muddy mark on his forehead. . . .

At that moment they touched land. Golets jumped onto the bank and drew the bow of the vessel into a little gap between the willows in the middle of the tangle of weeds. Then he helped her to step ashore and settled her in a little clearing surrounded by bushes. He did it with the care you would have for an important patient; or for a vase filled with water with a bunch of flowers in it, that you dread breaking just at the last moment. Or perhaps (the voice of the "little bitch" pierced the silence that enveloped her) yes, especially, for a person whose social standing made this riverside picnic somewhat inappropriate. "The Princess Arbyelina," the voice whispered. "That is what you still are to him. He is still susceptible to your body's added value."

Golets spread out a tablecloth and set down the bottle. From his bag he took two glasses, some bread, and a packet covered in grease stains. "Princess Arbyelina," she thought, picturing the life where the word had a meaning, where the people lived who knew her. The Caravanserai, Villiers, Paris . . . This world now seemed to her nonexistent, beheld in a dream long since dissipated. Now there was only the damp sauna of this July afternoon, the sweetish smell of the tepid, muddy water; this woman half reclining in the grass, with a glass in her hand that she raised to her lips from time to time, yielding to the pleas of a man who talked incessantly. A man who, when night came, would crush her breasts, penetrate her, fall asleep beside her. He already had all these actions imprinted in him, in his forearms, blue with their thick veins, in his fingers with broad, yellow nails. . . .

"And to think that last winter all this was under the snow!"

He was stretched out, his elbow planted in the earth, his legs crossed, and, without letting go of his glass, he extended his arm, indicating the fields beyond the river. She closed her eyes and signaled to him to say nothing more. A fragile night was forming within her in which she walked along, recognizing, with mournful felicity, a branch crystallized in the hoarfrost; a little frozen pond; but, above all, a floral tapestry of ice on a dark windowpane. . . .

It was Golets who roused her from her reverie. He must have thought her closed eyes—she had covered them with her hand to shut out the light more completely—were a sign of drunkenness. Without getting up he executed a rapid crawl and got behind her. He took her by the shoulders, tilted her toward him, slipped a hand beneath her back. When he met her suddenly opened eyes he froze: a glassy stare that expressed nothing, did not see him, saw nothing. . . . Detaching himself from her, he emitted, in spite of himself, a sort of moan of thwarted pleasure, almost a meowing. She got up, stared at the man crouching at her feet, then lifted her eyes toward the roofs of the upper town where they climbed up the hill, toward the flat curve of the river. . . . So after all, there was nothing in the warm, soft stuff of life but this whine of desire; this flesh forever hungering for fusion.

He picked up the remains of the meal, folded the tablecloth. And it was then that there was this moment of hesitation: should he throw away the almost empty bottle or take it with him? Already visibly drunk, he was brought up short by this ridiculous indecision. He stuffed the bottle into his bag, took it out again, examined it, perplexed. . . . These few seconds of uncertainty (she later felt it that way but no one chose to believe her) marked the start of that ticking away of minutes that preceded the end. If he had not delayed, turning the bottle over and over, if they had left a little sooner, or if he had ended up keeping the bottle, everything would have turned out differently. But he swung his arm, essaying a jocular war whoop, and threw the bottle into the water.

But with the intuition of drunken men, he must have felt as if there were a taut cord linking him to something invisible. His mood changed. He tried to joke. Now they were drifting downstream. Several yards farther on they caught up with the bottle that had not sunk; he gave it a poke with an oar, the neck disappeared, releasing a brief gurgling of air bubbles. He roared with laughter. And at once became somber again.

It was no doubt in order to cast off this obscure uneasiness that he suddenly abandoned the oars, stretched himself, raising his face toward the sky, and declared in a voice slurred by drunkenness, "Man is made for pleasure as birds are made for flight."

He half stood up and, shaken by the instability of the boat, lurched headlong toward the stern where she was sitting. She moved aside so as not to be crushed by this unbalanced mass, braying with laughter. He reached her all the same, hung over her, and tugged roughly at her dress.

At this moment she saw a twisted, rusty steel structure rising up out of the water and growing rapidly larger. It seemed to her that the boat overturned almost gently. . . .

She would never know if the violence with which Golets hurled himself at her and clung to her body was due to his drunkenness, his desire to save her, or his inability to swim. Perhaps he, in his turn, was trying to push away the woman who threatened to drown him. Or was it already the death throes? Nor would she ever know whether he had been wounded at the very moment when he fell or afterward, when he sank and resurfaced, already lifeless.

Whatever the reason for his brutality, by a macabre coincidence, Golets's gestures parodied the carnal act of which he had dreamed. He clasped the body he desired, did violence to it, tore off the upper part of her clothes, laying bare her shoulders and her breasts, lacerating the skin with his nails.

This savage struggle lasted scarcely a few seconds. He disappeared beneath the water and surfaced a little farther off, closer to the bank, at a spot sheltered from the force of the current. His body came to rest between a block of concrete, a narrow spit of sand, and the stems of reeds on which green and blue dragonflies continued to settle.

She swam, or rather allowed herself to be carried, surrounded by the tatters of her dress, as far as this sheltered spot. Just a few yards from the place of their shipwreck her foot touched the bottom. It all seemed like a game. And yet a few feet away from her floated this fully dressed body and the water around his head was turning brown.

On the bank two men could be seen running along, led by a boy who still had his fishing rod in his hand.

IT SEEMED TO HER as if she remained for weeks on that sunny riverbank, on the ancient tree stump where the first witnesses had found her sitting. There were no nights anymore, nothing but that interminable day, the muggy effluvia arising from the water, the smell of the plants and the mud; and the hot, slightly hazy light, more dazzling to the eye than glaring sunlight.

Interminably, people came and went, surrounded her; dispersed; timidly approached the corpse of the drowned man; made their comments. She recognized almost all of them: the Russified pharmacist, the director of the retirement home, the old swordsman, the nurse, the woman from the station ticket office. . . . She noticed that they all of them, even in these exceptional circumstances, remained true to their roles, to their masks. The nurse, with her bitter expression, did not fail to let it be understood that the mourning she wore was a good deal more worthy of respect than this stupid accident. The ticket office woman was constantly consulting her watch. The director managed the tragedy. The pharmacist moved from one group to another, happily taking part in discussions both in French and Russian without distinction. And beside the willow trees, mingling with the buzz of conversations, there rang out the merry "s-s-shlim!". . .

She felt herself to be the focus of dozens of inquiring—or quite simply curious—looks. These excited spectators were attempting, as they might have done in adjusting binoculars, to bring together into a single focus the Princess Arbyelina and this woman clad in water-soaked rags, a woman who made no effort to cover up her breast that was streaked with scratches. Some of them, those who felt they knew her better, addressed her in hushed voices—as if sounding out the silence of a bedroom to see if the person in there is asleep. . . . She remained motionless, seemed blind, inaccessible to words. Yet her eyes were alive, noting the new faces in the parade of gawkers, observing that the smear of clay on the man's forehead had disappeared, washed away, no doubt, at the moment of drowning. . . .

But what could she say to those who, like the director, leaned toward her and murmured questions that were unbelievable in their human triviality, supposedly intended to bring her out of her state of shock? Shock . . . shock . . . shock, the voices kept repeating in all the little groups. She should have told them about that smear of clay, about the impossibility of wiping it away that she had experienced in the boat, yes, her inability to wet her fingers, to touch that brow. Told them, too, about that unique fragment of beauty that had, by chance, sprung from that hopelessly ugly man—the phrase he had uttered a quarter of an hour before his death: "And to think that these water meadows were all covered in snow. . . ." But would they have understood? Perhaps only the old lady from the retirement home who suddenly went up to the corpse and removed a long strand of waterweed from its face. Whispered reproaches arose on all sides—nothing must move.

And nothing moved. The humid, stifling afternoon went on forever. The police arrived, the crowd regrouped itself. The days passed, but there were no nights. Always the same sun, the same lukewarm river, the same people, the corpse. The clothes it was dressed in gradually dried. And the scratches on the woman's breast ("On my breast," she said, but while recognizing herself less and less) closed up, faded. . . .

The investigating magistrate questioned her in his office—and yet she was still that woman sitting on the riverbank where nothing had changed: the drowned man, the gawkers, and, from now on, this magistrate bending over the corpse, feeling the sides of the boat, going from one spectator to another and then stopping face to face with the half-undressed woman. He called this woman "Madame Arbélina"; she became it and, at least initially, even felt relieved to be it. It was thus easier for her to admit that she had detested Golets, that the idea of killing him had often occurred to her. And that she had in fact killed him, even killed him twice over, for first of all she had not wiped his mud-spotted forehead (and that gesture could have changed everything!); and later on, when he did not know what to do with the empty bottle and the moment of his death was approaching, she had remained absolutely passive, an accomplice as the minutes fatally drained away.

One day she felt she could finally relate the essence of the case to this man who listened to her with such interest. Visibly the investigating magistrate was beginning to realize that he had in front of him not a certain "Madame Arbélina" but a woman who carried within her strange winter nights and terrible fissures that an ordinary object, an innocent word, could cause to erupt at any given moment. Encouraged by his understanding, she talked about the inexpressible beauty of the winter she had just lived through; about the tiny pond with the trapped fish; about the branch forever letting its hoarfrost crystals fall. . . . She lived again through those moments of silence and marveled to discover that her listener, too, went along with it more each day. She was certain now that she could confide her secret to him. . . .

So why did the stammerer suddenly appear, claiming to be Golets's best friend? Was she confronted by him, or did she learn of his existence thanks to the more and more numerous theories about the crime that had the Caravanserai, and indeed the whole town, in turmoil? She no longer remembered. In any event this Loo-loo's evidence turned everything upside down. Struggling painfully against his diction he testified: Golets knew that before the war Prince Arbyelin had engaged in a dubious traffic in properties in Russia owned by émigrés and so . . . The magistrate considered this new theory to be fanciful. Golets scarcely knew the prince and would never have been able to prove in what way these sales were illicit. . . .

It was she who saw in this testimony the destruction of everything she had built up, word by word, in her conversations with the magistrate. So Golets knew nothing about her winter nights. The threats he had made came down to that old secret of the estates sold by the prince. That was his ridiculous blackmail! While she, in her confusion, in her madness, had imagined this man lying in wait beneath their windows. . . . No, he had seen nothing. But in that case his death that she had so desired, the murder she had confessed to the magistrate, was totally gratuitous. She had killed him for nothing. . . .

Strangely, the magistrate listened to her this time with ill concealed impatience, frequently looking at his watch, acquiescing with a distracted air. And the clerk was absent. She insisted that she should be accompanied to the scene of the crime but met with a refusal, repeated her demand in categorical tones, explaining that they would be gathering crucial evidence for the truth, and finally she had her wish granted. Despite the late hour she went to the riverbank, found the exact spot where they had landed, indicated the position of their bodies on the grass, described the end of their meal. . . . And suddenly noticed that she was alone on the bank, that the sun had long since set and that her explanations were being addressed to no one. . . . In fact, they were being heard by several young ruffians who chased her, throwing lumps of clay at her and shouting obscenities.

It was probably on that evening, on the homeward path, that she met the stammerer. He told her they did not want his testimony either. And yet he had explained to the magistrate that Golets had kept himself to himself because he had a past to hide: as an army doctor he had been captured by the reds and had served in their army for two years. . . . Thirty years ago.

They were standing facing each other in a street in the lower town that was already almost in darkness. She, her hair disheveled from running, her dress smeared with the mud thrown by her pursuers. He, small, frail, his face distorted by the impossibility of speech. Both of them felt intolerably mute. Finally he was able to gain control of the air stuck in his throat and exhaled in a painful groan, "Y-you-you k-k-killed him!"

After this encounter she did not go back home. It even seemed to her as if she never again saw the house tacked on to the wall of the Caravanserai. Inexplicably she had become this woman lying on a narrow, white bed in a small room where there was a smell of medicines in the air. Someone woke her, forcing her to abandon the comfortable absence of unconsciousness. She opened her eyes: she felt no surprise at seeing a man of about fifty, an inaccurate portrait, aged and tired, of her husband, and a grave, tense young man—the future portrait of her son.

Their appearance transported her into a distant life, a forgotten city, and, above all, into another body. They seemed not to notice that she had gone and continued to address this pale, immobile woman, deprived of speech. It was her husband who did the talking. She heard him from the depths of her fog, smiled at him, understood nothing. . . . She had to sign a sheet of paper—the man guided her hand. When they took their leave her maternal instinct must have roused her from her unconsciousness. She heard her husband replying to her, "It's better like this. For him . . ." She understood that he was going to Russia and taking their son with him. "For a month or two," he said.

When the door closed behind them the memory of the previous days returned, or at least that of the cold, of the fragment of glass that had gone into the vein in her wrist so easily—a fragment of ice, it seemed to her, that put an end to the pain, to the stifling afternoon on the riverbank where the drowned man lay, to the clamor of the voices talking about her, forever talking about her. . . .

One night she was able to get up, went out into the corridor, and, advancing in a rapid ethereal glissade, passed through the echoing, nocturnal building. Despite the darkness the rooms in it were full of animation. She heard cries of joy, sad conversations, secret meetings, sighs. After she turned one corner the corridor took on a new aspect; she saw old portraits on the walls in their faded gilt frames. Through a half open door waves of operatic music spilled out. A woman dressed in an ample party dress walked ahead of her. A motley, laughing group suddenly appeared in a brief shaft of light and vanished at once at the end of a passage. . . . She already knew what there would be in the room whose door she slowly pushed open. The wood fire, the branches covered in melted snow, the big mirror, the bed that held the imprint of a body. She undressed and molded herself into the hollow, feigned sleep. A moment later a long, endless caress enveloped her, filled her body, began to dilate it. . . . She interrupted it suddenly. Within an armchair pushed against the wall a heavy profile stood out in which there glinted an eye that was at once malevolent and obliging. . . .

It was to escape this look that she hurtled along the corridors that had once more become monotonous. Hurried footsteps, sure of their strength, rang out behind her. The only refuge, she now remembered, was in that tiny room under the rooftops, the one whose narrow window looked out over a snow-covered forest. . . . She could already make out the little, low door, seized the handle, shook it desperately. Expert hands, almost nonchalant in their calm brutality, stopped her, twisting her arms. . . .

Her own cry woke her. So it had all simply been a long dream, tortuous and painful. The winter nights, that unspeakable love, the man hounding them from his armchair . . . She lifted her left arm—the scar was still red. Why had she done it, when everything was only a slow parade of ghosts? For she had learned, she did not know how (from the nurses' conversations, no doubt), that her son would not be coming back on the appointed date. Or perhaps he would not come back because she had opened her veins? Or perhaps she had wanted to die to escape the building from which there was no escape? For she was no longer in the hospital where her husband and her son had come to see her. . . . Or perhaps, precisely, they had gone away because they knew she was going to end up here? The cut vein, the building, their departure. Or rather: their departure; the cut wrist; the building one cannot leave. No, in yet another order: building; desire to die; their departure . . . How simple and insoluble it all is. And yet if I went to the window and if I saw it snowing, perhaps I could . . . Wait, first there was that fragment of glass, the blood, but there was no ice to stop it. . . .

SHE DID NOT KNOW that years were passing. Time wound slowly through the bowels of the building she was exploring, feeling her way, day after day. Not the building of the asylum, a banal, rectilinear construction where dwelled all those troubled souls, but the cavernous, changing building that had arisen in her sleep. Distilling the sounds, she learned to identify the music of a grand piano in a remote drawing room. She ran toward it, could already see the clusters of candelabra, caught the aroma of the food for a festive dinner. . . . But the rooms suddenly grew dark, filled with smoke and the fragments of windowpanes crunched beneath her feet. She made her way into a devastated restaurant where a man with a fur hat pulled down over his brow was playing a triumphal tune, from time to time wiping away the drunken tears from his soot-stained face with a rapid gesture. . . . She went out through a yard at the back, hoping to protect herself from the machine gun fire that suddenly started to riddle the wall. And found herself in a hotel room whose window opened out onto a hot southern night, onto the rustling of foliage in the humid, perfumed breeze . . . She wandered from one room to the next, occasionally ran into someone, embarked on a conversation with them and was never surprised if her interlocutor left her in midword, disappearing into a gallery that suddenly opened up at the end of a room. . . .

★ ★ ★

Among the people who came to see her there was a woman who never vanished unexpectedly and, as if to demonstrate that she was undeniably real, offered her her bony hand, kept warm beneath an angora shawl. She was the nurse from the Caravanserai, the one who used to be in mourning for her English fiancé. Strangely, she had preserved the memory of a certain Princess Arbyelina and came each month, despite a journey that took a whole day. She no longer spoke of the English pilot, her mythical beloved. No doubt, as even myths grow old, this unhappy princess was now becoming the new passion in her all-too-colorless life. . . . She would come on a Sunday, in rain, or in summer sunshine, making her way along the long avenue of lime trees, beneath branches sometimes studded with the first green shoots, sometimes gilded by October days. She explained to the others, gravely and sadly, that Princess Arbyelina had once been her closest friend and indeed her confidant. It was solely thanks to this new legend that Olga Arbyelina still had any existence in the land of the living. . . .

After the visit, the princess (the staff called her that without really knowing if it was her title or a *nom de folie*) would remain at the window at the end of the corridor, watching the figure disappearing down the avenue and observing the simple and repetitive life of the outside world. The drops of rain; the sky, blue or white with clouds; the trees, bare or green . . . Then she would move away from the window, follow a wall, and, as she turned the corner, plunge into a vast shadowy apartment where, in the midst of the sumptuous disorder of a bedroom, her gaze fell upon a great black leather armchair. Empty for the moment . . .

The meetings with the nurse from the Caravanserai and the few scraps gleaned from the chatter of the housekeeping staff taught her little of what went on outside the walls. Wars; the hardships of life; the pompous mockery of the commonplace; the banality of dying. Were these things more important than the falling of leaves? More reasonable than her wanderings through that endless mansion?

One of the housekeepers noticed that the princess filled dozens of sheets of paper with cramped handwriting and hid them in her bedside table. Her curiosity was fruitless: the notes were illegible, either written in an unknown language or, even in French, too muddled. As for the few lines that could be deciphered, they gave the details of a winter's day such as occur plentifully in everybody's lives.

One day, without having any notion of time, she guessed that the nurse from the Caravanserai would not come. In fact she never came again. Neither beneath the autumn rain nor beneath the branches bespangled with the first leaves. . . .

Finally after an indistinct cycle of weeks, months, and seasons, an icy morning arrived. At the top of an old wooden staircase, with high treads and a rail polished by many hands, the door opened, behind which there could only be that tiny room with the window looking out over a snow-covered forest.

SHE HAD TO BEND DOUBLE to creep toward that tiny window, a kind of skylight, dull with dust, covered in a tapestry of spiders' webs. With a piece of rag drawn from a pile of old clothes she wiped the window. Outside was the same avenue of lime trees but seen from much higher up, and that day veiled in a slow blanket of snowflakes. The ground was all white as well and the world beyond the boundary wall seemed half blotted out by filaments of snow.

She was not at all surprised to see a man appearing slowly in this swirl of white, in the middle of the avenue. She was astonished neither by his giant stature nor by the poverty of his clothes: you could see at a glance that the fabric of the long greatcoat of military style had been darned and patched. Beneath this worn garment a powerful but abnormally emaciated frame could be discerned. He was not wearing a hat, the snow had mingled with his gray hair.

His actions did not seem outlandish to her either. He stopped, set an old traveling bag on the ground, and went to scrape up a handful of snow from the seat of a bench. Then he carefully massaged his face, washing it with the ball of ice that was melting in his hands. Took out a handkerchief, wiped his brow, his cheeks. Picked up the bag and walked toward the entrance of the building.

She made no movement, only let her gaze travel around her, like one who wakes up in a strange place and tries to identify it. It was no longer a secret refuge lost in the labyrinths of that mansion of long ago but simply the top of the building, a narrow loft where she had acquired the habit of coming, prevented at first by the staff, who feared a suicide, then ignored by them. Broken chairs, old newspapers, that pile of yellowed paper from which she extracted the pages for her notes. . . .

Already a woman's voice was repeatedly calling her name from the bottom of the staircase. . . .

She knew in advance what the man who had just washed his face with a fistful of snow was going to tell her. He would begin talking at once, as he walked down the avenue, then sitting on the seat in a railway carriage, in a hotel room, in a café, later in some ephemeral dwelling that, for a time, would give them the illusion of a home of their own. . . . He would go on talking during all the years that were left to them to live. And the feeling that she knew it all as soon as he started speaking would never leave her. She would listen to him, weep, signal to him to be silent when the grief was unbearable, but all, absolutely all would already be known to her, endured a thousand times in the course of her nocturnal wanderings along the deceptive corridors of life.

She would know, she knew already, that the émigrés, the moment they returned to Russia, had been stripped of their luggage, screened, loaded into long boxcars. And that it was on the day of the first snowstorm that they had separated father and son. The adults had continued their journey farther eastward, crossed the Urals, traveled up beyond the Arctic Circle as far as the camps of the far North. Young people who had not reached the age of sixteen were considered still capable of purging their "bourgeois past" in reeducation centers. It was at the moment of separation that the father, after a solitary and futile rebellion, had almost died under the heavy rifle butts of the guards. . . .

She would also learn that Li had followed the same route to the North. And that her painted panels had been thrown into the snow behind the railroad station where they were sorting out the prisoners.

For a while the vivid colors of these panoramas were to be seen amid the frozen wastes: a pianist in tails accompanying a monumental prima donna; two vacationers beneath a tropical sun. . . . But little by little the local inhabitants had carried these panels away and burnt them during the great frosts at the end of the winter.

She understood that not knowing what had befallen her son was for her the only chance of believing that he was still alive. And the more improbable this hope was, the more confident she became. He was somewhere beneath the sky; he saw the trees, the light, heard the wind. . . .

One day she finally decided to speak in her turn. She knew that for the man to understand her she must tell everything in a few brief words and speak no more. And then speak again, until her words became fire, darkness, sky . . . Until that other life, the one they had so clumsily sought together, and that she had so briefly known, was finally made manifest to them in the fragile eternity of human language.

He opens the gate at the moment when the aureole of the streetlamps is beginning to waver and is extinguished. For some moments the darkness seems to have returned. I look back: the door to the keeper's lodge has been left open; and I can see the lamp that lit up his face all through the night. Our two chairs. Our cups on the table. And all about the little house dark tree trunks, the upright stones of monuments, tombs, crosses . . .

He stays beside me for a moment between the two halves of the gate. Then shakes my hand, moves away, and soon disappears among the trees.